YOKE OF THE VALE

LORIN PETRAZILKA

FATEBOUND BOOKS
A WOMEN-OWNED IMPRINT

Yoke of the Vale
First Edition
Copyright 2023 Lorin Z Pillai

All Rights Reserved. Printed in the United States of America.

Published by Fatebound Books
For rights inquires, please contact rights@fateboundbooks.com

FATEBOUND✦BOOKS

ISBN 978-1-7360622-6-5 (hardcover)
ISBN 978-1-7360622-9-6(paperback)

Edited by David Martin Lins and Paris Thompson

Cover design by Alberto Carranza and Lorin Z Pillai

*Dedicated to you,
the reader,
for your dedication.*

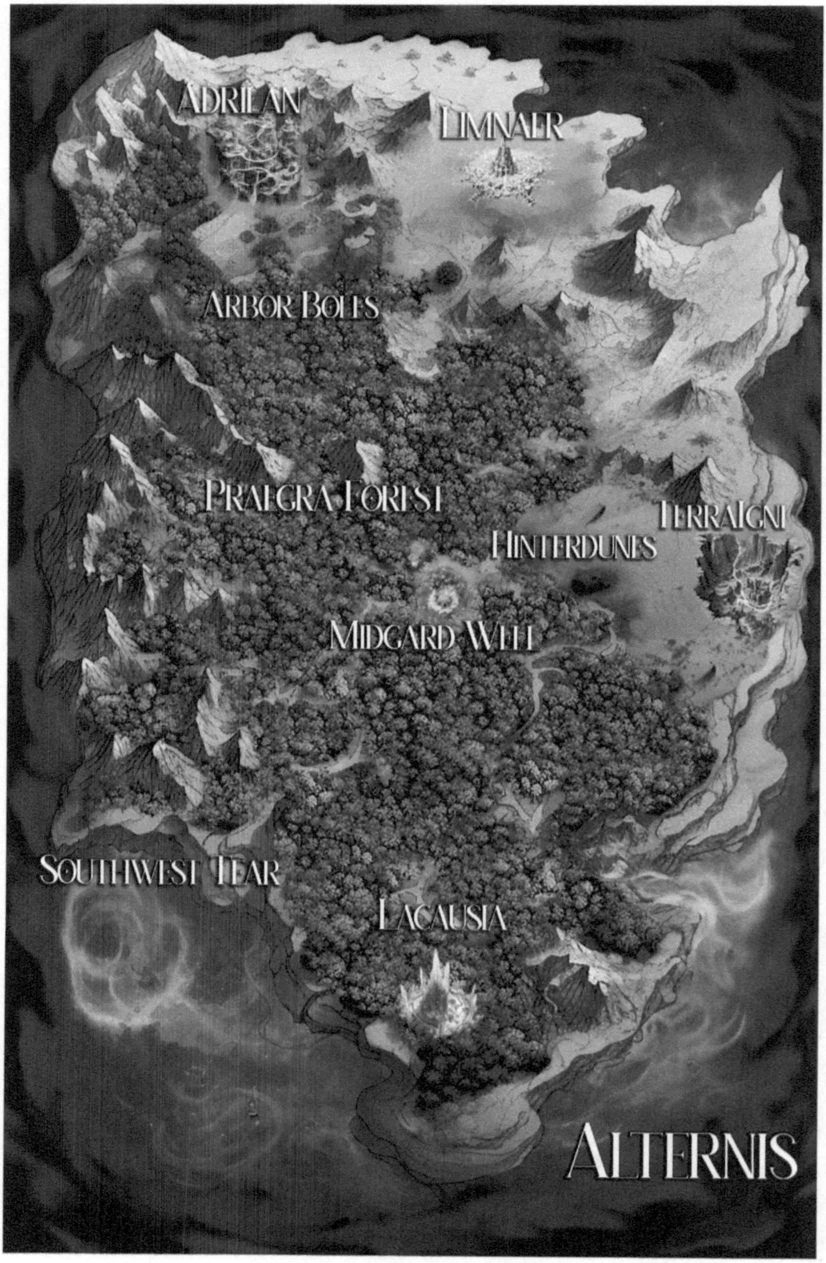

Adrilan
Limnalr
Arbor Boles
Praegra Forest
Hinterdunes
TerraIgni
Midgard Well
Southwest Tear
Lacausia
Alternis

TABLE OF CONTENTS

CHAPTER 1

The thin threads of cirrus clouds slipped through my fingers, as I lay back on my elbows on a narrow platform suspended high over the land. It jutted out from the farthest reaches of Limnaer, the floating Caelifae city far to the northwest of TerraIgni. An unnerving expanse opened below the precarious needle-like prong, one of many that bordered the entire edge of the stronghold in the sky. As we had approached the great citadel three rotations prior, the prongs had looked like glittering spikes on a fearsome crown. I realized now they were to prevent anyone without power over air to approach their city. The spikes were too narrow for our large winged horses to land on, and the entire city was constructed on the underside of a massive rock, held high in the atmosphere by funneled winds from ports along the sides and bottom. I cringed as I thought about how far down the ground was. But here out on the tip of the prong was preferable to being around Eiulans. He was the right hand to the king of TerraIgni and general thorn in my side. Being in his presence along with the Caelifae leaders at the city center was not appealing in the slightest.

My mind wandered as I looked down at the shapes the land made far below, with the border of mist blocking the view in a full, enormous circle at the edge of the expanse. I thought of my mom, of visiting my home once again. I imagined letting my hand drift through the tall weeds that bordered the rocky trails, which led away from where I had slipped through the Vale so long ago. I played back the memories of the last time I had seen it, the overgrown grass almost at the point where you could run your fingers through them without having to bend over, pinching the stems and making the seedlings pop off and scatter them in the wind. The smell of the sage brush beginning to warm in the Southern California sun. Lush, wild licorice growing on the trail edges, grabbing sprigs to chew on while I hiked near the forbidden edge of the forest. The delicate wildflowers bowing in the breeze, showing the verdant sign of spring before it became too dry and hot for them to flourish. The acrid smell of smoke still smoldering from the remains of my house.

I gulped as I thought about that last vivid memory. My home was gone, destroyed by Dashelle in a vindictive moment, a moment which had taken the final pieces of proof of a life lived with my family. The only proof which might remain probably resided at my Aunt Maureen's home in Ithaca, New York. A few scattered photos at her house was the most I could hope for. That and my mother herself, who had gone there to their parents' homestead after everything had been burned to the ground. What irony. What absurd, unfair irony. The largest wildfire we had ever endured in my hometown of Black Oak Grove had taken the lives of my father and sister years before. Yet our ranch remained standing when many did not. Then, I discovered that in this strange world of Alternis I have power over fire, albeit many times it was difficult to control. And then? That was the absolute clincher. The day that I went back to find my mom and tell her everything; it was then I discovered I had no power over fire when I returned home. I had returned to find that Dashelle had preyed upon my greatest fear and used that which caused me so much trauma, so much anxiety to take away what little remained of my human life.

I was already forced to return to the Vale anyway. But now I had nothing to go back to in Black Oak, even if the insistent demand of the Vale would subside long enough for me to enjoy a visit. Instead I was basically trapped here. There were a great many things I was lucky to have in this crazy, beautiful realm. But there were also a great many things that I missed. The true cost of the gifts the Vale had given me took some time to be felt and weighed. For each privilege came an equal price.

"Lily? Are you ready to come back yet?" Felix called to me from the edge of the platform. He must have had to search for a while to find me, there were hundreds of prongs that faced out from the perimeter of the suspended city.

I watched clouds wisp along my feet as I dangled them over the edge, toying with the drop off that loomed far below. I felt like I had found where the sidewalk ended, where the possibilities for different choices could split for different outcomes. The only problem with the current situation was that there were few choices I could make. I sighed and answered at last, "Yeah, I'll come back now."

My intention to clear Don'Li Calbaeric's name had not gone as smoothly as I had hoped. Eiulans was the one who had publicly—yet secretly—smeared him, which caused Don'Li grief for as many cycles as my mate's mother, Queen Deniza, had been unknowingly imprisoned for. Don'Li had been blamed for the event which led to her presumed death over one hundred cycles before. Eiulans made sure of that, and ensured that he was considered an outcast among every faction of the Fae. My great "idea" to restore Don'Li's reputation—after his death defending our queen's life—had backfired, as most matters of the Crown tended to when I was involved. Coming to Limnaer had proven to be more of a challenge than I had anticipated.

I stood up, then straightened my spine. If another verbal lashing was in order, I'd listen. The fact that I felt the blame was misplaced was irrelevant. I had come to make amends, and I'd see it done.

Felix eyed me as I approached. "I don't think I understand why they're being so hard on you," he said.

I sighed as we started walking toward the city center. "Who knows exactly. After all, this shit happened long before I became a princess, long before I was even born. But, I'm the only Ignisfae Royal here right now, so that makes me responsible regardless of when it happened."

"I guess. So, that brings up my earlier question again, why didn't Rannoch come? I know you wanted to be the one to clear Don'Li's name, but you didn't even want Rannoch to join the crossing. Dashelle *is* still a problem, after all."

I groaned. I didn't want to talk about it. About any of it. It was true Dashelle was still a real danger, though as of yet she still had not been sighted. Rannoch, and the warriors he commanded, would have been needed protection had we crossed paths with her. We managed to make the trek quicker and without incident as we could travel faster with only Dhiren and Dhirdre for companions instead of his contingent, even though we were forced to bring

Eiulans with us as well. "Not now, Felix. Can we just deal with the problem at hand? The sooner we do, the sooner you can work on training so that you understand your skills better. Have you seen the Caeli-Aedis yet? I hear their training temple is stunning."

"Nice subject change, Lily. You're so transparent. And no, you know I haven't seen it yet."

Fine. I looked straight ahead instead of bothering with a follow-up response. He was right, it was a painfully obvious attempt to change the subject to avoid his question. I studied the architecture instead. Our arrival had included a history lesson about how the vast city came into being, built during a trade partnership with the Petrafae. The massive, glittering columns of refractive labradorite had been grown out of the base of the disc shaped land mass, inverted and held in place while hundreds of Petrafae worked together to form channels for the Caelifae to funnel strong air currents through thousands of vents which would keep it perpetually floating in the sky. The major components and critical keystones were created by the Petrafae, while the Caelifae wove countless cloud-like connections called nubistela. In exchange, the Caelifae had helped shift the prevailing winds surrounding Adrilan, the city the Petrafae had begun construction on after they lost Lacausia Palace and the surrounding area to the Umorfae siege over five hundred cycles before, following the death of the Vale Born ruler Vitus Augustus. The redirected winds created a moat of sorts around Adrilan, the unapologetic current of it could only subside when a blockade was lifted in place. Then a series of stone steps had to be created in order to reach the city proper. Both mechanisms could only be accomplished by the Petrafae. And not by any single Petrafae, several were needed to open the locks to their great city. By the two factions of Fae working together, they were able to thwart future efforts of the Umorfae, should they attempt another border expansion. I scoffed at the thought of the Umorfae. I was convinced the way to tell if an Umorfae was lying was if their lips were moving. A vile group of takers and slavers, their beautiful exteriors masked true demons.

The stone of the city was indeed beautiful, and definitely sparkled as much as the Caelifae had claimed, refracting the occasional prismatic sheen found in labradorite. Though I had to wonder how much more brilliant it would be if the sun ever managed to break through the mist. The mist, the mist, the ever-present shroud which obscured anything beyond the vast borders. What was out there? There must be more. I had seen through it only once, when Rannoch and I visited Starcrest, it was his surprise trip to me when I was feeling homesick. I let out a pitiful, single laugh. There were easier times between the two of us back then.

"What's on your mind?" Felix asked as we walked. One of the many nubistela arches passed overhead as we entered the cluster of the city.

"The mist. I wonder what's beyond it." Not a lie, but not the whole truth, either. "I remember planning the Umorfae coup, at the map table in TerraIgni. The whole of Alternis was drawn as one big continent, no islands, no other continents like what we know back home. Isn't that weird?"

"Lily, *everything* about this place is weird."

"Hah! That's a fact." I laughed as we walked up the ramp to the palace center. My stomach dropped and my smile faded as I realized we were back already.

CHAPTER 2

The pointed, spear-like tops of the narrow palace towers had strung webs between them, glistening with dew drops in a geometric spirograph network. They tightened and coalesced the closer we got to the main throne room. We had arrived at the entrance too quickly for my liking. A few more moments to think would have been nice. It was already time to gather myself and restart the talks with Caelifae leadership. One of their own had been wronged by the Ignisfae, that was a reality that I had to keep in mind as I stepped toward the grand room which housed the dais. Telling myself that didn't make it any easier though, as I had to answer to Prince Ser'Ti and his Regent, Calria. Ser'Ti was closer in age to me than any Fae I had met aside from children, too young to rule on his own—even at thirty-five cycles old. It disheartened me to no end that at thirty-five he was not old enough to rule, yet older than me. We could have perhaps been friends, or at least related on a level of being young. Instead, I found him to be a preening brat raised with a silver spoon in his mouth. I might have said this is what comes from being born into royalty, but Kerenza and Rannoch were proof that it wasn't always true. No, for him, he was just a narcissist who loved to hear himself talk. Calria was level-headed, and seemingly tried to use her position to at least soften the negative impact Ser'Ti's words had when he weaponized them. Which, to me, seemed to be every time his mouth opened. I tamped down my feelings about him as I approached where he sat on the dais.

"Princess Lily, you have decided to return to continue talks, I see." Ser'Ti sneered from the throne he was perched upon, and I wanted to slap that look right off of his face. "I hope you will be more amenable to actually listening this time, rather than stomping away."

Blanching, I darted my eyes around the room. Eiulans was nowhere to be seen. It was hard to speak with confidence when I felt his judging, beady eyes upon me. So far, Eiulans was the last Ignisfae that had yet to turn to fully supporting me, in spite of the fact that he was King Ashwan's right hand and the king had renounced his earlier harshness toward me. I was glad Eiulans was not there to witness this interaction, should this round not go well.

I held my breath as I straightened up more. I needed to stay calm. Queen Deniza had taught me a lot about my Fire Bringing ability, it was no surprise that keeping my emotions reigned in was key to not losing control of the brimming power that simmered below the surface. Ser'Ti *was* a bit of a prick, but I couldn't let him erode the work I had done to keep a lid on the intense feelings that were rearing their head. "Of course, Your Highness. Thank you for your understanding and granting me some time to collect myself. I trust we are ready to move forward with positive discussions." We all knew he had granted me nothing, and I had left when the "discussions" became too heated. There was a lot of finger pointing, and a lot of blame thrown at the Ignisfae. I couldn't say they were entirely wrong, but it was difficult for me to separate the fact that I was there as an Ignisfae representative from who Don'Li was as a friend to me. Part of me did want to question why they had taken the word of Eiulans over their own kind back when the relationship between Deniza and Don'Li became known, but that would have done no good and would only have inflamed the situation further. I was not one who wanted to fan tempers and watch them burn. There was one person in particular I could think of who would probably enjoy that, and I did not want to be like her. Ever.

Ser'Ti hardened his face, knowing full well he had not excused me when I abruptly left before. I knew I had done at least two things with my response just now: thrown his shitty comment back in his arena, and not apologized for leaving. The choice was his for how to move forward. I had chosen to come to Limnaer without Rannoch or Kerenza, and I thereby represented the Ignisfae, so I needed to find that fine line to walk. The line of the diplomat that maintained a position of strength while finding ways to smooth the injustice. I didn't need to grovel for approval or forgiveness. But I *did* need to act with respect and dignity. I felt the color begin to drain from my face as I realized Ser'Ti may have been an arrogant ass, but he was right. I had stomped out. That kind of behavior was not exactly becoming of a princess. I held still and I thought over my next words carefully. "I would like to discuss what the Ignisfae can do to make amends. Don'Li Calbaeric was brave and honorable, and fought alongside the Ignisfae with the might and vigor of someone who was not nearing the Fading. He protected and helped me. I want to make things right not only for his name, but for us all."

The wind rushed around me, and suddenly Prince Ser'Ti was directly in front of me, having descended the dais in an imperceptible leap. "You know nothing of his name," he hissed at me, unnervingly close to my face. His prismatic eyes were all I could look at, and the brewing anger that was palpable in their depths.

Just as quickly, he was gone, my hair still rustling from his hasty departure. Calria cleared her throat. "I feel another recess is in order. We will reconvene in one rotation." She bowed, her robes skimmed the floor as she seemed to float away, curling her slender fingers toward her well-built male attendant, beckoning him to follow her.

I nodded, though there were few who even saw the reaction, as I was left standing on the vacant floor with my brother waiting in the background. The massive door at the end of the hall clanged shut, and all noise ceased in the great room. I frowned, my silly heart had hoped to connect with Don'Li's people, to lean into grief with them and to heal from his loss. I still hadn't gotten over it. I had been right there, I could have *done* something. But deep down, I knew he was ready to let go. There were some things he wasn't going to get in this life and he had finally accepted that. A mate was not in the cards for him. He did get to see Queen Deniza alive and healthy one last time, and Fade with his hand in hers, maybe that was enough for him. Thinking back on his Fading—the process of gently releasing the mortal coil that some in Alternis are lucky enough to go through when the end is nigh—I couldn't hold back a tear that brimmed at the waterline of my eye. I wanted to help him achieve what he wanted before that time came. He let the Fading take him before the spear could.

"Well he has a flair for the dramatic," Felix said, shaking me from my thoughts.

I grinned and turned to him, holding back my disappointment. I was suddenly appreciative that he was there. In truth I had been grateful during the whole trip to have him as my right hand for this endeavor, but now most of all. Because of his presence, the crippling weight of the failing mission felt a little lighter. After all, it was a diplomatic envoy and lives did not hang in the balance for it. It was words and assuaging feelings, damage control after the loss of Don'Li. While it mattered, the loss of life had already happened. This trip was meant to help those left behind heal. Healing may have had to wait, as the contentious meetings were dwarfing anything positive that might eventually come of them. Clearly Ser'Ti had something else getting under his skin. Like I always used to tell Josie, nine times out of ten when people unleash their "I want to speak to the manager" fury, it usually stems from something else that happened to them before they even stepped foot near the person they are verbally attacking. I nodded to myself, it probably wasn't me, he was just dealing with his own issues. I hated to think this, but maybe it was his youth, and his need to assert his power in spite of the fact that Calria could override him or lessen his impact.

"Let's take a rest, then go to the temple," Felix suggested. "I can learn there, and maybe we can get some perspective and figure out our next move."

"Definitely. I agree."

CHAPTER 3

Dhirdre and I walked to the Caeli-Aedis temple to meet up with Dhiren and Felix. We had split up for a bit, and I spent some time trying to nap in the guest room I had been given. In spite of the bed basically being a giant voluminous cloud with cumulus puffs edging it, I couldn't get any rest. I missed Rannoch, even though I was the one who had wanted to take the trip without him. I tossed around in the fluffy, buoyant softness, thinking of our parting words that I now regretted. Even the whisper-light mist coverlet didn't entice me to sleep. It all should have been like resting on a dream bed—it quite literally was that. It was like what I imagined you would describe to a child to make them feel like they were drifting off in the most peaceful way possible. A future child which Rannoch envisioned and hoped for and I—currently—did not.

"What has got you so tense?"

I nearly jumped as Dhirdre broke the silence. "Oh, just thinking about how I tried to get some sleep."

She looked me over, her eyes too sharp, too knowing. She nodded and averted her gaze forward after a moment. "Perhaps it is the end of the Pompa period. Some say it seems less exciting between a couple as things settle down after the first celebration of your union. Things become routine. I hear it is normal, if you were … worried."

I held back a reaction. Dhirdre was my friend, and I could talk to her, but I didn't want to say anything that might make her concerned. Rannoch was their prince and leader. Then again, Dhirdre was older than Rannoch, she could probably give me some advice. If Ser'Ti was considered young … I didn't even entirely want to finish that thought. "Maybe it's exactly that. What do you suggest I do?" In truth, I was starting to see that as much as I hated to admit it, I needed guidance in this area. I didn't have my mom close at hand to ask. Felix would listen, I was sure. But there was no way he could entirely understand. Plus, he had commented about me being impulsive, implying I was a fool to rush in. This problem would be a direct example for why I should have thought things through more. But isn't that what happens when you fall in love? Fools *do* rush in, it's impetuous, it's consuming. Reason and logic has little to do with the cresting tidal wave after one surrenders to the tortuously wonderful madness. Once feelings are admitted, falling in love is easy. Staying in love, that's the hard part.

"Have there been disagreements?"

I paused mid-step. I realized after I had asked her for advice, I had immediately slipped into a thought storm with little chance of resolving my own issue, and had nearly forgotten that I asked anything at all. *Consuming is right.* Even away from him our relationship had a tendency to hijack my brain. "Why do you ask?"

The corner of her mouth twitched up. I knew I had answered her question with another question, and the subtle facial expressions threw that fact right back. If I was going to ask her for advice, I'd need to open up a bit more. Without my mom here, I had very few people I *could* talk to about any of this. I might have been able to talk to Kerenza, but she was even closer to the situation because she was essentially my sister-in-law as well. I let out a resigned sigh. "Yes, we've been arguing. I don't want to say too much, because I don't think he'd be comfortable with me airing all our private matters, but things have been … tense between him and me." I frowned, he hadn't once pulled the thread that connected us while I had been in Limnaer, the link that allowed us to sense each other, or even sometimes send messages. It had been radio silence since I left.

She stopped, then turned to face me. "I know this is not easy to talk to me about. What I am about to say should remain between us. I had a similar conversation with Kerenza, after she mated with Kenneder. She did not have her maeder there to talk to, at the time we thought she was gone. There was no one else to fill that role for her, so I did. And my advice to her was the same, when things are difficult, you stay. It is that simple. If it is a loving relationship, and there is no abuse, you stay. You try."

My stomach tumbled with worry. Rannoch and I had argued, then I had left. I knew it was wrong at the time. I knew I should have not been reactive, I should have talked it out, but he was being stubborn. I was already holding back my emotions before Dhirdre started talking. Now, I felt my resolve wither, everything I tied up inside myself to keep it tamped down dissipated like the strange cirrus clouds surrounding us. "I know I should have stayed, but I was mad!" I shouted. Going quiet, I tried to collect myself to speak through the feelings. For all of my changes, all my efforts and steps forward to grow, to not slip into old ways, I was still sometimes beholden to them. *And goddamn, did that sound whiny when I said it out loud.* Once I heard my words—though they struck true to my emotions—they sounded pathetic.

I clenched a fist as the Caeli-Aedis doors came into view. They towered past a series of open arches, at the top of a long flight of cloud stairs with no risers. "You know what? After we see the temple and Felix gets started, let's go back to the main palace. I want to talk to Ser'Ti again. We're going to button this shit up with him, then we are leaving."

She looked confused for a moment, then understanding flashed across her face. "Back to TerraIgni?"

"Damn straight. Back to TerraIgni."

She grinned at me. "That is the Lily I know."

I nodded. *This is the Lily I am always becoming.*

CHAPTER 4

Felix was impressive with his skill, I watched with awe as he tumbled and sailed through the air. The small group training him were true masters. He had leveled up so quickly, it was a testament to their ability to teach. He had gleaned knowledge from their many cycles of practice. Though when I thought about it, he always had the innate ability with balance, it was like the addition of resistance with air simply gave him more time off the ground, more tools at his disposal to improve what he already understood. He funneled a burst of air behind himself as he ran up one of the arched buttresses. At first glance they looked like intricate architecture, but when you pictured them as ramps and runways, the space took on a new meaning. Instead of having sword training markings in a ring on the ground, as Ignisfae did in their training arenas in TerraIgni, there were markings suspended in the air. Illuminated, condensed vapors formed various patterns and concentric circles.

Felix glistened with perspiration as he dove through one of those rings, banked, then blasted in a different direction. He must have been training for some time before Dhirdre and I arrived. He aimed his staff through three tight circles that were spread out in a line, then sailed up to the next buttress ramp. The vapor curled around his staff for a moment before disappearing.

Dhiren clapped as Felix completed the course flawlessly. All goals caught with his stone staff, all marks hit. The four Caelifae nodded their approval, then spread out in a formation, creating a perimeter around him. They focused coordinated attacks on him, in ascending succession.

As I watched, I realized he had shown his skill and agility exhibition style, but now came the test to see how he could utilize those skills in battle. He dashed out of the way of the four-pronged attack, then inverted himself before shooting forward with his staff pointed at the abdomen of one of the trainers. He narrowly maneuvered himself out of Felix's path. Felix completed the move, then anchored himself near the top of the domed ceiling, giving me a thumbs up and a big, smug grin.

What an asshole, I laughed. This Caelifae was probably going to teach him a lesson for that one. Sure enough, he was by Felix's side before I even blinked. How did they do that? Sometimes the Caelifae seemed to have the ability to fold space, to be in two places nearly at the same time. It was less than a millisecond, and he had Felix pinned in place against the ceiling, with his staff slapped flat to the tiles from the Caelifae's foot. Felix was immobilized, and looked up to his trainer with a shocked expression.

I knew exactly what that move was meant to teach Felix. Rannoch had done something similar, teaching me not to congratulate myself when I was still in the heat of battle. Even if the battle in that case was mock, it should be treated with the same care that you would show a real one. Never stop to give yourself a pat on the back, no matter how small. I thought back to that time, when Rannoch and I had just begun our path together, all the things we had to learn, all the things we would do. The trials, and errors, and all the times that bridged those highs and lows.

I looked over to Dhirdre, who watched me with a small, knowing smile. She nodded once to me as Felix's trainer released him from the reprimand hold. They immediately got back to work, Felix properly in his place and humbled by their superior experience. I grinned, even if the intention of our visit to Limnaer was to clear DonLi's name, the secondary goal was for Felix to learn and grow in his skills with air. I could lift myself up on that, it *had* been successful, even if Ser'Ti hadn't been as easy to work with as I had hoped.

Dhirdre touched my shoulder, somehow she seemed to know that seeing Felix's progress was enough to bolster my confidence to be ready to approach Ser'Ti again.

I nodded. "Hell yeah, let's do this thing."

Calria rushed over as Dhirdre and I made our way into the biblio, the expansive library with sky-high glass windows overlooking the drop off to the world below. "His Highness Prince Ser'Ti is busy studying with his tutor. He will not be done for some time, and furthermore did not expect to meet with you until the next rotation. He may not react well to your appearance."

"My apologies for interrupting his study time. I thought perhaps a more informal meeting would be beneficial." Sometimes I felt so stiff, speaking formally and trying so hard. I held my imposter syndrome at bay as Calria eyed me. Ultimately, I *wanted* this to get resolved, even if it meant a little discomfort.

Ser'Ti was already glowering at us as Calria relented, then motioned with a quick swish of her arm for me to walk over to him. Dhirdre excused herself as I walked over to him, I had mentioned before arriving that I wanted to have a more riveting talk with him if possible. The prince glanced down at his textbook for a moment, pretending to carry on as I arrived at his desk. He made no effort to stand, letting out a disgruntled sound and dropped his hands to his lap, the book he held thudding as it struck his legs. "What is so important that you could not wait until our next scheduled appointment?"

"Well …" I looked around, "I am very interested in hearing about your impressive biblio here. I love books and reading. And in truth—" I paused, resisting the urge to fidget "—I gave it some thought and realized how much I could learn from you. You said I knew nothing of Don'Li's name, and it dawned on me how many things you must know. I am young and new to this world, and yet, have the responsibility of title. There's a lot expected of me, most of which I probably don't have a grasp of yet. I hoped I might learn from you."

He stared at me, his mouth open. Finally he smirked a bit. "You are trying to appeal to my vanity."

I returned the smirk. "Is it so obvious? I thought I delivered that rather subtly."

His jaw dropped further, looking stunned. I waited, trying to read him as his whole expression changed, I tried to figure out if I had made him angry, or just confused. I never could tell when a joke would land with the Fae. And Ser'Ti in particular, with how our prior conversations had all ended with terse words, I started to think there was no other route when speaking with him.

He threw back his head and howled with laughter. "All right! I give in," he laughed again, wiping a tear from his eye. "Please, sit down." He closed his book, then motioned to the chair next to me with it. His tutor, who stood nearby over his shoulder, left after Ser'Ti silently dismissed him with a quick jerk of his chin.

"Phew!" escaped my lips as I sat down, I couldn't deny the relief as the tension dropped. I had broken through to him, he had finally removed that invisible barrier.

Calria ordered a capuli cart delivery that an attendant dropped off, complete with a small carafe for cream and beautiful cloud-white porcelain cups. He poured two cups, then offered me one.

"All joking aside," I said as I accepted the cup, "I *do* want to learn from you, and I do love books. I've been learning how to read in your language. Many of our words sound the same but the letters look totally different." I glanced around at all the carefully bound books, each one a work of art. "Your biblio here is gorgeous. Where I'm from they're called libraries. Yours could rival some of the most beautiful ones I've only seen pictures of."

"Pictures?" he asked as he raised his capuli in a short salute.

"Oh, yes, where I was born there are devices called cameras that can take images that can then be printed out."

"Like that?" he asked, pointing to a black-and-white ink sketch of the main palace that was framed in crystal and hung in a recessed focal point.

"No, not quite. That's a drawing, done by hand. Very well done of course, but a camera can take an image immediately, everything in range of the glass lens on the front can be captured and recreated without an artist painstakingly putting down the details on paper. Light, shadows, forms, all of it is captured the moment a picture is taken. I'm not a photographer—someone who professionally uses cameras—so I'm probably not the best person to describe it. But that's the basic idea."

"Unbelievable, are there many of such devices where you come from?"

"Yes, a lot of technology and things that you would undoubtedly find incredible. Modern conveniences, automation, vehicles that are made of metal and other materials that can transport you quickly to places. It's a really long list, actually." I stared out the windows for a moment, thinking about how different the two worlds were, how much had changed for me and how something as commonplace there as taking a picture was an impossibility here. And yet, the reverse was also true, so many things of Alternis were simply dreams and fantasies on Earth. *I mean, technically I'm still on Earth, just in a different frequency.* My brain started to hurt as I once again tumbled down the mental path of the time shift and matter resonance differences of the two worlds, occupying the same location in space while being barely connected by tears. Rips in a tenuous fabric between worlds which few could pass. Tears in the Vale. The phrase alone frustrated me, the Tear that took and gave at the same time. It yoked me to this realm like a workhorse. The Tear that asked no permission, gave no explanation as it rushed me through its passage. The Tear that beckoned Josie, that beckoned me. The same one that made my relationship with Rannoch possible.

"With such things in your former world, I am surprised you would want to be here, a part of this one."

His words ripped me out of my thoughts. I took a moment to evaluate his comment, the look he gave me felt razor-sharp, his tone ice-cool. It definitely felt like a test, or laced with some ulterior motive. "There are things I miss there for sure, mainly my mom—my maeder, and technology was nice. There are also things I don't miss. Bills, taxes, being busy literally every single day, I mean, rotation, and if I took any time off I felt guilty. In reality I feel more at home here, more settled in my spirit I guess. But, it's hard being away from my maeder."

"I am surprised King Ashwan would send you here under diplomatic relations, someone seemingly divided in their loyalties, and essentially a newcomer to this world."

I took in a slow breath through my nose. He didn't even really respond to what I had said, it felt like he had that comment loaded and ready to go. I could *easily* unleash on him, the fire pricked at the surface of my skin, demanding to be released. It was yet another test. Would I stomp away again? This time I had shown up uninvited. No, I would *not* take the bait. "It is true I am a newcomer, which is one reason I had said I wanted to learn from you, if you were willing. As to why the king sent *me*, in truth, he didn't. My visit was not with intentions of securing a large trade deal, or some sort of alliance for military purposes, it was more of a personal matter. And with how close the *matter* was to King Ashwan, and his children, it really makes perfect sense that I was the one to come. And to say I am divided in my loyalties, I think that is a bit unfair. I said I miss my maeder, I believe many would feel that way given the situation."

His expression lightened, and felt notably less cold. "I can relate to missing your maeder. But your maeder still lives, unlike mine. Like beckons to like, after all. Only the Tears separate you."

I stared at him, bewildered. "What does that mean?"

He shook his wispy white hair with a gentle flick. It reminded me so much of DonLi's. Even some of his facial expressions were reminiscent of him. "Well, I do not know all that much about Vale Born in general. Your kind bridges the two worlds. But I do know that here, like beckons like. We are naturally drawn to those we resonate with. Caelifae to Caelifae, that sort of thing. Your connection to your maeder, well you had to have been drawn to her, for her to be the one that gave birth to you. She may be there, in the human world, but your connection to her is not severed."

Like beckons to like. I wanted it to be true, but I had no way of knowing. Whether it was true that our connection remained was not the issue at hand right now, and I needed to remember that. Perhaps he had provided me with some insight, or false hope, either way I was there for a different reason. "You mentioned I knew nothing of Don'Li's name. I would very much like to know more about him. I think of my friend with fondness, and want to honor him by knowing his history better."

I waited as Ser'Ti slowly lowered his cup. I had chosen my words and tone carefully, picking a conversational path that would, hopefully, equal Ser'Ti being a bit more forthcoming, rather than ominously shouting at me that I don't know what I don't know.

He spoke at last. "I will tell you if you agree to one thing."

CHAPTER 5

My invisible heckles instantly raised. I didn't know if it was because too many shady tactics had been used by others in the past, but his request for "one thing" in exchange for information about Don'Li put me on high alert.

"It is nothing illicit, I assure you. You said you wanted to learn. I have realized that I do as well. I study every rotation here in my biblio, yet even with the many thousands of books there is some knowledge they will not contain. These devices you speak of intrigue me. I want to know more, perhaps I can be the one to usher in growth to a new era. I am moving toward leadership here, and am trying to figure out what my purpose will be, aside from stewardship. What will I be remembered for? This question has been on my mind a lot lately. What can I help us build toward?"

Ooof. "The Fae then would have magic *and* technology? That sounds like a potential recipe for disaster. Aside from the moral implications of introducing otherworld technology, I would only be able to describe it, not create or replicate it."

"But the ideas are there. Even if you cannot make the devices yourself, ideas alone can be enough to push forward and grow," he countered. "It may spark a seed of change without you divulging anything other than what different technologies are possible."

"You sound like a human. Build, invent, grow, grow, grow."

"We Fae do everything slowly with infrastructure, perhaps we need a balance? Not as fast as humans, but not as slow as we have historically been. With your help, we could encourage that growth. I have to ask myself, why would we have this link between worlds? Barely attached, yet a few individuals are able to cross the boundary. Why would it exist as a possibility if we were not meant to learn from each other?"

"The connection is nearly a one-way ticket, I can only be on that side of the Vale for a short time now. They have no knowledge of this world and no opportunity to learn from it, so I wouldn't say we can learn from each other." I sighed, he was really angling for this technological advancement, which I wasn't even equipped to teach them. I nearly shuddered, thinking of the Fae going through some sort of industrial revolution, like teenagers who just got the keys to the car. It could be a near-disaster. I thought for a moment, then it dawned on me how he could potentially achieve what he sought, without too much involvement from me which may or may not be questionable. "Have you heard of Yantzen J'Dun?"

"No, should I have?" he asked as he poured us more capuli.

"He's the oldest Ignisfae there is. He's an inventor, and brilliant, really. He invented a special device that can see through the mist to the space beyond. In the human world we'd call that a telescope. Currently he spends his time thread painting in the TerraIgni bazaar, but if the offer were intriguing enough to him, I bet he'd join you here and tinker. He thinks about things with a different perspective, he's more inquisitive to what's out there and what's possible. I can make the proposal to him. And I can give some starting points on invention possibilities, but beyond that I'd personally trust Yantz to take the helm. Deal?"

Ser'Ti smiled. "Agreed."

Finally, *finally* things seemed to be going better with Ser'Ti. As long as I could convince Yantz, it would be perfect. If Ser'Ti wanted to usher them into a technological era, so be it. But in truth I didn't want to be a part of it for more than one reason. How would such things change this world? It wouldn't be right for me to prevent it, but I also wouldn't want to meddle in their natural course. The sooner I could step aside, the better. I had to ask myself how much what I wanted from him was worth. It was clear though that Ser'Ti was motivated, and that might mean if I couldn't give him what he sought, he might try to find another who could. On a personal level, I had grown to love the lack of machines and automation. It was an endearing, peaceful aspect to the sometimes brutal world. Modern conveniences were also synonymous with things that needed upkeep and management, aspects which I didn't love about living in the human world. The brilliant delusion that those conveniences equaled an easier life was perpetuated by industry and money. But really, it didn't matter what I felt about it, this world could become more advanced with or without my input. That was something that would take a very long time, and I had more pressing matters. Such as getting on with this conversation, then getting myself back to TerraIgni and working things out with Rannoch.

"So, Don'Li. I would love to know more about him, and his name. Your comment when we last spoke, it left me thinking about that."

He put down his cup. "Yes, his name. His disgrace affected

more than just himself. Anyone of rank related to him had to distance themselves, and I believe that the whole dramatic event was a contributing factor in my maeder's death."

I almost spit up the last sip of my capuli I had just taken, then carefully set my shaking cup down. "Your … maeder?"

"Yes. I am known as Ser'Ti Zan Cireclos, but I *would* have been named Ser'Ti Calbaeric Zan Cireclos."

I searched his face while I processed his statement. "So Don'Li was-"

"My avunculus. My maeder's sibling. Her only one, in fact. She was far younger than he, though she was considered old by the time she gave birth to me. My faeder said she thought I would return joy to her life. Sadly, I never knew her, as she did not survive my birth. She had been in a long sadness due to Don'Li's scandal, it left her lonely and filled with despair. My faeder never recovered from her death—it is difficult to recover from losing a true mate—and he Faded to be with her when I was twelve cycles old, leaving Calria to raise me. I realize now he stayed as long as he could, until it became too much to bear to carry on, I suppose. He made sure everything was in order for me and that I was well cared for. But, still, he left me just the same."

My emotions swelled, bringing heat to my skin, the fire asking to be let out. When I was angry, the fire demanded. But when I felt sorrow, it requested release. I pushed aside the feeling, releasing any flame would be the least helpful thing right now. Ser'Ti's beautiful cirrus hair would probably evaporate right in front of me.

"I understand what your intentions were with coming here," he continued, "and in some ways I can appreciate it. But it also inevitably dredged up a lot of wounds."

I couldn't help but relate some of his feelings to myself, and also think back on how I had arrived in Limnaer thinking it would be as simple as a magnanimous gesture to restore Don'Li's reputation. I hadn't even thought about how others were truly affected by his actions, and then by his loss. "I'm … sorry. I didn't know about all of these intricacies, and how his life might have impacted yours. Thank you for telling me."

He merely nodded his acknowledgment.

I hadn't liked how he treated me in our first conversations, but it all made a lot more sense now. He was hurting, and perhaps even a little lost. He'd been given the privilege and responsibility of ruling, with no direct family to guide him. My arrival was another painful reminder of the manner of his loss. "The choice is yours on how you proceed, he was your family member and your subject. I came to set the record straight with the truth of his life, or what I knew of it, and I have done that. In the meantime I think it would be best for me to return to TerraIgni."

"Do me a favor. When you take that conniving worm Eiulans with you, punish him for his lies."

I blanched. I really disliked Eiulans, I was pretty sure there was nothing redeeming about him. But I did not want to be the one to exact punishment on him. I didn't even think I was qualified, how could I determine what would properly mete out justice? It wasn't in my skill set.

We said our goodbyes and I excused myself. I was so ready for this trip to be over, it had been an emotional rollercoaster. But at least I felt like I was returning to TerraIgni having done something. It wasn't quite what I had expected, but we had made progress, and I had grown in the process. I thought about everything as I walked over to the section of the palace that housed the guest quarters. It was a solid twenty minute walk through the pristine architecture, which gave me time to think about how I could do as Ser'Ti asked, what punishment would be fitting for Eiulans.

Eiulans. I hadn't seen that rat bastard since the first meeting with Prince Ser'Ti and Calria. He had managed to both skulk like a weasel *and* glide into the throne room with an air of self-importance when we first arrived. Did he have no understanding of the misery he had sown? He was one of those types that always left me feeling like I had to get him off my skin, having to rub off the invisible residue his slimy persona left behind. Him being occasionally lecherous definitely contributed to the feeling, with him leering at Fae maidens like they were tasty morsels. More than once I had to subvert him away from Tanzara, my loyal assistant in TerraIgni. I could tell that having to tolerate being in Eiulans's presence was a distasteful part of her job.

I knocked on his door. He had kept to himself after the first meeting when Ser'Ti had unloaded on him. The prince had made it *quite* clear he held no positive opinion of the king's right hand, and was moments away from striking him down on the spot. I kind of wished Ser'Ti had, I would have loved to see Eiulans get the smack down. There were probably many who would have gotten some kind of satisfaction at seeing that. But, I was there to foster something positive, not encourage pisssing matches.

Where is this fucker? I pounded on the door again. It was possible he had gone to the main hall for a meal. I turned to head that direction, when I noticed the trace of blood coming from under the door.

CHAPTER 6

Amber blood. Unmistakable Ignisfae amber blood. I hammered on the door with my fist. "Eiulans! Come to the door if you can! Make a sound! Anything!" I couldn't hear any movement coming from inside his room as I paused to listen. My hollering alerted guards stationed nearby around the corner. They flew down the hall on a hurried gust. "Open this door immediately. He may be injured," I ordered as they arrived.

They fumbled with the lock until it released. Dhirdre came peeling through the corridor a moment later, right as the door swung open. "What is going on?" she asked as the guards filed into the room.

The trail of blood snaked along the pale stone floor. It looked thick and slightly dried.

Old.

"It's Eiulans. I don't know what happened."

He lay near the entrance to the bedroom in a motionless heap. "Oh shit." I raced over to him, placing my hands carefully on his shoulder to turn him over. I had already unwound my healing thread, but there was no need. His vacant stare looked past me into nothingness, his skin cold and his mouth twisted in a pained expression.

He had been dead for hours. Perhaps longer.

"Oh Gods, how did this happen?" Dhirdre asked.

I looked him over, he had several wounds to his torso shaped like pointed ovals, and two more to each bicep. "He's been stabbed several times. The lacerations are kind of rough. Whatever it was wasn't smooth like a blade, though they're shaped like sword wounds. And there's a little bit of stone rubble around each one."

Dhirdre gasped. "What is that?"

I looked up to find her pointing at the wall, which was partially hidden behind the bedroom door. Peering around the jamb, I saw large letters crudely swiped onto the surface, with amber drips running down and crusted in place. I stood, walking over to the chilling statement written in Ignisfae blood.

"What does it say?" she asked from behind my right shoulder.

I spun without answering her, looking over the room. Could the killer still be in here? "Search the area," I ordered the guards.

At that same moment, Ser'Ti charged into the room, with Calria right behind him. "What is going on here?" he demanded. When he saw Eiulans on the floor, his eyes shot to me. "I told you to punish him, not kill him! And you could have waited, now we have to deal with this mess."

"I didn't kill him! I came to talk to him and found him dead. It happened probably a rotation ago at least. I'm not sure when."

His gaze drifted to the wall behind me. "What ... is that blood?"

"Yes. It says "I'll get what's mine." It's written in English, my language." I groaned and rubbed my face, not wanting to believe what the truth most likely was.

"Oh no," Dhirdre said as her expression changed, realization dawning on who it must have been.

"What? Tell me now!" Ser'Ti demanded.

"I believe this was done by Dashelle, the Vale Born who bargained with the Umorfae faction led by Opius," I answered. "She has been in the wind since her escape. This message was for me. All guards should be put on alert and the city should be searched."

"In the wind. Is that some sort of joke aimed at the Caelifae? That is not tactful considering you have brought your problem with her upon us." Prince Ser'Ti folded his arms.

"I didn't mean any offense, that's a saying from the human world. It means her whereabouts have been unknown." My skin prickled with heat, I fought hard to keep the fire at bay. Juggling the emotions of flames that literally wanted to leap out of my body while navigating a diplomatic situation was a challenge I didn't need. It was like spinning plates of the finest porcelain.

I took a beat, and took a breath. "But you're right, this is primarily my problem. I'm shocked that she was able to come here, and that she somehow knew my location. She has no abilities like the Caelifae, as far as I know, so how she even got to the city is a mystery. There's a lot to unravel from this incident, but I think it also shows that your borders need to be shored up. She shouldn't have been able to get here, much less get so far into the castle."

Ser'Ti's nostrils flared, but then closed his eyes and inhaled sharply. "I agree. Tighter measures are called for. It makes me wonder if she had help. How else would she have made all the way up here?"

I thought for a second, she had managed to use her skills to safely traverse a pit that was hundreds of meters deep, maybe the reverse could be true. "Dashelle may have been strong enough to get here alone, she does possess the powers of four Vale Born," I said, trying to swallow the lump in my throat. One of those Vale Born was Josie, my lifelong friend who died at Dashelle's hands. She had taken Josie's powers, and the powers from two others by murdering them. I pulled myself back from the downward spiral of despair, then looked around, focusing instead on the scene of the crime. Two deep marks in the wall pulled my attention.

The prince followed my line of sight as I stepped over to the gouges. They were the same shape as the wounds in Eiulans's body.

"Think she missed?" he asked, peering closer to inspect the marks. "No, there's blood on them, a small amount but there is some on the edges," Ser'Ti added as he ran his finger along the jagged opening.

"And more bits of rubble. Look at the placement." I turned around, then backed up to the wall, placing my body in front of them. The damage lined up to my arms if they were slightly outstretched. "She pinned him here. Perhaps she interrogated him before she killed him." I frowned. I would have liked to think better of the former Hand of the King, but knowing Eiulans he probably spilled as soon as she demanded—if he knew the answer.

"What information would she want?"

I snorted. She had made her intentions known the first time we met face to face. It was pretty obvious to me what she would want. "My whereabouts, or Felix's for that matter." I covered my mouth with my hand and shrieked as I realized Felix knew nothing about all of this. "Felix! Alert the guards in the training temple!"

We arrived at the training temple nearly breathless, in spite of the assistance lent by the guards, who funneled air currents from behind to get us there quicker.

"Felix!" I shouted as Dhirdre and I burst into the massive arched rotunda, followed by our escorts.

Felix lingered by the far wall with Dhiren, dropping his propped up elbow and spinning to me. "What? You scared the shit out of me, Lil! What are you doing?"

I looked around, the Caelifae trainers were putting away training weapons. Other than them and the guards we had arrived with, the place was empty. No sign of a disturbance or of Dashelle. The ten escorts fanned out and began searching, some blasting up to the ceiling to get a look from above. Sounds of additional guards searching the area could be heard through the open archways.

"What's going on?" Felix asked, watching the sudden influx of Caelifae investigate the structure.

"Nothing good. There's been a murder."

"What?" He snapped his eyes back to me.

"Eiulans has been killed. It was Dashelle. We figured it was her, at least." I recounted everything as quickly as I could. Dhirdre pulled Dhiren aside so I could speak in private with Felix.

He asked a few questions, but was mostly silent until he spoke at last, "We need to leave."

"Yeah, but before we do, we need to talk to Prince Ser'Ti in the great hall. His people were moving the body to prepare it for transport."

"Oh man, I didn't even think about that. We have to bring him with us."

I nodded, folding my arms across my abdomen. This was all a terrible mess.

"Wow, you actually seem upset that he's dead. I have to admit I'm surprised," he said as he looked at me skeptically.

I stared at my brother. "What do you mean? Of course I'm upset!"

"Well, it's no secret you two didn't get along, and him being dead does potentially make your life easier."

I paled. *Unbelievable.* "You seriously think I killed him? And then what, made it look like it was Dashelle? You really think I'm capable of outright murder?" My stomach clenched, I felt like I was going to throw up. How could my own brother think I was comparable to someone like Dashelle? I was a flood of raging emotions; dismay, sadness, anger, confusion. I screamed, the fire finally finding its release and churning toward the ceiling in a plume of heat. As my temper simmered, I glanced around. All the guards had stopped what they were doing. Having a Fire Bringer in their presence was most likely new territory. They quickly averted their eyes and got back to work. I collected myself before I continued. "I'm sorry. The fire has been irritating me to get out for days, and you're not the first to suggest I killed him. It really upset me, because, well actually the thought terrifies me. What if I'm perceived to be like Dashelle? How much would it take for me to be more like her? I didn't kill him, in truth I'm not upset he's dead.

I'm even more annoyed with him now. Unfairly perhaps, but even in death he's causing problems. What I would have liked would have been for us to turn over a new leaf and grow to respect each other. I'm all about redemption, but some people are beyond that possibility. I hadn't really decided if he could be redeemed or not. And it's obviously not on the table anymore. Further than that, I now have to deliver this news to King Ashwan. How will he react? We were on tenuous terms as it was, even if he has been trying harder recently."

"Whoa, Lily, slow down." He regarded me for a few moments. "I didn't think about what I said, I don't really believe you could do that on purpose. But, crimes from heightened emotions are not uncommon. It took a total of two seconds for anyone who had seen the two of you interacting to know you hated him. There has to be some other explanation, it doesn't seem possible that is was either you or her."

"All right, I get it. It doesn't fully add up. But I do think it was her. Maybe this is part of her twisted plan. Now I'm questioning everything. Why would she do this? To make me feel vulnerable? She can get to me anywhere, is this to hunt me before she takes what she wants? Is it to wear me down by making me hyper vigilant, always looking over my shoulder? It sure feels like some sort of mind game. I have to wonder what information she could have possibly gotten from Eiulans. Frankly, he didn't know our next moves because I didn't trust him with that knowledge. I realize how far-fetched it sounds to say that it was Dashelle that did this. She came here? To Limnaer, unreachable by Fae unless they possess the power of air *and* the knowledge of how to reach it? That alone makes it pretty hard to believe. Then she kills Eiulans, writes a message in blood, then dips? Just gone? "Killed me an Ignisfae. Peace! I'm out." The only thing this crime served was to scare me." *It sure as fucking hell worked.*

Felix put a hand on my shoulder and gave me an understanding look, then guided me toward the exit to the temple. "We'll figure this out," he said. I glanced back to see Dhirdre and Dhiren fall into place behind us. They had become my friends, Dhirdre was a trusted advisor, and Dhiren was now Felix's mate—practically a brother-in-law to me. Did they believe it was Dashelle, or did they think the evidence pointed to me?

In spite of the three of them being right there next to me, solitude pushed me away across a formless expanse. Wandering cold and alone in an emotional wasteland, I could sense the subtext in their wary glances. They weren't sure if it was Dashelle or me that killed Eiulans. I could feel it, I knew it to be true. Aside from that, Rannoch still had not caused the slightest tremor in our bond, not even when terror surely surged through me at discovering the murder. How did he not feel something from me at the time?

I was so busy fretting and feeling sorry for myself, I didn't notice we had arrived back at the main hall, to have one more parting discussion with Ser'Ti. I stifled a groan. We had made progress with our discussion in the library, but it seemed everything that had happened after that had undone all the positive strides toward a better relationship.

The doors were open, and armed guards lined the corridor. *This ought to be fun.*

CHAPTER 7

Safely away from the city—and guided by far too many Caelifae for my liking—we neared the point where we had left the equus, our horse-like companions. The parting talks had gone significantly better than I expected, however there was the weighted undertone which I took to mean "get your shit and get out." Eiulans had been prepared for transport, and a contingent of guards were assigned to escort us. Prince Ser'Ti had ordered them to see us safely beyond the borders, which I assumed meant ensuring we were out of the range of being able to have Felix even think about trying to use his skill to get us back to the floating citadel. It didn't matter what reassurance I gave him, he wanted to make damn sure we were not coming back there. Though he definitely wanted us gone, we had at least smoothed things over. The relationship wasn't great by any stretch, we were heading back with a body after all, but it was a lot better than it could have been. However, the extra blast of wind funneled by the guards to aid the equus as we left felt like an unsaid "don't let the door hit you in the ass."

Maybe I was self-sabotaging again. Maybe not.

We flew into the mist as the guards all but disappeared from view behind us. Had I accomplished my goal? I still wasn't entirely sure. The one thing I was sure about: I had left Limnaer with more problems than when I had arrived. And now I was flying toward a problem I really needed to fix. Now.

Had I pissed Rannoch off so badly that he was distancing himself from me? It sure felt like it. I shouldn't have left him in TerraIgni as I did, I knew that now, but I did come to a resolution in my mind regarding him and me while I was away. And if I was going to be resolute about the problems we needed to discuss, I needed to stop questioning myself constantly and undermining my own progress. I had not gone through all this shit to be my own undoing. Losing my dad, sister, and Josie, having my former life essentially end and a completely different one start, being captured by Opius and nearly killed by Dashelle, attempting to save the Syrenni by handing myself over to the Umorfae, Don'Li's death … all of it was enough to make anyone question their life and their choices. Everyone, *everyone,* has their days where they have their doubts. Days when those doubts sow the seeds of internal destruction. I may have stepped down that path for a moment, but one glance at that well known, well-worn walk, and I knew that was not where I would allow myself to venture.

I was Princess Lily Mae Brennanfalk, goddammit. I didn't need the title, but I was ready to rise to the occasion.

Traveling from the farthest north western reaches of Alternis to the farthest east was exhausting, long, and grueling. I was so thankful for my equus, Zephyrine. I ran my hand over her mottled gray-and-black silky coat. What a champ she was, without her and the other equus our trek would have been downright brutal. Having a herd of giant flying horses as allies gave us an edge I didn't think any other Fae had. Only some of the Ignisfae rode equus, and the ones that did were a force to be reckoned with. Wielding the power over flame and able to travel at speeds the Caelifae could barely manage, as well as being honed hand-to-hand combat fighters made them formidable. Thinking of Ignisfae's skill, I couldn't help but let my mind wander to Rannoch. They are a powerful race, but Rannoch … he *emanates* that raw power. Every movement of his is quick, assured, and exactly the amount of energy needed to execute a perfect maneuver. In some ways that always seemed like a secondary power to me, that he knew when to exert more force, an understanding of the precise limits and capabilities within him. For someone so powerful, he was also so tender, that was one of the most endearing aspects of his qualities. That, and he never seemed to abuse his power. Power of status *and* gifted power from the Vale. He wasn't without fault though. Not listening to me about the possibility of childbearing was troubling, my readiness for that big step should be a key factor. I had clearly said I wasn't ready, then we got into a blowout argument. They *were* things that needed to be said, however I didn't understand before then that he was basically ready for a pregnancy to happen, and that in his mind it would simply be a matter of when, on a biological level. He hadn't even considered that I might not be mentally there yet.

Aside from that, we were still a relatively new couple, and I was still pretty new to the world. It was all so much to process. The prospect of preparing for motherhood terrified me. Selfishly,

I wanted it to be just us for a while. And really that wasn't even selfish. It probably made good sense. Lots of people have children on the younger side back in the human world, by the time you're in your forties the kids are pretty much on their own and you can still feel young and able to do things. There were arguments for either having them younger or older. But in the end, it's not about logic, it's not really about whether it makes sense or not, the time needs to be right. Who knew how many hundreds of years I would end up living, what was the rush? Life does find a way, and with how Rannoch and I would sometimes shred our bedroom, life might do exactly that. But as I had started to learn a new cycle—because being Vale Born apparently meant having a brutal period, what the fuck—I had learned when I needed to use the contraceptive tea sold in the dark recesses of the TerraIgni bazaar. There was no way to know if it actually worked properly with my physiology, but I was pretty sure that it did. Rannoch had found out about the tea, and wanted me to stop. That, and the fact that he wasn't listening to me about being ready was what led to the blowup.

If what I was doing was harmful, I may have been more willing to hear him out. But what it boiled down to was a man telling a woman what she should or shouldn't do with her body. In his opinion, I shouldn't take the tea, and I should get pregnant. That was a big slap in the face for me, the person I thought I knew suddenly had a side I didn't expect. And I hated to say it, one I didn't like. I was his mate, and I would listen to reason to an extent, but what he had been spouting before was not reasonable.

We had things to talk about, that was for sure. But at least I was ready to talk, unlike prior to my leaving. I loved him, and I was willing to do the work to mend this issue. Mend, but not cave to it.

He needed to hear me and respect my feelings and beliefs about it. I tightened my fist in Zephyrine's mane as I affirmed to myself that we would work this out.

"We are nearing the descent zone for TerraIgni," Dhiren's voice cut through from the lead position. I was glad I had just unintentionally tested my hold in her mane only moments before, he scared the crap out of me when he announced our impending arrival. It had been silent for hours. I might have jumped enough to fall off when he suddenly spoke up.

I looked around, trying to pick out anything of note for how Dhiren knew it was time. How they learned to judge the mist was beyond me, somehow Dhiren always knew when to exit. I supposed I would understand eventually, so far everything was identical in every sense of the word, no distinguishing landmarks could be seen from where we flew. Perhaps it was the time it took to travel to the various locations, if you did it enough times you might feel when it's time to drop below the cloud-like layer. I guess it didn't matter now, we were nearly home, and my reunion with Rannoch was rapidly approaching.

CHAPTER 8

We landed to little fanfare, our arrival was announced by the blasting of the fire basins held by the massive fifty-foot tall rock sculptures of Ignisfae warriors, which was expected, but other than that it was the quietest arrival I had seen so far. My heart thudded in my chest as I dismounted, I could feel the tug through the link that bound Rannoch and I together. My face fell after I hopped down, I could sense him, but I could also tell that he wasn't nearby.

He hadn't come to see me.

I looked to the entrance, to the craggy canyon-like opening that led from the equus valley back to the citadel. A form filled the passage, backlit by the soft shafted light. Rannoch may not have come to welcome us, but his father had.

King Ashwan strode toward our group, unaccompanied by Queen Deniza, I noticed. I smiled, he *was* making an effort to be more welcoming toward me. It was small gestures like this that were paving the way for a better relationship between us. He had even opted to greet us without his robe over his wrap clothing, he had been trying to be less formal around Rannoch and me, even going so far as to allow Rannoch to omit the title when addressing him. King Ashwan walked a little more than halfway to my position, when his eyes drifted past me and he stopped in his tracks.

Ohhh shit.

I had been so focused on Rannoch that I had completely forgotten about Eiulans, *and* conveniently forgotten I needed to tell King Ashwan about his murder. I looked over my shoulder as Dhirdre, Dhiren, and Felix guided Eiulans's covered body down from where he was strapped across the equus that had ferried him home. Attendants arrived with a stretcher, which they gently placed him on. They all stepped back with heads bowed as King Ashwan walked the remaining distance to our group.

He said nothing as he looked over each of us, the unasked question of who was under that wrapping must have resolved as he finally looked back at me.

I bowed my head, then lifted my eyes to meet his. "King Ashwan, I regret to tell you that Eiulans was killed during the diplomatic envoy."

He said nothing, but his entire face tightened and I sensed angry questions bubbling through his gaze. Who, how, when?

I took a steadying breath before I continued, "As far as we could surmise, the Vale Born known as Dashelle infiltrated the city. She murdered him, seemingly after interrogating him. I found him deceased in his room, quite a long time after it happened. The city was searched for her presence, but she could not be found."

He was still. Utterly still, and silent. I wished he would say something, even if he shouted it. The silence was worse than any yelling might have been. His eyes narrowed on me momentarily, it was a millisecond, but I saw it, and I felt it. It was a flash of doubt, of something not adding up for him. That nearly imperceptible facial expression speared my heart.

He didn't believe me either.

Everyone knew Eiulans and I didn't get along, and here was the perfect opportunity for me to get rid of him; away from his home city and with no assigned Ignisfae guards, Eiulans was a sitting duck. Right now the only one who could remotely corroborate for me was Dhirdre, she had arrived at Eiulans's room moments later. I had no blood on me, wasn't in any sort of heightened emotional state—other than the one I was in from finding a dead person. But when hard-pressed for details, what could she say for sure? She hadn't seen me find him. Further than that, it had happened well before then, who's to say I hadn't snuck over there when no one was looking, and then conveniently discovered him later.

My eyes widened. Could I have done it? There were things that had happened before to me, traumatic things which I only remembered parts of. And some things not at all. Nothing existed in my memory of the funeral for my dad and Maris. I remember sitting on my bed before it was supposed to start. But nothing of the actual service. I remember the wake, and the delicate madeleine cookies that were arranged on a porcelain platter. Weird little details like that, but other than that all I had was people telling me about it. Could I have gotten into an argument with Eiulans and lost control?

No. No, there was evidence of punctures from something made of stone, and if I had truly lost control to the point that my memory blacked it out, how could I possibly have reigned in the fire? I would have been a living candle. The room would have shown signs of that.

I realized my brain had completely gone on a tangent, wondering if I was in fact the murderer after all. I looked back at

King Ashwan, who eyed me with caution. "There are details to tell you, my Lord," I said, trying hard to keep strength in my voice, "evidence and what the nature of his death was."

"We can discuss this after you have recovered from your journey. And I expect you would like to reunite with Prince Rannoch before then. I trust you have much to talk to him about."

My resolve to maintain my composure finally broke. "Of course, Your Highness," I said shakily.

He eyed me. "Is there something wrong between you and my filio?"

I opened my mouth to answer, which was when I felt that familiar tremor, the one that resonated from deep within me, whenever Rannoch was near. A tight string inside struck a harmonic chord in my soul, pulling me to his presence.

"No, Faeder," Rannoch's voice answered from behind me. My knees went weak as he continued, "she and I have much to talk about, but nothing is wrong."

I turned to look at Rannoch, my emotions swelled as I took him in. Feelings crashed against each other in a surging tide, I felt the indicative burn of my skin as my hands heated, I knew it was mere moments before they would erupt. It wasn't always anger that caused them to do that, any heightened emotion could manifest it. And since I was experiencing roughly seventeen simultaneous reactions to his sudden arrival, it probably shouldn't have been a surprise.

"I will excuse myself," the king said. "But we will need to discuss what happened in further detail. I expect a full report. You, Dhirdre, and Dhiren will explain the circumstances. At *great* length."

I looked back to King Ashwan as he departed, an order of an unset future meeting was his only goodbye.

Rannoch took my hands in his, pushing the rising heat back down with an effortless use of his skill. It always took him so little, when for me it was practically boiling over and rearing for release. Easy to let go of, nearly impossible to reign in.

"I missed you, Lily."

I wanted to blurt out all my feelings, all the things I was previously mad about, all the things that had happened. And I was *still* mad, he had to have felt something of what was happening while I was away, and yet I could feel that absence. Thoughts tumbled through my head as I thought about how he never once checked in on me. Was he not worried?

"I felt you the whole time," he said. "I can feel your anger and disappointment with me right now, but in truth we stayed connected throughout your whole trip. You never let go of our link, and so it remained. I made my best effort to keep my distance so you could have your space, but I always knew more or less how you were faring. I know about Eiulans. I can't say I'm sad that he's dead, but the nature of it does concern me, and more concerning that Dashelle seemingly got so close."

"Well then why didn't you say something to me through the link? Anything! Instead it was radio silence from you." I threw down my hands, which sparked and sent plumes of flames to the ground, turning the sand in a small radius below them to glass. I didn't know if I was angry all over again, or glad that he actually had been making sure I was okay from the background. The last of what he said settled in my mind. "You … you know it was Dashelle? I mean, you don't suspect me?"

He shook his head, and my hands sputtered out. The air left me, as I realized how truly devastated I had been by the subtle, and sometimes not-so-subtle implications that it had been me that killed Eiulans.

"No, I don't suspect you. I think we were connected the whole time, though I admit it could have slipped here and there. And even if we weren't connected, I would not suspect you." He paused, his eyes searching my face. "Why did you leave, Lily? I understand you are mad and were frustrated by our disagreement, but you didn't give us the chance to finish working it out."

"You weren't listening to me, you were making assumptions about what I want for myself. I shouldn't have left, you're right. But in a way I felt like it was the only way I could be heard. I'm not ready to have children. I get that you're ready, but I'm not. And you weren't hearing that." I folded my arms, hoping that by tightening my limbs to my chest I could stop further spouts of fire. It was enough that we were arguing all over again, I didn't need the distraction of flames shooting out of me. For all my training I had done with his mother, I clearly still needed more guidance.

He stepped forward and pulled my hands free, holding each palm in his broad grasp. "I will listen, I am listening. I'm sorry you felt the only way to get me to hear you was to leave. Please, come back with me to our quarters. It's been agonizing being there without you. I've spent every rotation in the forge because I couldn't stand to be in our rooms while you were gone and angry with me."

It felt like my heart split in two, held together by raw, painful sinews. I squeezed my eyes shut and wrapped my arms around him at last. I had been so, *so* isolated. Or at least I had thought I was, cast out on a lonely island surrounded by treacherous seas. Somewhere far off, on the main land mass was everyone else, including Rannoch, who all thought it was perfectly reasonable and even expected that I would simply want to get pregnant immediately. Even Kerenza was surprised I didn't want that for myself right away. In every face I had seen while visiting the bazaar or walking the red stone streets of TerraIgni, I saw the expectation from the citizens. I couldn't even visit Yantz for a threadpainting lesson without encountering it. In all honesty, why wouldn't I want a break from all of that? And at the center of it all Rannoch had stood as an unaware beacon, reminding everyone of what I was not yet willing to do. I was tired of being mad, and I was tired of feeling alone. I couldn't say I was entirely wrong for leaving, because he hadn't been hearing me, and now he did.

I leaned back to look at him. "I want your promise that you will listen to me about my choices, Rannoch. I know and understand we will have growing pains as we learn to live together. But this issue is so critical for us, for me. I already knew what your choice was, but mine was that I wasn't ready yet. No one heard me, and because you also didn't, you then didn't back me up when others questioned it. That left me feeling abandoned in a way."

"I hear you now, I promise I do. I think I may have misunderstood. But I understand now." He pulled me further into his embrace again and rested his chin on my head. "Will you come with me back to our quarters?"

Gods, I really did miss him, too. I felt like it was the first time in far too long that blockades had been removed. The locks that had been slid in place by either me, him, or the circumstances now felt like they opened, allowing the familiar rush to churn straight through me. I didn't say yes aloud, or nod, I told him in our intimate way that no one else could hear. I spoke through the link, and said exactly what I wanted to do when we reached our rooms.

CHAPTER 9

His lips crashed into mine before the heavy embroidered fabric door shut to our rooms. I pushed it all the way closed and fumbled with the loop latch, trying to manage to pull it taut without tearing myself from him. Our kisses were frantic, heated, and untempered.

It had been too long, the gap between us finally lessened. While the link had never faded, the veritable ocean that separated us before because of our disagreement had now narrowed to something passable.

He backed through the front entryway, his hands never leaving my waist, the nape of my neck, my backside, until he scooped me up from behind and encouraged me to wrap my legs around him. It was as if now that we were unburdened and close, he couldn't bear to not be melded with me.

I tugged at the linteum wrapped around me, forcing the yards of fabric to release. I kicked the last of it off of my foot as we reached the bed.

Our bed.

He lowered me to the plush coverlet, his flame-filled pupils the brightest light in our suite. I loosened his asymmetrical wrap from his shoulder, then tugged at the ties on the waistband of his wrap pants. My breath caught as he brushed his mouth to my collar bone, sweeping his lips to the side to graze my bite marks. The bite marks he had given me when we swore our commitment to each other. His canines pricked at the visible scar, tempting me.

There's nothing quite like your first bite. It's really the only bite. After that it's the memory of it, toying with it and sending the playful reminder of everything that happened for that first true joining. Even the gentle nudge he was doing with his teeth was nearly enough to send me over the edge, past the precipice where I would fracture, then coalesce to shatter again.

And again.

Rannoch's lips moved lower, running his tongue over the crest of my tightening breasts. Lower still. I had been so untouched for so long, my thigh muscles drew in to shield myself a little as he licked gently at the apex between my legs.

Rannoch laid down on his side, pulling my legs over his hips, cradling me as he reached up to nibble the shell of my ear. I hadn't said anything, not out loud nor through the link, but he had sensed enough that I was not entirely ready for him.

I smiled, he was patient, and would take all the time needed so that it was perfect. He always did. His hand found my breast, with light circular motions he caressed, running his fingers down to my hips and brushing his thumb over the sensitive nub of my center. I swelled with each pass he made, each gloriously taunting pass.

Moving again to nestle his face between my legs, I was finally ready to let my knees drop open for him. He was careful, considerate, and slow. So wonderfully slow, sometimes brushing with a soft, supple tongue, sometimes lightly sucking.

He would wait when it was clear I was becoming too heated,

too virile, my fiery hands gripping our sheets, before continuing to taunt my now begging flesh.

I need you now, here.

I pulled him to rise to meet me, desperate to get him closer. I wanted his lips on mine while he was inside me. I wanted to feel his solid size, making me stretch to the point just before pain. I wanted to share breath as I could see the effect I had on him, just as he could see the same for me. To breathe in unison until the waves of release crashed at last. I didn't want my undoing to happen any other way.

His eyes locked with mine as our breath stilled. I was molten for him with slick heat, aching for him to finally be as close as we could be, the ultimate joining.

It was just like the first time, when he entered, every inch was agonizingly beautiful. I gripped his back and guided him further, until he was seated all the way. I arched my back, catching his lips with mine as we waited, holding fast to the moment.

Rannoch pressed in, and every nerve in my body unfurled in cascading pulses, sending a surge through me so strong I cried out. It only took one motion for him to evoke that sensation, and yet he kept going. It released again, my eyes squeezing shut as, for a moment, it became too much. His breath quickened, and his shoulders tensed the way they always did when I could tell he was trying to hold on longer.

I leaned forward and licked the ridge of his piked ear, the very thing I knew that would send a shiver straight through him, the part that if I touched I'd better be damn ready for the absolute wrecking he'd want to unleash.

Rannoch's whole body hardened and his corded muscles in

his forearms flexed as he pulled powerful strokes, letting out an unbridled sound as he came.

His arms almost immediately wrapped around me, holding me tight as we both shuddered.

Even with Rannoch sleeping by my side, my dreams were unsettling. I dreamt of the Maeder Tree, she wanted something from me, but I couldn't tell what. Her words sounded garbled and indistinct. I shook it off and got out of bed, leaving Rannoch asleep in the covers.

I decided to make us both capuli in our kitchen. In truth we didn't need a space to make our own food, we could always go to the banquet hall. But sometimes it was a comfort being able to cook together or make a "cup of hot" as I liked to call it. I arranged a plate with small rolls I had quickly warmed with my own fire, spread with a delectable percala fruit jelly I had become obsessed with. It was somewhere between a strawberry and citrus flavor, but grew on a dry tree in small bunches and had to be made into preserves to be able to enjoy. Eating them freshly picked would result in a bitter, chalky mess. But with a little time and boiling, it became sweet and flavorful. I took a bite and closed my eyes.

I had missed my home with Rannoch, missed him, and the things I held dear in what was now my safe space. I tightened the belt on my plush robe, made from the fabric I wove with Kerenza and Rannoch from my first Praetexia, the revered Ignisfae holiday when all citizens weave together. Rannoch had the cloth put through an extra process afterward which made it luxuriant and soft, then ordered a custom-sewn robe, matching blanket and pillow for me to lounge with while I read on our balcony. Reading the Fae language was slow going, but I had been making progress with learning it and even found some novels I was starting to understand. There were a lot of things I had been learning, strange customs such as never saying thank you to any Fae, they found it "lessened the sincerity of the generosity." But the biggest learning curve had been living with Rannoch.

One hundred and sixty-five cycles meant a long time to become set in your ways. And it's not like he was the only one who was difficult, I knew I was, too. Mundane things got under each of our skins: how long the capuli cups sat unwashed, whether the bed was made, when I left my clothes on the floor. He didn't like having an attendant clean up after us often, and I agreed with that whole-heartedly. Tanzara only rarely brought in her crew to deep clean. They were all things that could be adjusted to, it was when there were bigger issues that things could get heated, the small things added to the pile when there was a more glaring upset.

Rannoch sauntered out of the bedroom, wearing his favorite loose pants, the low slung waistband tied off with one measly thin string. I handed him his capuli, thinking about those pants, how they showed off his bare abs, and the muscular line in them Josie would have pointed out as his "cum gutter." She really was the worst, always saying the naughtiest shit to make me turn red and then I'd do everything in my power not to explode in nervous laughter. Gods I missed her.

"What is it?" he asked as he sipped. His muscles gleamed in

the early light.

"Oh, just thinking about things, too many things, as usual." I smiled as I took a sip to keep myself from giggling, or ogling. I set my earthenware cup down. "I think we need to go back to the bedroom."

We didn't even make it to the doorway before I yanked that silly little string that held up his pants.

Octobo ventured out of his little home nestled in the wall of the balcony, when I sat down to lounge in my favorite chair. He kneaded his furry paws on the floor as I pet his head. I had to admit I'd grown to love the funny spider. It took some time, but I had warmed up to his persistence. Rannoch had told me, when I first met his friend, that Octobo was "very respectful," which I had scoffed at. But I found it to be true. He never climbed up on me, because that would be too much, and certain spaces that he realized were mine he steered clear of. He wouldn't jump up on my chair, even if I wasn't there, and the aranea, as they were called, never got into our bed. I had made the rules when I first met him, and he respected them from the beginning. I smiled as he nudged my hand a bit more. Reaching over to the small table nearby, I picked up my water glass then carefully poured a small drop on his head. He danced around, showing off his water hat as I laughed.

The succulents and potted citrus trees were verdant and overflowing. Overlooking the rugged, red rock canyon walls of northwest TerraIgni, there was nothing that inhabited the canyon face across from us, every balcony on the outward side of the fortress had a broad sweeping view of the jagged, steep wall.

Octobo scuttled over to Rannoch to greet him as he came out of the living area. He brought a fresh cup of capuli and handed it to me.

Specifically skipping the "thank you," as I had learned to do, I accepted it and said thank you with my eyes. His eyes twinkled at me in return, and I felt a pulse through the link between us. The sensation of relief came in waves, I thought there was a part of him that worried I would stay away a lot longer. He pored over my face, then sat down on the lounge chair edge next to me, his expression shifting to a more serious one. "What is it?" I asked. "I can feel a question burning." And I could feel that the question that was nagging in his mind was one that might upset me. I sighed and set the cup down, waiting.

"It's just that … I know this is not going to be a welcome possibility, but, I'm wondering how it was probable Dashelle made it all the way to Limnaer, killed Eiulans, and then simply left."

My blood went cold. He *did* doubt what I had said happened after all. I felt like such a fool, a stultus—to use their phrasing of it—to think that he had believed me.

"No, it's not what you think, though you still won't like it," he rushed to say. "I'm wondering, could it have been Felix? You said the words were written in your language. He reads and writes those letters, too, does he not?"

I moved my body as far back as I could on my chair, regretting the details I had told him on our walk back to our shared space. It *couldn't* have been Felix. For one, what was written would have no context for him. It simply wouldn't line up. And then there was the residue of rough stone weapons. He had no power over stone, but Dashelle did.

"You know he hated Eiulans, too. Eiulans made no effort to refrain from remarks about Felix and Dhiren's relationship," he offered.

"Yeah, well, Eiulans was a fucking bastard. He had a lot of people who didn't like him. That doesn't mean Felix killed him. He was training in the Caeli-Aedis temple for a long time, I don't even know when he would have had the chance."

I gulped as it started to dawn on me, he did have time. When we had separated for him to go to the training hall, and a few times before that. It was possible, timing-wise. Character-wise, no. Felix was far too moral to do something so outright violent, even if he didn't like how Eiulans treated him. And then of course the fact that he lacked powers over stone apparently used to kill Eiulans ...

Stone.

I remembered with dread that some of the weapons in the training hall were made of stone. I had even asked about them. It was because wood can have tiny amounts of air in them, enough that a trained Caelifae can push them to their will to some degree, and the stone weapons were heavier so they built muscle quicker. Wood weapons were introduced later, when a warrior had advanced to the needed level. And finally steel. Felix had been training with stone weapons.

I replayed the moment I told Felix about Eiulans, unless he had seriously worked on his meager acting skills, he had shown true shock at the time. And he had asked me if I had done it. If he had killed him, there was no way he would implicate me in his place.

"I can feel it, Lily. I can sense you thinking about the possibility."

"That's not fair. Don't read me through our link like that. I *considered* it, because you're right, it's a good point about the message in English. But then I started to go over each detail and imagine Felix as the killer. While there is the slight possibility, I truly don't think he did it. First of all, the message doesn't make sense if it was written by him. What words would he have swiped into the wall? Surely something else. The way he was shocked when I told him about the murder, the way he questioned me. If he *had* done it, he would never in a million years—cycles, whatever—want me to take the fall for it. In fact I think it would be the other way around. If I were implicated, he might even go so far as to falsely confess so that I didn't take the blame."

He looked thoughtful, then he looked sympathetic. And it was not a welcome look. It was one that said "Poor Lily, so easily fooled." Maybe I was being reactive, and assuming thoughts that he wasn't thinking. I specifically did not tug on the link to find out for sure. I couldn't chastise him for doing it, then turn around and use the link like that myself.

"My sweet, I know you want to give the benefit of … what is that phrase you say?"

I gulped, I didn't want to finish the phrase for him. My heart sank as I realized my intuition of that facial expression may have been correct.

"I think you want to think the best of your brother and not allow yourself to face the possible facts of what he might be capable of."

I stood quickly, not wanting to hear another word about this. He was wrong, I had actually considered it, and quickly weighed the facts in my mind. I opened my mouth to snap at him, but tempered myself and balled my fists to prevent any fire from leaping out. "I think you need to consider the fact that I have known Felix my whole life, and you are still getting to know him. In the interest of not damaging the relationship you are still *building* with him, I'm going to forget you said that. I need to take a break from this, I'm mad right now, though it should be obvious. Before you freak out, I'm taking a break from this conversation. I'm telling you because I know I promised to stay, but sometimes people need a break. I'll be back later. I'm going to visit Kerenza."

I didn't wait for his response as I left our residence.

CHAPTER 10

I stormed down the halls, muttering to myself as I recounted the interaction. Maybe he thought he was being logical. And, sure, consider all the facts and don't eliminate anyone until there's proof to show it *wasn't* them. But if Felix was being considered, then I had to be as well. Shit, maybe it could have even been Ser'Ti or an operative of his. He made no effort to hide that he hated Eiulans. With the news that came to light about Don'Li, how much Ser'Ti had been affected by that disgrace and how Eiulans was the one behind spurring the rumors more, it was fair to say that Ser'Ti also had motive. He could have exacted his revenge. But, there was no way in hell I could even pursue that without evidence beyond a reasonable doubt. Who knew if there was such a thing as diplomatic immunity in this crazy world, but I had to assume that was the case. You don't go accusing a royal of murder. Plus, there was the matter of the words written in English, which to my knowledge he didn't know.

Perhaps I was further upset that Dashelle had us chasing our tails and she hadn't even been seen. My breath quickened thinking about her. I hated to admit it, but I was terrified of her. I may have beaten her before, but then she went so far as to go back to the human realm and destroy my former home. I stopped walking in the middle of the hall. She was unpredictable, malicious, and probably driven mad by having the power of four Vale Born dammed up inside of her. Of course the last fact was her own doing, *and* she wanted more. Worse still was that one of those Vale Born was Josie, bound up within a madwoman. What if Josie was somehow still conscious while her power was used to do evil? If it was psychological warfare Dashelle intended to commit, she had achieved it. I didn't know what she would do next, or even if she was involved in this murder.

The hallway stretched before me and distorted, making me doubt my sanity. Was this all her doing? I didn't know left from right, or who to trust now. I clenched my fists. Kerenza, hopefully she could provide some guidance.

I arrived at her room to the sound of scuffling and laughing behind the heavy fabric door. I knocked on the wall several times. The door folded back finally, revealing a partially dressed female with her hair a mess and still giggling.

"Greetings, Lily. I gather you have come to visit Kerenza." She could barely get her words out without slurring, the whole room smelled of wine. After a moment, I recognized her. "Hello, Zia. I didn't realize you'd be here. Uh, sorry to interrupt." I glanced around, hearing water splashes from the bathroom.

She motioned for me to come in. I tried not to show the surprise on my face at seeing Kerenza's place so disheveled. There were empty glasses knocked over and clothes scattered about. It looked like Kerenza had not had the place cleaned in awhile.

"Would you like to sit down? Kerenza should be out soon." Zia grabbed a linteum that had been tossed carelessly over the back of a chair, then tied it on as she quickly headed toward the door. She bowed her head in a subtle nod to me, then left.

Kerenza came sauntering out a moment later. "Lily! What a nice surprise."

I blinked, the vapor coming off of her was enough to get me high. "Wow, that's strong." I fanned the air. "What have you been drinking?"

"Vocafortis. After the vinirubrum ran out. Want some?" She picked up a carafe of clear liquid and poured herself some more into a dirty glass. It had a small amount of old vinirubrum in it, discoloring the clear alcohol to a murky pink. She tipped the bottle at me in a silent question.

"Kind of early isn't it? I'm okay, I don't want any."

She shrugged and flopped down on the settee to nurse her drink. "I thought you liked drinking."

I tried not to visibly cringe at the off-putting color in her cup. "I do sometimes. It's just too early for me right now, and … do you want me to get you a clean glass?"

She shook her head. "It tastes about the same, I do not really care."

I looked around again. "Where's Emblyn?"

She stared down at her cup as she swirled it. "With my maeder. She has been taking care of her for a while."

I watched her for a moment, it felt like there was something in that statement, something that weighed heavily on her. I decided to not push it, and changed the subject. "So, Zia?"

"Zia!" Kerenza exclaimed as she immediately perked up, suddenly seeming far less drunk. "We recently reconnected. I will say, she has been the one bright spot in my life of late. I did not remember you had met her before. She and I … we were together, long before I was mated to Kenneder. We had decided to go our separate ways back then, but always remained amicable. We have been spending many rotations together lately."

"I'm happy for you. You deserve to be with someone that makes you smile."

She beamed for a moment, but then her face fell. She threw back the remainder of the contents in her glass in one gulp. She barely reacted to what must have burned the shit out of her throat. "So, you seem like you have something to tell me."

I nodded. "Right, I almost forgot." How the fuck could I almost forget? I shook my head and continued. "Something happened on the trip to Limnaer. Eiulans was murdered."

She had been starting to pour herself more, when she almost dropped the bottle at the news I had unloaded. "Dead? How? Who killed him?"

"There's some mystery to that, I had my immediate suspicions that it was Dashelle who did it, but it's unclear who killed him. From my perspective I still believe it was her, but others have their doubts as it would be so unlikely she would be able to even get to Limnaer. And then she wasn't seen by anyone after that. Because there's nothing else evidence-wise to place her at the scene, it's been difficult for me to prove."

"So, what makes you think it's her?"

I explained all I could, the letters in blood on the wall, what was written, the manner of his death.

She nodded as she listened. "So, who are the other suspects then?"

"Well that's where it gets dicey. Frankly, it could have been any one of us. Rannoch suggested it was Felix, which really pissed me off, but I kind of get it. The thing is—"

"Everyone hated Eiulans," she finished my sentence as she watched me carefully. "Being the Lesser Culus and all. He earned that nickname."

I half-smiled. As distraught as I was, I did appreciate that she always called Eiulans the Fae equivalent of an asshole. For as much as I agreed with the ideal of never speaking ill of the dead, Eiulans was one of the few who didn't deserve that honor. "Even Ser'Ti had a good reason to kill him. *I* could have done it. Dhiren could have. There are certain things which eliminate others from being considered a suspect, mainly the words written in English and what was said. If it was Felix, why would he write that? Or me for that matter. I don't know. I don't have an answer. It's all just," I let out an exasperated sound, "it's all a cluster fuck!"

She smirked. "Sounds like it. Well, big picture, Eiulans is gone. Whoever did it did us a favor, as dark as that truth is. He was nothing but trouble for all of us, except perhaps my faeder. I imagine he will be angry."

"Yeah, he knows already. I saw him briefly. He demanded answers, but wanted them later. I think he didn't want anyone seeing him react. At some point I'm going to have to go before him. Who knows how that will go. Things had been better with him before this, but … well we didn't need this hurdle. I would have much rather found a way to not hate Eiulans, to get on better terms and maybe stay out of each other's ways. It was perhaps foolish to hope that, or baseless optimism at the very least. This whole event is making me question everything. Sorry to unload, I needed someone to listen."

Kerenza nodded. "Glad to." She looked at the bottle, reaching for it again. "Are you sure you will not have any? Join me for a while, we can talk more."

"None for me now. It … uhhh … well it seems like you've been drinking a lot lately. Is everything okay?"

She didn't say anything, poured more, then didn't bother recorking it.

"If there's something you want to talk about, I'm here. Now or another time. Whatever you need, I'm here for you, " I said.

"I just want to drink. Nothing more."

"Okay, it's just a bit concerning. Where I'm from this can be a real problem, and can even damage your body terribly if you do it too much. It's addictive and can be hard to quit."

"If that happens perhaps I will just go to the Midgard Well, toss myself in and let it heal me." She grinned.

"So your big plan if you hurt yourself with this is to fly your equus for rotations on end to get to the Well? You, the most highly skilled female warrior in TerraIgni would put yourself in the position of *needing* to go so far to undo what this might be doing to you. Distance aside, there are real risks of running into enemies. Dashelle. Umorfae. That witch woman, the Pythonissamul. I could keep going. Continuing to drink like this is worth all that?"

"Maybe. Or you could heal me, if you are so worried about it. Not like you are so perfect. You drink a lot sometimes, too."

"I do sometimes. I'm not perfect by any stretch, I don't claim to be and I'm not trying to … look I'm worried about you right now." I paused, debating about how to proceed. "Drinking for fun is one thing, but this doesn't feel like it's for fun. I don't mean to judge. Maybe I shouldn't have said anything, but would that have been the right thing to do? I don't know. I just want you to know I'm here for you."

"Well, I am going to continue talking to my friend vocafortis here, so if you do not mind," she motioned to the door.

I opened my mouth to say something. I was stunned into silence. It all felt like a set up for an "Am I the Asshole" self-questioning situation. If I had to ask, maybe I *was* the asshole. I headed to the door. I could accept that I was. I said the uncomfortable, I said what I felt. Maybe I was a dick for it, but would I be a worse person for not saying anything? She had always been one to indulge, but this was beyond that. I could feel she was masking something, numbing something. She had been through hell when she lost Kenneder, and under constant stress and worry when Emblyn was taken. Perhaps she needed to hide from her feelings. I could certainly relate to that. I had hidden many times, it was still a pattern I fell to when things were difficult.

I let myself out of her quarters without another word. Dismayed, worried, and disappointed, I left the inner keep of the fortress to the outer ring where the bazaar was. There was at least one more person I hoped to find who might give me some perspective.

CHAPTER 11

The familiar smells of barbecued, skewered meat and citrus permeated the air as I walked along the bustling cobblestone street of the TerraIgni bazaar. Woven awnings sprawled over the wide walkways. The streets were expansive enough for carts or vehicles, yet everyone walked wherever they went. The warm day kissed my skin with bright indirect light, baking the area in a rich earthy hue. People stopped and stared, some bowed in greeting. I realized it was probably the first time many of them were seeing me unaccompanied. I hadn't even thought about it as I made my way. Now that I noticed how many paused to watch, I felt bare and obvious. I did my best to smile, but in reality I wanted to escape back to my quarters. There were too many; too many eyes and individuals focused solely on me.

I arrived at the threadpainting booth. Opulent textural images covered the walls, including a massive piece at the back that was hidden by a draped canvas. The rear end of someone swayed back and forth as they were bent over, rummaging through stacks of finished landscapes. A distinctive male voice hummed a made-up tune while his long, brightly colored woven vest made of thick yarns brushed the ground. After finding what he sought amid the soft paintings, he stood and held a blank canvas in his rough hands.

"Lily, my filia!" Yantz's face lit up as he noticed me. "I had been wondering when you would be back. I was just about to start a new piece, sit down and start one with me! You can tell me of your adventure to Limnaer." He turned back to all the paintings stacked behind him, checking the canvas covering the largest one.

"I was hoping to talk, not work with thread today."

He assessed me with a look, his glance keen and quick, but I could feel he gleaned a great deal in an instant. "Some threadpainting will do you good. I imagine you saw some splendid sights while visiting the Caelifae, why not put your ideas down? It may help to order your thoughts. We can work and talk."

I relented. Making progress with thread was usually his price for my curiosity or my need for his guidance. He loved to be inspired by the world around him, and sometimes it meant experiencing it through my eyes. To him it was a fair trade, and he always said his excitement about the world was what kept him in it, kept that sprig of youthfulness growing even if his body looked aged. Being the oldest living Fae known, he had some tricks up his sleeves to keep the Fading at bay. "Okay," I smiled, "I did see some pretty rad views from way up there."

"Rad," he repeated with a quirk of his lips, "I never tire of your speech, my filia!"

I grinned as I started picking out thread; shades of aqua, some green, and a small amount of variegated grays. I selected a small canvas, something I could possibly finish in one long sitting. Yantz always preferred the larger formats, images that took many rotations to complete. He liked that I worked smaller, yet another reason to have me work by his side, he had told me before he learned from my knack of taking on what I could complete. I figured I defaulted to smaller because it was less intimidating, less of a blank canvas staring at me. He always had a way of making my choices sound like they were out of good sense rather than reasons of more negative connotation. I could learn from his way of thinking and be a bit gentler with myself.

I drew the first thread through, leaving the unseen tail a "decate long", a length of about an inch as Yantaz always advised. It took me some time to get a feel for the Fae measurement system, but now it was easy and second-nature. I could go based on feel alone after practice. Part of me still wanted to knot the end and pull the thread all the way through, like my grandmother had taught me when I was a child, but Yantz insisted that leaving the tails on the back created a work of art all its own. The owner could display it front or back, depending on their mood.

I thought about all the views from the great city in the clouds, the horizontal spires that spiked outward in a ring around the entire perimeter, the limitless expanse that Ser'Ti's great library looked over, the stunning arching architecture of the Caeli-Aedis. Any one of them would have been good choices to create a threadpainting of. I started working without thinking, letting the thread and my subconscious guide me.

"I think you would be interested to meet the new leader of Limnaer, Prince Ser'Ti Zan Cireclos."

"Oh?" he answered absently, already absorbed in a new work of art.

I pulled through the blend of gray, working upward on the canvas. "I told him a bit about you. He's very interested in inventions. He has ideas, or rather, he's looking for those with ideas so that he can fund them. I actually think you would like him, once you get past his reactive nature."

"Reactive? Now who do I know like that?" He stopped working for a moment to look over his shoulder at me with a big grin on his face.

"Very funny." I worked through the rest of the gray on my needle, then added more. "In all honesty he seems different from most Fae that I've met, somehow forward thinking and planning for progress. He was especially interested in the Starcrest telescope." The mention of the incredible mist-piercer made my heart twang, I suddenly missed Rannoch. He had taken me there so I could feel a connection to my home still, to look at the stars and the moon. It was the only way to see through the mist in Alternis.

"Well I do not want to go about remaking Starcrest viewing scopes for neighboring dignitaries. That does not interest me."

"I know and understand that. He's thinking of other inventions, whatever you can dream up. Sounded like a great way to have access to whatever materials you wanted in order to create things." I didn't look at him as I continued embroidering, adding more layers.

"Do you want me to go?"

"Not really. Here's the truth: I had promised him I would mention it to you. If anyone can invent things with what we have access to here in Alternis, it's you. I wanted to talk to him about Don'Li, and to get more information about his history. It was my trade in a way, my peace offering. I said I would tell you about the possibility of going there to tinker, but the decision is yours. I did think you would be interested, which was the other reason I brought you up."

"Hmm, it does sound somewhat appealing. I have always wanted to go to Limnaer."

"Then there you go, you have an open invitation. There is, however, something else I wanted to talk to you about."

Making sure no one could overhear, I proceeded to tell him about Eiulans's murder and the subsequent investigation, which I was weirdly heading up even though I realized technically I could be the culprit. And the fact that I was biased as hell because my brother was also a suspect. It was all sorts of messy and I needed someone else not involved to weigh in.

Yantz mulled everything over for a few minutes, even stopped working to think things through. "It sounds to me that however unlikely, Dashelle cannot be excluded as the perpetrator."

"Right, that's what I thought, too. It's crazy, but I don't see how we can just say she wasn't there simply because it's hard for her to get to Limnaer."

"But," he continued, "unfortunately, I have to say that, given the facts, you cannot be excluded either."

My blood turned absolutely frigid. Any semblance of fire within me sputtered out. I knew that I had unrealistically hoped that Yantz would simply say "Of course it was Dashelle, that bitch!" But I didn't think he would outright consider me as possibly being the one who had done this.

"You have mentioned to me that you have had lapses in memory in the past," he added gently.

I wanted to cry. Or scream. Maybe run away. It was all true, I had and had told him about it. It wasn't impossible that I had done it and I had far more access than Dashelle did, who was, for lack of a better term, the lone gunman in this situation. How could she have gotten there? I couldn't manage any words as I sat there staring off into the crowded street.

"I do not know anything, my filia. All I can do is listen and try to be objective. I know you to be good. Do I think you are capable of such a bloodthirsty act? No, I do not. I do, however, know how unkind Eiulans was, and how he derived pleasure from inflicting emotional pain. He was a terrible Ignisfae, one that somehow rose in the ranks. I think it is possible he tortured you with words to the point that something could have happened."

I crushed my eyes shut, I couldn't bear the thought that Yantz could think I might have done it. I had admitted it to myself I could have, and even admitted it to Rannoch and Kerenza as well, but hearing the words out of Yantz's mouth somehow stung so much more. I turned back to my canvas, and started angrily stitching. I wanted peace from this situation. I knew we needed answers, and I knew it wasn't for some altruistic reason. I didn't need to solve Eiulans's murder for him, for justice for him. I needed to solve it for myself.

A hand to my shoulder made me jump, as I realized I had lost myself to the threadpainting.

"Looks like you have nearly finished, my filia."

"I suppose. I feel like I haven't even thought about what I was doing." My mind had rambled while I worked, oscillating between every emotion imaginable. By the end, I was spent, but at least had delved into facing myself a bit more. I didn't think I killed Eiulans, but now I was that much more resolved that I needed to prove it. They needed to know just how ruthless Dashelle could be. I already knew, but maybe the Ignisfae didn't. They had been largely separated and offset from the terrible things she had done. There had been Ignisfae losses during the final battle with her, and the imprisonment of their children by the Umorfae separatists had been a result of her deal with Opius. But other than that, they didn't grasp the depth of her capabilities.

"This doesn't look like Limnaer," Yantz commented as he studied at my work.

I looked at my canvas finally, then was startled to realize what I had spent my time creating. "Oh, I didn't know ... how did I do that?"

"You must have really submitted to the will of the thread. It is a beautiful version of the Maeder Tree."

I had dreamt of the Maeder Tree, she had been asking me to do something, trying to send a message, but I couldn't hear her. Now I had unknowingly recreated her image. As I looked at it, it almost felt like she did have a message for me and it wasn't just a dream.

"It is magna work, perhaps your best so far." He lifted it up, inspecting each stitch. "We should give it a place of honor."

I smiled a little, then suddenly I missed Rannoch terribly. I was reminded of the first time he had introduced me to Yantz, the first time I tried threadpainting. Maybe it was the self-reflection I had done while I worked, maybe it was the time I gave myself after we last spoke. I hurriedly thanked Yantz for his time and guidance, then rushed back home to find my mate.

CHAPTER 12

I went to push open our woven door, only to find it already slightly ajar. I paused, listening for a moment. Rustling sounds from inside made me uneasy, I could feel it wasn't Rannoch, that much I knew. I cautiously opened it, peering in to see if I could see anything. A moment later a face appeared out of my bedroom hallway.

"Lily!"

I gasped and backed up a step. "Tanzara, you scared the shit out of me!"

"Oh, I am sorry, I thought you knew I would be here. Rannoch had asked me to come and see that everything was clean and in order."

I was still catching my breath a bit, realizing the whole situation in Limnaer had left me hypervigilant. Dashelle had—supposedly—reached what should have been unreachable. All she would need was the power of one Vale Born who had the gift of fire. With that Dashelle would be able to cross the Hinterdunes. Who's to say there wasn't one she had managed to find and kill? Which would mean TerraIgni wasn't as safe as we all assumed. There were more tears to the human world, two that I knew of for sure, probably more. Someone unexpected could slip through at any point. Unexpected and *unsuspecting*, if such a person crossed paths with Dashelle they would likely have no idea how deranged she was.

"Lily?"

"Yes, I'm sorry, I'm okay. I was just startled, that's all. It's good to see you, Tanzara," I managed at last. "Is Rannoch here?" I already knew the answer, I couldn't sense him nearby through the link.

"He was leaving as I arrived a quarter rotation ago. He was going to the forge."

The forge. I had only heard about it. He had yet to show it to me. I decided I would go and find him. I had been curious about where he went to release his frustrations, and where he created such remarkable things. Weapons, shields, items for the home such as bowls or helpful things for the Ignisfae, whatever Rannoch made at the forge was always crafted with the utmost care and precision. My own sword was made by Rannoch, a selwaer which had once belonged to Kenneder, Kerenza's mate. I remembered how I had marveled at the careful details and etchings on it when I first saw it, and the precise balance of it. Rannoch was a true master, and I had never seen where or how he did it.

I quickly said my goodbyes then left. As glad as I was to see Tanzara, I didn't want to hang around and chat.

After making my way through the fortress center to the southern outskirts and crossing the guarded boundary, I headed across the sandy expanse toward the smoking cliffside forge. The stream of smoke could always be seen emanating from it if you stood on one of the southern-facing terraces, and the high heat distorted the atmosphere surrounding the rocky entrance.

I walked into the arched entryway, taller than it looked from a distance. There was no one in sight, but I could hear the pounding of hammers and the whooshing air from some sort of great bellows. Along with the pounding, there was an extra layer of sound, like rhythmic drum beats and chants. I wound through the serpentine hallway, the rough natural walls reminded me of the passage to the equus valley that lay to the east of the fortress. These hallways however, were more twisted, sometimes doubling back in hairpin turns. Fortunately there seemed to be only one route for the entrance, so I had little chance of getting lost on my way in. A bright red glow crept from around the corner of an end wall up ahead, and a blast of heat seeped from it as well. I cleared the last corner and was struck by a barrier of sizzling dry heat. My hair blew back from the arid blast, as the enormity and depth of the forge left me in awe.

It was dozens of levels tall, most of them subterranean, with irregular arched openings dotted sporadically across each section. The large hollowed out recesses were rooms in which scattered Ignisfae worked. Flows of molten ore poured in streams from spouts, like vividly glowing treacherous falls. Each swing and subsequent clang of hammers was followed by a drone of voices, it reminded me of their favorite holiday, Praetexia, when we had chanted and woven the iconic Ignisfae fabric. Every inaudible word had moved us through the work, it all became a fluid rhythm. This chant—while it equaled the flow of Praetexia—carried a virility and strength that somehow pulsed through the whole forge. The entire place felt alive with power. It called to the strength of the flame welling inside me.

A fireball erupted from below, blasting upward in a churning plume. I covered my face with my bent arm and staggered back a step, waiting for the heat to subside before I trusted lowering it again. My skin was starting to bead up with sweat from the intensity. As the heat dissipated, I hazarded peering over the edge to see where it had come from. Rannoch locked eyes with me from below. For a split second I worried he wouldn't have liked that I showed up unannounced to the forge, but I quickly felt a euphoric tremor through our link.

He wasn't just happy I had come to the forge, he was ecstatic. My heart leapt at seeing him.

Without tearing his eyes from mine, he set down the hammer he had been swinging. Rannoch stepped forward to the ledge over the fire-filled lake at the center of the forge and put his hand out, scooping up something unseen from below. A rush of liquid flame and lava pushed a narrow platform up, which he jumped onto, then he scooped again to call another. My jaw dropped as I watched him climb a staircase of rock and molten ore toward me. I had never seen an Ignisfae display such power before. Fire was an integral, natural part of their lives, usually it would be demonstrated in a more subtle nudge or pull. Mainly an aid for mundane tasks, it was used as an extension of a gesture resulting in a plume of fire, the way I had grown accustomed to seeing their skill used was apparently a mere inkling of its potential. In battle I had watched him and Kerenza use considerable force with their gift, but this, this was a demonstration of how much control he had over what was otherwise dangerous and unruly. Like a chaotic stallion broken to the will of its master, the lava obeyed his every command. The air felt electric around him as he ascended the stairs to me.

Rannoch was laser-focused, his body shifted and moved while he climbed, though his head remained perfectly still as he kept his sights on me. He hopped off the last stair, his gaze never once leaving mine.

Unsaid words hung between us for a moment, but I didn't want to talk. I was over anything he had said and I didn't have the need to resolve prior conversations. Seeing him, being near him again, it was enough to light the fires that burned within me. My breath quickened as I looked at him, his skin glinted in the warm light. Now that I was almost close enough to touch him, any terse words that had ever been were swept away like they were never uttered. It was only me and him, and the ever-thickening cord between us that called insistently to be pulled tighter, closer.

Another round of chanting from the background caught my attention. I realized how many—seen and unseen—Ignisfae might be nearby.

"They won't hear us," he said, taking another step toward me. His pupils sparked with flames as he got closer, his tall, piked ears twitching. "There is a secluded room nearby, they wouldn't see us, either."

"Reading me through the link again?" I asked with a playful smirk.

"I don't need to use our link to know what you want right now."

My whole body flushed at those words. My reaction caused the air to twang like a tuning fork, and he moved as fast as lightning.

I didn't even see him close the distance between us. His arms surrounded me in an instant, one hand reaching lower, tugging my leg up from behind my knee. It always stunned me when he moved that fast, faster than I could blink. I gasped as he trailed his nose along my jawline. The mating bite in the nook of my clavicle ached, demanding him to run his lips over it. He seemed to sense it, as he slid his teeth along it, pricking the healed wound lightly with his canines. Heat flared to life in my core, the throb at the apex of my legs grew stronger as he nudged against me.

His grip on my bent knee tightened, and his other arm around my waist pulled me closer and lifted me up slightly. I felt the wind blow my hair forward for a moment as my toes dragged on the ground. The cavern blurred in horizontal lines, and a glowing haze rushed past.

My back pressed up against a stone surface which hadn't been nearby before. I could feel we were now in an enclosed space. I only wanted to look at Rannoch. His gaze was locked with mine as he pushed further into me. I hiked up my linteum, not bothering with untying it. He didn't wait, and he didn't ask. There was no need to. I was already demanding as I reached down to guide him in. He filled me completely as he sheathed himself. One of his hands was between my shoulder blades to protect me from the rough surface he hoisted me against, the other pulled my leg higher, opening my hips more.

Any previous thoughts or worries fled my mind. Whatever I might have been thinking about was blasted away by Rannoch's closeness, by his grip, by his sheer power as he flexed into me. I curved around him, calling him in deeper, harder, faster. All his corded muscles held me in place as he pinned and unpinned me in rapid succession. I met him stroke for stroke, mirroring our motion. The only sounds were those of our shared, quickened breaths, the guttural rumbles from deep within his chest, and the building moans from me. The whole world narrowed to the two of us, our bond tightened as we rode the swelling wave, the crescendo ramping to a fever pitch.

I clenched hard against him and unleashed a moan as I exploded off the precipice we had reached, the surge spilling across every nerve as it emanated outward from my center. I felt it all the way down to the tips of my toes, which curled as Rannoch took another long plunge.

I was nearly quivering, but he didn't stop. He hardened further inside me, my heartbeat pounding as he descended to the hilt again.

As he withdrew slightly, I finished backing him out, then flipped around to face the wall. His hands found their way to my hips, as he guided me back onto his massive length. He pumped several times, angling himself into me deeper. One of his strong, broad palms reached up, cupping my breast.

It was his undoing. A wild sound escaped his mouth as he came, his fingers clutching my hip. He fell forward, his other hand releasing my exposed fullness to plant against the wall for support. A single sob worked its way out of me, the enormity of the pressures that had been wearing upon me finally caused me to crack. The release we shared opened that crack a little more, allowing it to unfold.

It quickly turned to a satiated, settled exhale as we attempted to catch our breath. He rested his cheek on my back, his hair trailing down my skin as we soaked in the afterglow. As my own emotional rupture had split more, the divide between us healed completely. The issues had been there, but they now lay bonded below layers of our solidified link like they had been hammered in the forge we reunited in.

We stayed joined, our bodies rested against that warm rock wall, listening to each other. His mind fed me snippets, thoughts of pleasure and relief. Relief at feeling melded back together again, at being able to conquer whatever was in our path because we had each other. We had now weathered storms, both between us and externally, and I knew that through it all, our love would triumph.

I moved at last, shifting to make it easier for him to pull himself free. I turned around to face him, looking in those remarkable cognac eyes with embers deep within them. Something tickled my leg, and I realized the tail of my linteum wrap dragged on the ground. I let out a small laugh, at some point without my noticing, he had untied the top portion of my dress. It was only held together by the waist tie.

He ran his thumb over my bare shoulder, brushing past my mating marks. "I'm so glad you came to the forge, Lily. I didn't know how long you…" *would want to be alone.* His mind finished the sentence that he didn't want to say aloud, perhaps afraid that mentioning it would remind me that I had needed a break and wasn't happy with what he had said.

I caressed his arm. The truth was, with our last conversation neither of us had been wrong. We both said how we felt, he said what he thought. Even if it made me mad, he wasn't wrong. It was logical to consider the possibility that Felix had done it. And I didn't think I was wrong for the feelings I had about it. "I'm glad I took some time to think. I've been under a lot of pressure, and then with Eiulans's murder … it's all been intense and sometimes

I don't know if I might be losing my mind. I feel like I don't know the difference between up or down right now. Taking some time to myself to order my thoughts helped, at least a little."

"I'm sorry for the difficulties."

"What happened in Limnaer has me questioning everything. But when I really look at it, when I look at the facts and look at you, I know what's real. I also know that I need to solve this, and to clear those who may be suspects—myself included."

He nodded, then tucked a lock of my hair behind an ear, grazing it lightly as he moved his fingers. "This is all very serious conversation considering what we were doing just a few moments ago."

A delighted shiver passed over my body. My pointed ears were probably half as sensitive as Rannoch's, what he felt when I touched his must have been intense. My toes curled into the warm earth. I nuzzled in closer, feeling his warmth, his dewy skin against mine.

The tip of one canine peeked through his slightly parted lips as he half-smiled, half-growled in approval. His arms wrapped around me tighter. He always had a way of picking up even the slightest physical cue from me.

I squeezed him back as I let all the love and devotion I felt for him shine through our link. "So, do I get the honor of a tour of the forge?"

Glee surged through our connection. "Yes! There's so much to show you!"

I couldn't hide my smile. It was hard to believe he was over a hundred and sixty-five cycles old, his reaction felt akin to an excitable teenager. "Have you ever shown someone around here?"

"Kerenza, twice. She got the idea in her head that she would make some weapons. But she lost interest pretty fast. Other than that, not really. Dhiren comes here with me sometimes, but even he doesn't enjoy it like I do. No one else has shown curiosity, aside from the ferrars who work here."

I tossed the loose pieces of my linteum across my collar bones, crossing them just under my neck. "Ferrars, you mentioned them once a long time ago. Who are they?"

He reached behind the nape of my neck, knotting the ties for me. "The Ignisfae who are metal workers. If you think your selwaer I made is beautiful, wait until you see what they can do. I am a learner compared to them." He finished dressing, then walked toward the exit with me as I adjusted my linteum.

"Uhh, I didn't notice that before." A churning flow of lava apparently covered the only exit.

Rannoch chuckled. "There are several rooms closed off that way. Our usual doors don't hold up over time here, the heat is too high. Even though our fabrics are specially woven to withstand flame, the forge is too intense." He pushed his hand forward, then used his force to invisibly move aside the curtain to reveal the multilevel forge beyond. He held it open long enough for us to pass through, back into the main chamber of the forge.

I recognized the area we had been in before, the edge of the rocky dropoff to the molten lake far below was a short distance ahead. I could see several working ferrars swinging their hammers in alcoves across the way, sparks flying with each swing as they chanted.

"Let me show you where I usually choose to work." He held out his hand and beamed at me, walking toward the ledge he had come from previously. I smiled, I could feel the swell of his emotions that I wanted to see where he liked to create metalwork.

He reached over, calling up a step like he had used before. For a moment I thought he was moving the stone, but then realized it was actually the lava from below the rock that he manipulated, asking it to push the platform into place for us to step onto. My stomach dropped as I took a shaky step on the surface. Instead of calling up the next step down, he wrapped his free arm around my waist to steady me, then guided the stone down with his other hand outstretched to the forge floor. My blood rushed as we descended, holding tight to him. I may have become somewhat more comfortable with fire, but flaming pools of liquid metal was a lot more intimidating. Fire powers or no, any mistake would undoubtedly equal an immediate injury or death.

Don't worry, I've got you.

I looked up at him and felt instantly more connected. When he reassured me through our link I always knew the truth of his words. Somehow, it was a more unfiltered, honest form of communication. Learning to use it when I invited it had been a process, I certainly didn't want someone else in my head at all times. But when it was a silent, equal agreement to share thoughts, there was nothing more pure. I looked back down at the stone, at the flows of lava pushing up from below. For a moment I wished I was strong enough to do the same, to pull the lava to my will. But I felt no tug from it. Usually with nearby flames, I could sense them, I felt their power and my connection to them. The flow of the lava was too chaotic and powerful, I could of course feel the heat it emanated, feel the push of it below the rock surface we stood upon, but it didn't feel like a source I had the potential to control.

You can do it.

For as much as I trusted our link, I still couldn't grasp that his words might be true, I just didn't *feel* like it was there like I did with open flame.

It will bend to you when you really need it to.

We reached the bottom, then jumped down onto stable ground. "When did you learn to control it?" I asked, trying to steady myself after the unnerving descent.

"When I really needed to. On my first visit here, I was about twenty cycles old. My maeder was long presumed dead at that point, and I needed to find something to focus on. I was being taught by a ferrar, when a new flow burst through the wall." He pointed to a spout nearby. "It came shooting down toward me, it would have burned me, but I held up my hands on instinct with all my might. It listened, and veered away from me. The spout has been active ever since, and it's the one I always use to fill my crucible. I have a respect and connection to it, it hones my blades. I think it's why the weapons I make retain a spirit, of sorts. The same way the selwaer greets you after you selected it as your own."

I looked up at the powerful flow coming out of the rock face. I couldn't imagine commanding it, but I could feel its strength. "Amazing, Rannoch. I don't know how you do it."

He accepted a thick rimmed cup from an approaching Ignisfae, which was welded to a sturdy, long rod. "You will know once you do it yourself."

"What?!"

He took my hand, then wrapped it around the handle. "Just place it in the stream and collect some. Do it with intent, with the knowing that you will forge something with it." He released me, and I stood for a moment holding the empty vessel.

All right then, smelting, or whatever. Man, my life has gotten nuts. Who would have ever thought I would be here doing this? A girl from the rough chaparral hills of Southern California, a horse woman who lived a wonderfully uneventful life. Until a wildfire changed the course of my life, of many lives, then my best friend went missing. One thing after another had led me here. But in truth, now I was home. Along this confusing, unbelievable path I had found my course to my new home. My home with Rannoch.

I realized I had already filled the cup and was pouring its contents into a mold, which was either a short dagger or a long knife. It wasn't long before I was breaking it free from the mold with Rannoch's guidance, and pounding it with a hammer. Each swing resulted in sweat beading on my brow, but the chant of the ferrars had me submitting to the process. Somehow, the will of the hammer took over, and a blade was being forged. I felt like I was merely the link between the two, the hammer and the blade, but the power passed through me like a current and I was merely the conduit.

My former life, my current one, both flashed in my mind as I pounded the edges sharp, heating the metal then pounding more, before forcing it into a water bath to cool the metal quickly.

With Rannoch's help, by the end I had my own small dagger. He showed me how to etch it. I decided to call her MJ. M for Maris, and J for Josie. In truth, it was not a beautiful dagger. It was not well-made, it was created by an inexperienced hand. I couldn't expect it to be as fine as the blades the expert ferrars made. But it was mine.

Who knew how long I had been working away in the forge, by the ache of my muscles and the layer of dirt on my skin it was probably a long time. I opened my mouth to say something to Rannoch, when a voice came from above.

I looked up, and realized Dhiren was calling to us.

Rannoch guided me back onto a rock platform, then we ascended to meet Dhiren at the main level of the forge.

"The king has demanded an audience with you, Lily."

My stomach clenched. For a little while, at least, I had pushed Eiulans and the mystery of his death to the back of my mind. The inevitable inquest with the king was finally at hand. I sucked in a breath. "Okay, Dhiren. I'm ready to get this over with."

CHAPTER 13

After quickly cleaning up, I changed into a fresh linteum then headed to the center of the fortress, where King Ashwan held court. I was glad we had swung by our quarters first, I hadn't realized how covered in soot I was until I saw myself in the mirror. If I wasn't so nervous about our meeting I might have laughed. Sweat lines streaked through the dark layer crusted on my brow and cheeks. People had stared as we walked through the bazaar, but they always did, so I had paid them no heed.

I adjusted the brilliant gold edge of the asymmetrical, cream-colored wrap, making sure it draped nicely off my shoulder as we neared the entrance. I had chosen it intentionally, the king seemed to have a preference for the look. Rannoch wasn't summoned, but he accompanied us anyway and dressed to match me. We also wore our gold circlets, rather than our full crowns. The king had gifted me my crown, but I opted for the more understated version, fashioned from dainty sculpted flames of gold. I would have chosen no crown, but again it was something that pleased King Ashwan, so I usually obliged when it was a more official meeting.

Rannoch's presence was a comforting support for what would

likely be an interrogation, or an emotionally charged conversation at the very least. Felix looked uncharacteristically nervous, but Dhiren was there to reassure him, as was Dhirdre.

We entered the gilded doors to the throne room, unlocked this time. I remembered the first time I had seen the king, the massive doors had been locked and Eiulans had made Rannoch complete the complicated unlocking sequence. My interactions with his father had improved over time, but that was not the case with Eiulans. It was always tense, and filled with disdain from both sides. As I walked in without him hovering like he was Ashwan's gargoyle, it was a stark reminder of how it made the outcome between us appear: Lily the victor and Eiulans the unfortunate soul, in the long running tussle of one-upmanship.

The large room was empty, save for the king at the far end on his throne. In much the same way when I had first met him, he sat as still as stone upon the dais and waited. Dhiren closed the doors behind us, then we proceeded toward the imposing figure. My mind raced and heart thundered in my chest as I thought about how to even begin to explain it all.

Especially since I didn't truly know who did it.

The look on the king's face pained me as we stopped in front of him. For as much as he put up a façade, I could feel his agony. Maybe that was it, more than how he looked visibly. I could *feel* his pain. Which I thought was strange, as Eiulans was a horrible man.

To everyone except King Ashwan.

I didn't understand their relationship. Eiulans seemed to be nothing more than a yes man for the king, with a layer of constant scheming underneath. Every word was laced with venom, every interaction had some ulterior motive. To me, frankly to all of us who didn't currently sit upon that dais, he was a wretched, wicked soul. But there must have been another side to him, why else would King Ashwan care so much? The king had been isolated for a long time, granted it was self-imposed. But a long time nonetheless. Perhaps Eiulans was all he had.

"We have gathered to discuss the most distressing and unfortunate death of Eiulans Penferna," the king's booming voice shook me out of my thoughts. "When someone of such an esteemed rank is taken before their time, a death which resulted in preventing him from Fading, we are duty-bound to investigate. The loss of Eiulans will be felt throughout TerraIgni."

I tried not to shift where I stood. I had a hard time believing that anyone other than the king felt that way.

"Princess Lily, you will now explain the manner in which he died. I would advise you to be honest, and thorough. The Gods themselves watch over the proceedings in this throne room."

As if I needed more to worry about, now I also had to be concerned with beliefs in Gods I didn't understand or even know much about yet. I sucked in a breath, then recounted all I could with the sequence of events. When it came time, I held my voice strong as I declared the list of possible suspects, in order of likelihood. Having to admit that I was second on the list out loud to the Ignisfae whom I had finally turned over a new leaf with, hurt in a way I couldn't prepare myself for. It was like letting my own father down, coming clean about something I was ashamed of but could not shield myself from those piercing, astute eyes.

"You, Lily? You would have done this?" The heartbreak seeping from him was unbearable. It wasn't so much the loss of a friend that wounded him, but a betrayal. He had let me into the fold, and now

Eiulans was dead.

"No! No, I wouldn't have. I don't think I would have anyway. What I would have wanted with Eiulans was to cultivate a better relationship. I meant that I couldn't in good conscience eliminate myself from the list. I can't say for sure that I *didn't* do it, not yet anyway. But I swear to you, I will find his killer. And if it was me, I will atone for this crime."

"Dhirdre, is this true?" the king questioned.

She nodded once. "It is, my King. Aside from the possibility of it being the Vale Born, Dashelle, we could find no other explanation. We must consider all possibilities."

He shook his head and pinched the bridge of his nose. "You do not understand, it *cannot* be Lily. If it were, it could rip this familia apart. It could call into question my leadership. I appointed you as princess, Lily. It will have been *my* mistake at letting you in. One that I may have to revert to keep the peace."

My mouth dropped and I nearly collapsed, but I managed to keep my spine straight. At first the crushing weight of that possible outcome stripped me down to something small, and helpless. What would it mean? Cast out of TerraIgni, my new home, and forced away from Rannoch? Or would he insist on coming with me, only to wither in the Hinterdunes by my side. My eyes welled.

Then, just as quickly, I became angry. Really angry. To the point that my blood practically boiled, and fire leapt from my hands, my arms, my chest. His words "my mistake" echoed in my mind. After everything, I might be considered a mistake? The people of TerraIgni could so easily turn on me? I was instantly aflame. The fire was suppressed the moment it appeared. I snapped my gaze to Rannoch, who looked at me apologetically. I realized with dismay, he wasn't only there to support me.

He was my insurance policy.

He was there to make sure I remained calm and did not do exactly what I had just done. He may have been holding back the visible display of my fury, but it was barely contained beneath the surface.

The king eyed me warily as he continued, "In accordance with our customs, we must perform the pyre ceremony, and burn his body to release him to the aether. As you were the one to find him, you will be required to light it. No one is to speak of the nature of his death outside of this room. Is that clear?"

Rannoch held up a hand. "Must she light it? That seems unnecessary."

"Yes. It must be her. She will light it. It is our way. If we are to navigate this and save face, she must do her part."

"But, Faeder, she has been under tremendous pressure. This may be too far. The question of who committed this crime has weighed heavily on her already fragile state."

I had to stifle my already overflowing feelings. I knew Rannoch meant well, that he was being protective, but it felt like he was treating me a bit too much like lace, like something that would come apart under too much pressure. Though, burning Eiulans's body was the absolute last thing I wanted to do. A fire sweeping across the landscape took over my vision. All I saw, and felt, for that moment was the powerlessness at the unfolding scene before me. I could do nothing as my dad and sister perished. My breath quickened, the people that surrounded me in that throne room felt like they were miles away.

I closed my eyes. *Three, two, one. You are safe.* The idea of setting him ablaze terrified me, I couldn't deny that. But here, in TerraIgni, in Alternis, I was not the Lily Brennanfalk who was powerless. I was not the Lily that could do very little against a surging firestorm. I was the Lily who could barely *contain* her power. I was the Lily that could do something. And I was the Lily with something to prove.

"I'll do it," I said with cold resolve.

Rannoch stared at me. "Lily, we can find another way. It does not have to be you."

"I realize there may be another way. And I will admit that I don't *want* to do it. But, if it will mean something to the people, if it will mean something to your faeder, I will do it. I will take my place and perform the rite. Though, I don't know how to do it, I'll need your guidance."

He nodded once, though clearly unhappy with how I accepted the king's order. In truth, I wanted to do right by King Ashwan. I didn't like or understand Eiulans, but he meant something to the king. If for that reason alone, I should do as he asked. Simply because he was Rannoch's father and was hurting. If he had a reasonable request, I should do my part to make my best effort to do it. As far as I could guess, it sounded something akin to a Viking funeral, setting a platform on fire to usher the departed soul to the other side. I knew very little about the Ignisfae's beliefs. I had been learning more with my reading, but it hadn't been my main focus. I should have committed more time to it. Now I was having to learn on the fly. *Nothing like a trial by fire, pun intended.*

I inhaled sharply, trying to alleviate my discomfort with my internal jokes wasn't helping much. For as altruistic as it sounded to simply do as the king asked, I still had to burn a fucking body. A body which I found, *and* I was a potential culprit of the reason that he was dead.

A slam on the arms of the throne snapped me out of my thoughts.

"The pyre ceremony will commence in one-half rotation. Dhirdre, I would like you to focus your efforts on preparation. I want all of TerraIgni in attendance."

My blood went cold. It was a strange sensation to have both my skin on the verge of flaming out while my blood simultaneously felt like it dropped ten degrees. Having everyone watch me perform this rite—a rite which I had ultimately no damn clue about—sounded as close to hell as I could imagine.

"I suppose we should go get ready," Rannoch leaned over to whisper to me.

All I could do was nod at him, as the king excused us to prepare for the dreaded event.

CHAPTER 14

I flopped down on our bed, as Rannoch gave specific instructions to Tanzara out in the main living area. I gripped the covers and wanted to pull them over my head. I'd even accept Octobo jumping in the bed to comfort me. Nuzzling a ginormous spider sounded preferable to what we were about to do.

I must have mentally projected my thoughts, because Octobo came scampering in. I sighed, I didn't *actually* want him in my bed, but I would be happy with a cautious petting of his furry head. I reached down and stroked the top just above his compound eyes. In spite of myself, it did make me feel better. He leaned into my touch for a moment, before scuttling back to his hidey-hole that was in the wall of our tiled terrace. Maybe I should go out there with him, some rest on the wide balcony would do me good, spend time listening to the breeze through our potted citrus trees and percala berry hedges. Both were preparing to bear fruit again. I did love tending to them mindlessly, ironically doing that helped order my thoughts.

I got out of bed, intending to avoid Rannoch and Tanzara's conversation about what I should wear to a spectacle where I would dispose of someone's remains. I edged past them, not making eye contact as they were finalizing details.

"I will return from the Tower shortly with the items," Tanzara was just finished saying to Rannoch.

I was instantly on alert. "The Tower? What for?" Spending time on the terrace was immediately abandoned.

"For your crowns, the Firestar gem crowns and something you may not be familiar with, the Purification Scepter. They will both be needed for the pyre ceremony."

I groaned. The Firestar crowns were of course beautiful, stunning actually. And when I thought about it, of course that's what we would be wearing for the ceremony, they were the most stately crowns in the lot. They were also the most unwieldy and uncomfortable. The thought of wearing mine for any length of time while trying to perform something I wasn't familiar with sounded like enough of an anxiety-inducing reason to try and back out.

But I couldn't back out, wouldn't back out.

I realized Rannoch was carefully appraising me, as my mind rambled along until I came to my own resolution. *You better not be listening in on my mental committee.*

His eyes rounded momentarily, then he almost laughed. *Sorry, you project things and then say "don't listen to me!" It's a little hard when you are practically shouting.*

I smiled. It was probably the first smile I had allowed since Dhiren had appeared at the forge and told us we had to go to meet with King Ashwan. "All right, I get it. I just didn't want to have another argument about whether or not I should be doing this," I said aloud to him.

Tanzara looked momentarily confused, then her expression changed. "I sometimes forget you can hear each other's thoughts."

She shook her head and chuckled. "I will return shortly." She disappeared out our front door.

He waited, searching my face. "I do not want you to do something that will be difficult for you. If we are keeping the nature of Eiulans's death a secret, why does it have to be you who does the rite? It could easily be my faeder who performs it, or even Dhirdre. There is no one to say who was the one it must be according to our beliefs. The Ignisfae as a whole will not know the difference."

"But your faeder will, *he* will know the difference, and I know this matters to him. For that reason alone I think I should do it. Further than that, he *ordered* it. For me to then not do it would inevitably be problematic for my relationship with him."

Rannoch's expression darkened. "Your relationship?"

I wanted to ignore his subtext, but it had been clear to me that Rannoch would likely have daddy issues for a long time. One hundred and sixty-five cycles of hurt from his faeder would have a far reach into the future, even with King Ashwan trying to make changes. "Yes, where I'm from he'd be what's called my father-in-law. And that makes him the only father, faeder, I've got now. He's asked this of me. And he's said that this will matter to the people of TerraIgni. Don't forget, I'm the outsider here, I'm the one who's different. I have no context of how important this ceremony is or what to even do for it, but I'm going to do it even if it's uncomfortable for me. And this isn't me being altruistic and trying to do the right thing. In a way I am, but also remember what your faeder said. He said he may have to revert the title he gave me. That's some serious shit! What would become of us then? What would become of me?"

"I did not think you really wanted the title. All of your …

your thoughts on it made me think you felt it was more like a burden than a blessing."

"Maybe it's both. I don't know. Maybe deep down I'm a lazy girl who would rather sit on the terrace and read, or an introverted one who would rather just ride my horse, in this case my equus, with no one watching. An arena full of thousands upon thousands of Ignisfae watching me light a dead person on fire while I'm wearing a crown I can barely keep on my head does sound like the opposite of what I'd be comfortable with. But I've already spent enough time running. I ran from the problems of my former life, and now I have this life. I can't say this life is a burden, the responsibility of the title is hard, but even you have admitted to stepping aside sometimes to just be yourself. Like when you go to the forge. You aren't the prince there, you are one of the ferrars."

He looked thoughtful for a moment. "That is true."

"Simply because I need a break from it sometimes doesn't mean I don't want it or am unwilling. Yeah, this ask from your faeder is *a lot*, I will admit I've already had flashbacks of the fire that I watched kill those that I love. But I can do this. Plus, I have you to help me. You'll be near me, right?"

"Definitely."

I stepped forward and hugged him, burying my face in his chest. He wrapped his arms around me and held me until Tanzara returned.

The deafening sounds of all the citizens of TerraIgni overwhelmed me as we stepped onto the platform. Dhirdre and Dhiren stood to the side, dressed in the same deep red satin silk as Rannoch and I. The hem of my flowy skirt licked in the wind like tendrils of flames, as we waited for everyone to assemble. I made an effort not to shift too much, trying to keep the Firestar crown in place as I subtly adjusted the wrapped top portion of my dip-dyed dress. It was a brilliant yellow gold fabric which had been partially submerged in deep red color, allowing the material to soak it part way up. It created a stunning gradation from gold on the bodice, to a horizontal strip of rich orange at the waistline, with the majority of the long dress being an eye-catching crimson hue at the base. It made me think about Kerenza and how she had explained the lavish fabrics of her home, all that time ago when I had first met her. I looked around for her but she was nowhere to be found.

"Shouldn't Kerenza be here?" I leaned over slightly and whispered to Rannoch. He nodded once, but if he was concerned, his face didn't show it.

King Ashwan appeared a moment later. For as distraught as I could feel he had been at our meeting in the throne room, he might as well have been wearing a mask of stone at that moment as he prepared for the rite to begin. The mask of a practiced king ready to be what his people needed to see, regardless of how he may have felt.

With a flick of his robes, he ascended the stairs to join us on the platform. King Ashwan took center stage while Rannoch and I stayed closer to the stairs at the side, in front of Dhirdre and Dhiren. I adjusted my shoulders and clasped my hands in front, ensuring I was stoic for the start of the proceedings.

The crowd hushed as he waited for all to settle. I realized that most of the citizens—maybe even all—didn't know why we were gathered. To my knowledge Eiulans's death hadn't been announced. The king looked around, waiting for the right time to start.

He held up his arms in a wide V as he announced, "You are all probably wondering why we have assembled. We have come together to send Eiulans Penferna to the aether." He lowered his arms, then bowed his head in reverence with one fist to his broad chest.

A murmur swept through the crowd, I looked around trying to discern the nature of their reaction. Did the people of TerraIgni have any idea what Eiulans was really like?

I heard a scoff from over my shoulder. I tried not to turn too fast, lest my crown might topple over. Kerenza had made her way onto the platform without my noticing, and now stood next to Dhirdre. Truth be told I was relieved to see her there, but I wondered if there might be any repercussions for being late. Hopefully King Ashwan didn't take notice of it.

"In accordance with our ways," the king continued after the crowd quieted down, "the one who first attended his body will perform the Purification. Princess Lily will light the fire to release him, so that he may walk with his forefaeders in the aether and be free from his duty to those of us who are left behind."

I sucked in a breath, but made sure to keep my posture straight and face neutral as the king's glance swept to me. There was a loud clang, and the sound of unseen doors opening from behind the dais echoed throughout the plaza. A slow drum beat started from large, hide-covered pans that were along the left and right sides below the stage. A rising single note played by some kind of stringed instrument started. More of the same instruments joined, creating a harmonic effect. After a moment, a shining gold platform came into view, being carried by ten pallbearers. A box with cutouts along the sides was inset and raised on the platform, on top of which rested the shroud-covered body of Eiulans. They walked the heavy looking platform slowly to the front of the stage where a ramp had been erected. After they had climbed to the top, they walked the platform into position behind the king.

"Ignite the monuments," King Ashwan proclaimed. Within seconds, the massive statues of Ignisfae that surrounded the square were lit one by one, the flames reached high in the sky from the bronze basins the statues held in cupped, raised hands.

A double line of sixteen more Ignisfae walked out from where Eiulans had been brought from, each group of four carrying an extremely thick-walled, large chalice set atop pronged platforms. They gripped the handles that jutted out from each edge, still struggling with the apparent massive weight of what looked like giant smelting cups—in spite of the fact that every one of the Ignisfae were some of the most muscular I had seen of their warriors. They ascended the ramp, then placed each large chalice at all four corners of the platform. I noticed a spout or horn-like shape angling down from the corners of the platform, which pointed into the chalices.

"Princess Lily," King Ashwan's deep voice resonated loud enough for all to hear, "approach with the Purification Scepter."

I turned to Dhirdre, who now held the weighty golden staff, angled across her chest. She offered it to me. It was heavier than I expected, I had to engage my muscles to keep it steady, then walked over to stand in front of the platform. I could barely make out Eiulans's face under the gauzy covering. I gulped, trying to steel myself for what was about to come. Rannoch had instructed me on what to do before we had arrived, so I was at least prepared. It wasn't complicated: light the end of the scepter, raise it for all to see, then place the lit end into each opening below the raised portion Eiulans was laid upon. Start below his head, move down to his feet. There were seven openings in total. By the time I would be lighting the one below his feet, he should be nearly consumed with flames. That was the totality of my part of the process.

I moved into place to begin when the king was ready to give his command. I tightened my grip on the intricately detailed staff, adjusting my hand placement to be able to release one hand in order to light it. The tip of it had a bezel set gem, with an open box below it which led to a filament in the center of the shaft that would carry the flame.

"With the flame of our Gods, Eiulans may burn brightly once again. He shall be purified of this world, and ready for the next. Light the Purification Scepter, Princess Lily."

I released my left palm and let my fire free. It erupted into a fireball that shot high into the air with an initial brilliant burst. It had been begging to be released for awhile, it was no surprise there was some fury behind it. The entire crowd gasped. I turned my attention from the scepter, glancing out at the crowd, then back at Rannoch.

He cringed a little. *I should have told you not to Fire Bring.*

I sighed, realizing I should have called a flame from the closest torch and formed the conduit from the torch to the scepter, rather than Fire Bring to ignite it. The people knew I was a Fire Bringer, but as it was a fairly uncommon skill, it probably startled them to see it as a live demonstration. *What's done is done.* I had already released the fire, there seemed to be little point in closing it off in order to collect it from a brazier or torch instead. I ignored my misstep and angled the scepter into the flame which still spewed from my hand, lighting the end. It burned so white-hot I had to squint my eyes for a moment. The filament inside the core must have been something like magnesium, based on the brightness. It didn't seem like a fiber wick the way it ignited. I faced the masses of people, holding the burning torch high overhead.

I don't know if I expected cheers, but the awed silence surprised me. Not a sound could be heard from all the Ignisfae clustered in the massive square, nor from the people that stood on the battlements that surrounded the walled city made of red stone, and not even from those on the terraces that overlooked the expansive area. The only sound I heard was the crackling of the scepter which was about to begin the process of burning Eiulans away.

I turned, looking at his body for one moment. I almost wished I could care about him, that I could have liked some part of him. I tamped my thoughts down, because you're not supposed to speak ill of the dead, so I tried not to think disparaging things either. Stepping forward, I inserted the scepter into the first port. It responded with an immediate bright white fire of its own. I moved toward his feet, lighting each opening in the platform one by one. As I finished lighting the final port, he was already engulfed. The fabric sizzled away, and I saw his face for a moment. His skin bubbled before peeling away from his bones. I wished I hadn't looked, I'd never be able to remove the image of what happens when fire meets flesh. Just as quickly, the entire platform was ablaze with unbearable light. The thinner, gold-like metal he rested on started to buckle and warp, beading up in rivulets that started to run down toward the corners of the larger bronze platform that the pyre rested on. The melted metal began to collect in the chalices, filling them with brilliant liquid gold.

The fire burned brighter still and heated further, causing me to back up farther away from the pyre, closer to the crowds. His body was already gone, he was nothing more than embers in the air or ash mixed with the molten ore. The narrow platform had melted down to a puddle, the last of it draining off the spouted corners of the thick block it had laid upon.

The chalices were nearly full, and the brightness began to subside. That was when I finally heard something other than the hissing and crackling of the pyre. Whispers, so many whispers started to creep in through the din. "How did he die? Why was the princess the one who attended him? Could she be responsible?" Questions and musings of the gathered Ignisfae started to make their way to my ears, carried on a wind that felt malevolent. I turned, trying to figure out who was talking. I looked around wildly, I moved so fast and had to steady my crown as I searched the crowd. But I couldn't tell who it might have been, it looked like no one was speaking. They all seemed to be reverently waiting.

A hand clamped down on the scepter, causing me to snap my head back to the stage. King Ashwan had reached for it, but I had yet to let go. He nodded to my hand, which still gripped the burning staff. His face was void of any emotion, though I could feel some level of displeasure. Maybe it was the Fire Bringing that I had done to light the pyre. Maybe it was that his friend died and I was the only one who might know anything, and yet I had little information to offer. Maybe it was that I—a hybrid outsider—was now bound to his family and we were shielding a potential scandal.

I let go and he swung the Purification Scepter into the air, holding it aloft as the last of the flames sputtered out from the tip. "Eiulans Penferna has been released to the aether. Ferrars, come forward to collect the molten ore. What remains of him shall be crafted into a brazier and hoisted over TerraIgni, so that he may always burn brightly. We will now rejoice in the life he lived. I invite you all now to eat, drink, and burn brightly in his absence."

Tables laden with food and beverage were brought out, platters of appetizers started to circulate through the crowds, and servers carrying libations offered up rounds to all. I looked to Rannoch, who waited dutifully near the edge of the stage to escort me off. I tried to sidestep whatever disappointment the king may have felt as I walked toward my mate. Kerenza had already exited the stage and was getting drinks for herself and Zia.

I'm proud of you.

I almost stumbled when he said those words to me through our link. I nodded, appreciative of the sentiment. I hadn't done it perfectly, but I had finished it. I had done as his father commanded, and I held strong throughout. I took his hand and smiled as he guided me over to the closest table for refreshments. Though my stomach was in knots, a little vinirubrum sounded like a good way to end the ceremony. Tanzara was there ready to accept my crown, and had my more comfortable circlet ready to set in my hair. Lifting the Firestar crown off was a relief, I didn't realize how much my neck had been straining to keep it on straight.

I had to resist clinking my drink against Rannoch's, though I had taught him about giving cheers to someone, it might come off as strange to anyone watching. And I could feel many eyes on me still, though the ceremony had ended and people were beginning their revelry, there were quite a few Ignisfae who still peered at me with curiosity. I didn't need to bring more attention to myself by displaying a human custom. I took a sip and thought about the differences between the cultures, big things such as funeral traditions, and small things such as sayings or salutes of recognition. Even in the human world there wasn't one way of celebrating someone's life, or one way of dealing with their mortal shell once they had passed on. I wondered what other races of Fae did for their funeral services. I decided I should commit more time to reading about Fae traditions and history.

"You look lost in thought," Kerenza said as she sauntered over. She had already finished her first drink and was onto the second.

"I am. I'm just thinking about what was done in the human world for when someone dies, versus the ceremony we just had."

"Hopefully the human custom is for a party after the ceremony, like this one. I may not have enjoyed Eiulans's company, but I can certainly raise a drink to him!" She grinned, then downed her whole cup before motioning to a server for another.

"It seems you need little reason to raise a glass," Rannoch muttered.

She shot him a searing glance, before shifting her attention to Zia, who was at the nearest buffet table loading a plate. She lifted a shoulder to her brother and gave him one last haughty look, before heading over to Zia. A moment after, Emblyn appeared and rushed over to her maeder, with Queen Deniza trailing not far behind to greet her.

"I had been wondering where they were," I said, turning back to Rannoch.

"They were here, but a little ways away. My maeder was trying to keep some of the unsettling parts of the ceremony a fair distance from Emblyn, after everything she went through. She is still such a young filia, after all, my maeder has been making an effort to give Emblyn back some of that innocence."

I nodded, then it struck me that Queen Deniza had not been present for any of the discussions surrounding Eiulans and what happened in Limnaer. "Did she know about Eiulans before the ceremony started?"

"Yes, I went to speak with her after you and I had … after you went to see Kerenza. I realized I should tell my maeder. Suffice it to say she has a very different perspective than my faeder does."

I raised my eyebrows as he took a convenient swig of his drink with a conspiratorial smirk. "I'm sure you wouldn't be surprised to hear she hated him too. Naturally, she is not upset over his death."

"Right, that makes sense." Of course she did. I didn't know what happened all those cycles ago, when Deniza was pushed to the point of looking for comfort elsewhere, and ended up with Don'Li for a time. It's not like she did the right thing back then, but I could see Eiulans playing a role in her systematic isolation before anything had even happened outside of her relationship with King Ashwan.

A familiar male voice cleared his throat behind me. "Lily?"

I spun, finding Felix standing awkwardly near the stage.

"Are you okay?" I asked as I reached forward to clutch his shoulders, looking into his eyes to try and ascertain his current state.

He laughed a little. "I was going to ask you the same thing, to make sure you were all right after the ceremony. It couldn't have been easy. It wasn't easy to watch."

I paused. "Oh, Felix, I'm sorry. It must have been hard for you as well. I'm glad you're here, though. Come on, let's have some fun."

The musicians who had played the funeral dirge notes started up with a lively beat, and before long feet were stomping and everyone was dancing. For as somber and serious as the service was, the wake was the complete inverse. The mood had lifted as we moved to the beat.

I lost myself to the rhythm, the striking of the drums and the fervor of the strings. I danced with Rannoch, I danced with Felix. I danced with anyone who ended up in my grasp. Sometimes it was an unknown Ignisfae female who got too close and I scooped her up into the round, sometimes it was a male. It felt as though we had cast aside our ranks to dance with whomever was nearby. Felix and I danced like we did after the battle with Dashelle, when he had swung me high into the air. Rannoch alternated spinning me, then holding me close. I did an exotic circle dance with Kerenza, Dhirdre, Tanzara, and Zia. By the end, we were all laughing and sweaty.

The event had started to wind down. King Ashwan had long since left with Queen Deniza, with Emblyn at their side. Kerenza left with Zia. Even Felix and Dhiren weren't dancing anymore but quietly talking nearby. I was exhausted to say the least as Rannoch offered his arm, heading back to our quarters, our safe space, sounded pretty perfect to me.

CHAPTER 15

The night didn't end after the wake, tired though I was, I reveled in my time with Rannoch. Sleep claimed me eventually, as did the dreams that followed. Though Rannoch had done his level best to brush aside any dark imagery that could have sprung up in my mind—by planting new images in me, *deeply* in me—it wasn't enough to clear the shroud of uneasiness. There was the obvious: the phantom, murderous Dashelle who could be anywhere in Alternis, but then there was the less obtrusive Maeder Tree. Once again she haunted my dreams, calling to me, demanding something of me. What it was I couldn't tell, it seemed tied to Dashelle, was it Eiulans's murder, or something else? There was an insistent need, a pull. A responsibility that she wanted me to carry. Yet another yoke to hook across my shoulders. But every time I saw the Maeder Tree in my dreams her words had no clarity, it was like listening to them through water. And like looking at her through mist.

I grimaced, glancing out across the expanse of the ravine as I tried to settle myself on our terrace. I had startled awake, *again*. The dreams wore me down almost as much as some of my realities. I pushed it all away with an exhale, I had learned through therapy to have patience with myself. That healing would take years, and unsettling dreams would be a part of life. Knowing that didn't make it any easier, though. I kneaded my thigh, my legs folded to the side in my comfy terrace chair. I had been reading some books Rannoch had procured for me. With another fresh cup of capuli set beside me and a veritable stack of books to choose from, it was as close to heaven as I could imagine. The light was waning as we approached the dark rotations, what would equate to afternoon lighting was the perfect atmosphere to sit on the terrace and either read or look at the stunning natural beauty of the canyon wall. It was still strange to me to have an entire day retain roughly the same amount of light. I didn't know if I would ever truly adjust to having the passage of time not be indicated by the amount of light in the sky. Twenty-eight rotations to go from dark to light, then back to dark again would probably always feel off.

Rannoch came out to check on me. "I was going to return to the forge, I have something I'm working on. Need anything before I go?"

I smiled and patted my obnoxiously large stack of books. "Nope, my friends here will keep me company."

He set down another full carafe of capuli with a side of cream, kissed my head, then departed.

I settled back into my seat to begin devouring as much Fae knowledge as I could consume.

It could have been an entire rotation or longer by the time Rannoch returned. It was definitely darker out, and the placement of my leather bookmark in the carefully hand-lettered pages told me—at least in some manner—how long I had been reading. I had managed to skim an entire book, and was currently studying a book on maps and military strategy.

The book detailing some of their religious beliefs was hard to follow, and turned into more of a saga from an age past which held little relevance for me. I had decided I would need to ask more specific questions to a living Fae, rather than rely on histories written in a language only slightly legible to me. I had gleaned that each race of Fae had their own main god, and each god had several deities which served them. The Fae were not only competitive with each other, but with their gods as well, always boasting who would best who in a fight. However, once the mist had rolled in and shrouded their realm, gods were no longer accessible. Vitus Augustus had supplanted their gods, though he didn't force them to renounce those gods. Instead, he illustrated how they rarely, if ever, did anything for them anyway. It was one way he had taken hold of the realm, by promising real actions. A major difference between what I would identify as the two eras, the time preceding Vitus and the time after, was that although the races were competitive prior to his arrival, they did not war with each other. And the lessening role of the Gods in daily Fae life, it was diminished to momentary references to them, rather than dutiful prayer times. Religious leaders were also done away with, I would guess they had been systematically killed so they didn't get in Vitus's way. He did however seem to bring some positive advancements: irrigation, plumbing techniques, and inventions—which to me seemed almost Roman in a way.

I thought about Yantz. He had mentioned once that he made

Starcrest so that he could use the telescope to pierce the mist, to see through it to the Gods' realm. He was the oldest living Fae after all, he would be the perfect one to ask. He was born hundreds of cycles after Vitus had died, but maybe he knew more history that he could share with me.

I frowned. He probably did, but it would most likely only add to my education to better understand Alternis, rather than helping me with my immediate problems. I thumbed through the pages of the book on military strategy, as I slowly realized my answers for these problems would not be found in books, and would not be found in TerraIgni for that matter.

Rannoch appeared in the doorway, holding a tray piled with miniature tortams and a creamy dessert topped with percala berry preserves. "I brought your favorite, come and sit with me?"

I smiled and stretched my legs, then stood to head inside. I did love those little wrap appetizers, filled with stiff cheese and tangy bulb vegetables. I sat down at our table for two while he poured us juice. I filled up on the tortams while he talked about the forge and asked questions about the books. For as grimey as he was after a visit to hammer out whatever he was currently working on, he was never so beautiful to me. His face was smudged, but he glowed with pride from his work. I had to admit that his enthusiasm was motivating, his spirit exuded a sense of self that made me want to find my own inner stability. To find my own goals to work toward.

In some ways I had begun to discover what my goals were. With the eventual positive result of wrenching the Syrenni free from tyranny, I had started to achieve that goal of being a force for change. We had all worked together and made a huge impact by freeing the Syrenni from the Umorfae's iron grip. By comparison, this task of clearing my name and confirming that Dashelle was the perpetrator was so much smaller. The lives of many did not hang in the balance for this issue.

It was just me and her.

It finally dawned on me that *that* was what I was so terrified of. I had been afraid of becoming her since I learned who she really was. At what point would I not be Lily anymore, my actions easily mistaken for hers? Killing as naturally as she did, one heartless, deft swipe of a sword after another. That was the true fear. Not that I could have killed Eiulans, but that I could be just like her. I had been fighting against that possibility since the battle with the Umorfae in the waters outside of the cave, when I had killed for the first time. I didn't know who she was at that point, I didn't even know she was female back then. It was the ideal or the distillation of that person that terrified me. I couldn't deny the capability within me to become like that. To think otherwise would be foolish. To get to the point where I was comfortable with killing, and to become mad with power.

I looked at my glass of juice, thinking about the abilities I had. I lifted my hand, pulling a runnel of liquid from my cup, letting it swell and fill into a globe suspended in the air. I pulled until the cup was empty, letting the ball hover as I thought about everything. I closed my eyes as I felt my magic well leveling out, tempering the current that flowed through me. I so rarely used my water ability in TerraIgni, it brought about negative feelings from Ignisfae in general, as it was an Umorfae skill for the most part. I only let it out around those I was closest to. I opened my eyes and looked at Rannoch, who pretended not to notice the large rotating orb of red juice suspended in the air near him.

He tore off a bite of a tortam. "Got a lot on your mind still, I gather?"

"Am I so easy to read?"

He let out one small huff of a laugh. "You only do that when you're really deep in thought," he said, using the remaining bite of his tortam to point at the sphere.

"It does help me to let it out, holding up the liquid is almost peaceful in a way, and it eases a little of the building tension inside me," I answered, shifting my gaze to the deep spectral reds within the sphere. "I—"

A loud knock outside our wall startled me. I lost my hold on the orb at the same time a female yelled for Rannoch and me.

Rannoch hollered as red liquid soaked what little clean area was visible on his wrap pants. "Damnatus, Lily!"

I jumped up to run to the door, wiping the drips from my face. "Sorry, that scared me!" I reached the door with Rannoch a few paces behind, then unhooked the loop to unlock it and threw open the heavy closure.

Zia stood breathless on the other side. "Come quickly," she panted. "Kerenza needs you."

CHAPTER 16

We raced through the fortress to her quarters. I tried asking Zia what was wrong but she was too panicked to explain. We reached the door after a breathless run, before she turned and held her hand up to Rannoch.

"I think you should wait out here, she asked for Lily."

Rannoch opened his mouth to protest, but quickly shut it before nodding once. I gave him an apologetic look, then I entered behind Zia.

I blinked, forcing my eyes to adjust to the darkness in the room. Zia rushed into the bedroom. I followed and watched as Zia knelt at Kerenza's side. Her hair was soaked and she shivered in the covers, trying to peel them off in her fevered state.

"Kerenza, Lily is here."

Kerenza's eyes fluttered open a little, and she whimpered. I clasped my chest, I could *feel* her pain, it was an overwhelming sense of both physical and emotional distress.

"Kerenza? Are you okay? What's going on?"

She clenched her eyes shut, then turned away. "I quit drinking vinirubrum and vocafortis. I finally realized the hold it had on me. Well …"

"I told her it had become too much," Zia spoke up. "We got into an argument. Things escalated, but eventually she decided—"

"I have a problem," Kerenza interrupted her. A spasm overtook her, and she stopped speaking for a moment as she shook. "I knew I did, but I did not want to admit it." She started quivering again.

"That's good that you quit. You're very brave to take this first step and to admit that you have a problem."

Kerenza shook again, her body probably revolting against the lack of alcohol. "It hurts so bad," she whispered.

"I'll try to help you." I knelt down next to Zia, who promptly stood.

"I will be out in the main room if you need anything, so that you can focus on helping Kerenza."

I nodded to her. "Can you tell Rannoch that I will be here for some time, that Kerenza will need me for awhile? I'm guessing Kerenza isn't quite ready to see him." Kerenza managed to nod her agreement.

Zia dipped her head, then left the room.

I cast my hands over Kerenza's body, sending soothing pulses to the ache that permeated her, lessening their severity.

"Talk to me, tell me things." Her voice was feeble, but she seemed to speak through the pain. "I keep seeing dark imagery. Horrible, grotesque things. Talk to me about things I have never seen. What is it like to be human? Is the world much different there?"

I sighed. "In some ways it's very different, and in others I see a lot of similarities. Words that come out of people's mouths can be as bad as what comes out of their culuses."

Kerenza snorted a laugh, quivered, then sucked in a breath.

"Tell me more." She closed her eyes and clenched her fists. Whatever she was going through, it was intense. I could feel the pain, but it was hard for me to pinpoint the source. I recognized the similar physical reactions post traumatic stress disorder had taken on me, dealing with this sort of withdrawal must have been painful. I rubbed in between her shoulder blades, along the peak of her neck muscles. I didn't know all the right things to do, what steps I might be missing. I had never tried to help someone out of alcohol withdrawal, I was probably missing a part of the process which could help ease her.

"My body hurts, my hands will not stay still. I feel like the only way I will feel better is to have a glass," she said, shaking as I clasped her hand. "Please, tell me more. Even if it is not good things. I want to hear the truth of the world you came from. Anything to distract me from this."

"What hurts? Tell me and I'll do my best to ease your pain as I talk."

She rubbed her shoulder and neck, then her lower back. "Here and here. My skin hurts also, little pin pricks all over. And the shaking, I cannot stand the shaking and sweating."

I nodded as I moved onto the bed with her. Placing my hands on her exposed back, I started to rub, and cast out my healing threads. I caught one beautiful glimmer of the golden cords, before my sight changed and my vision turned in, clouding over so that I could see inside her body. I thought for a second of what to even talk about. "There are oceans there. Huge bodies of saltwater that are so big you can't see the edges of them, with massive creatures that live in it. Aside from that, you can see the sun on most days, it's bright and sometimes obnoxious, but watching the sunset is one of the most beautiful sights you'll ever see. The world itself is beautiful. Sometimes the humans make it less so. Wars never seem to stop. We have so many of them, sometimes because of only one man, so many people die. Misinformation is spread through some of the media—the people that are meant to disseminate news. I think they're fed idealized snippets of what's going on, occasionally hitting some truth and other times just making it sound like it will be all okay and "look at this rescued puppy! You're happy again." It can feel pretty manipulative."

"Puppy?" She asked as she shook once more, this time quite a bit less.

I smiled. "Yeah, puppies are wonderful, baby dogs. Four legged creatures nicknamed "man's best friend," they have this distinctive breath when they're little that I swear is made specifically to make humans sleepy." I thought with a smile for a moment of puppies that had grown to adulthood on my family's ranch, grown into loyal friends that also had a job to do there. "Dogs are definitely one aspect of the human world that makes it better. Other animals, too. Life as a human isn't easy, many times the people in power are doing things you don't want, are hurting others or killing, and you feel powerless to stop them. But also, humans can do beautiful things. Art, literature, dance, there are so many ways they express themselves."

"Sounds a lot like the Fae honestly."

"I agree. Maybe we have closer roots than we know. I know I have questioned how I could have been human, when other humans have done such awful things. Surely I couldn't be as bad as the man in power of a huge country that decides to take over his neighbor, killing many of them and his people in the process.

But then, I turn out not to be truly human, but am the same as someone equally vile, so I know it's not impossible for me to become like that."

Her shoulders contracted and she withdrew into a fetal position. "You are not Dashelle, Lily. You are good." She flushed and a wave of sweat was evident.

"It's my greatest fear that I will become like her. The power is strong, and I feel like I can never underestimate it or I could lose control."

Kerenza tried to hold my hand, but her tremors were too strong. Sweat beaded on her forehead and dampened her linteum. "You *are* g-g-good. Fuck! I cannot believe I did this to myself. I did not know this could happen. I feel like a stultus. How did I let it get this bad?"

"You aren't a stultus, this isn't your fault. Alcohol is a tricky bitch. I guess it can sneak up on you and make your body think you need it. And now, technically, you do. Your body is addicted to it and it's protesting not having it."

"I miss Kenneder so much!" she cried, tears flowing down her rosy cheeks before they plopped on the bed. "Vinirubrum dulled that raw feeling, lessened it, for a little bit anyway. I hid from that truth when I drank it, the pain could go away and I wouldn't think about it every second. I watched the whole moment he died play out before me, and I could do nothing to stop it. And now, it is back again for me to have to watch it in my mind over and over. I cannot breathe when it happens, and I cannot shut it off. When Emblyn was taken, I could not function without drinking. It was the only way I found to deal with that stress."

"Oh gosh, Kerenza. That all sounds awful." I cast my hands

over her arms, soothing down the involuntary jitters. It quieted slightly, but didn't go away completely. I'd have to probably ease those at the source: her brain.

I pulsed carefully with my palm at her temple, not wanting to affect the balance of her inner workings. I could see a radiating nerve bundle sending thousands of signals in a cascading ripple, could feel her calm down through my hand laid on her arms that it was working. I stayed after a moment to make sure the nerves wouldn't ramp back up again, and realized I saw a dark mass hiding within the surface of her brain. It had a strange, misshapen, star-like jelly substance. I prodded it, it didn't feel right, like it didn't belong. I realized she may have had some brain trauma from the withdrawal. I carefully pulsed it, shrinking it down, lessening its blockage of whatever it was clogging. I shrank it into nothingness, then retreated back to myself.

She closed her eyes and shook hard, trying to speak.

"We should talk about that later. Right now what matters is getting you through this."

Kerenza's face scrunched and tears squeezed out of the corners of her eyes. She nodded at last.

"I'll stay with you the whole time, I promise," I said.

Her clammy hand gripped tighter to mine, as I laid on my side next to her.

I was awoken by Rannoch's hand on my shoulder. "What is going on? Why is Kerenza trembling and sweating?" he asked.

I raised my finger to my lips, realizing that Kerenza had finally fallen asleep. I unwound a healing thread and sent it into her temple, checking her condition. Tremors were still evident, but they had lessened considerably. I backed the thread out and it snapped up inside of me, my vision returned to normal once I had released the white-gold magic.

I crawled out of bed as carefully as I could, motioning to Rannoch to follow me to the living area.

Zia was asleep on a wide, tufted settee. I shooed Rannoch to walk further, I didn't want to disturb her either. We walked out of the quarters and into the hallway.

"Will you tell me what is going on? I have been sitting there with Zia for what felt like half a rotation. What is wrong with her?"

"I … can't tell you. It's not my place to say. It is Kerenza's choice to tell you, I'm sure she will when she's feeling up to it. Right now I need to go back and be with her."

"You will not come back to our rooms right now?" He looked like he could barely process what I was saying.

"No. I promised her I would stay with her. She's having a tough time and she needs all of our support."

He pulled his head back, and I could feel he was instantly upset. "I have *always* supported her. Are you seriously implying—"

"I'm sorry, Rannoch. I didn't mean to imply anything. You are definitely supportive of her. I mean that she needs my support right now in a way that she hasn't before." I paused, hoping to shift the subject. "I didn't realize you were waiting there for so long."

He dropped his jaw. "How did you not know? My mate, whom I am tied to, can feel heightened emotions from, is in my sister's room helping her with … *something*. Whatever it is that you're doing is troubling to you, all of which I can feel part of through our link. And you think I would just leave?"

My eyes rounded. He was right. I was unaware that he would spend all that time worrying without the knowledge of what was going on. "I—"

He lifted a hand to stop me. "I'm going back to our quarters. I guess I will see you there *eventually,* maybe then you'll tell me what's going on."

Rannoch turned, then left, leaving me stunned. The time I spent helping Kerenza had shifted my focus away from any of his needs. It seemed I was currently only capable of navigating one relationship at a time, and that wasn't going to work. It wasn't that he was needy, it may have been that I hadn't entirely adjusted to sharing myself with someone else. I puffed my lips. It was yet another reason to button up this mess with Eiulans and figure out what the hell had happened. It was taking up too much of my reserves, there wasn't enough of me to go around. My time I spent isolating after so much trauma had happened in my human life clearly had repercussions with how I was able to manage things now.

I would do it, at some point. I had to. It wasn't avoidance again. I assured myself of that as I went back into Kerenza's room to stay with her until I was sure she was better.

CHAPTER 17

I awoke in Kerenza's bed, with her not in it. My dreams had not been haunted by visions of the Maeder Tree at last. Perhaps I had been so spent from using my healing skill on Kerenza that I had no mental space for it. Remembering the previous dream made me wonder why they kept happening. I scratched my head with all of my fingers, ruffling my messy hair further.

I heard voices in the other room, so I eased out of bed and stretched, then poked my head out of the doorway to see where she was. Kerenza stood at the entrance to her quarters, bidding Zia goodbye. I tucked back in just as she leaned forward to kiss her, I didn't want to intrude. Kerenza came around the corner a moment later.

"Bonus mane, Lily. The Fae do not usually give thanks, but … I feel that I must. It is rare that we do, so I wanted you to know how truly appreciative I am of what you did for me."

"Of course, I'm just glad you're feeling better. You seem more like yourself," I noted as I looked her over.

She nodded and sighed. "I imagine it will not be easy, but I am ready for a change. Zia has helped remove all vinirubrum and vocafortis from here. And she has pledged to not indulge in it around me as well."

"I will, too. I'd gladly support you in that."

She smiled. "Truly?"

"Definitely." My thoughts shifted to my mate. "I should return to my quarters. When you feel up to it, will you talk to Rannoch? He wanted to know what was wrong, but I didn't tell him. I didn't think it was my place to say."

She grimaced, but nodded her agreement before bidding me farewell.

As I walked back to my home I thought about my dreams. Only when I spent myself completely were they untroubled. More than that, they were a void. Maybe that's all I was capable of, either dark dreams or all out blackness. I supposed it shouldn't be a surprise, given some of my experiences. But my dreams lately had seemed like more than that. They seemed like messages. Whatever they might have meant was still a mystery.

I arrived at my quarters to find Rannoch cleaning up an apparent mess that had happened while I was away. I panicked as I looked around. There were things scattered on the floor, the furniture was out of place, and something ceramic had shattered. "Did someone ransack our house?" *Oh my God, she's here. She's found me and she's come to kill us!* "What happened? Did she—did she find us?" I clasped my neck in fear.

Rannoch turned to me as he held a broom in his hands. His piked ears angled in a way I had only seen once before. His face, his whole demeanor was off. His expression reminded me of a time I did not want to remember; when we had been captured by Opius. At the time Opius had revealed Rannoch's involvement in a plan that Rannoch had engineered, along with Naiya's help to subvert the Umorfae. Part of that plan he had hatched was to split me off from Opius, so that Opius would not have a Vale Born to manipulate. The look he gave me was reminiscent of when that truth was made known. Did he look … guilty?

"What happened?" I repeated.

He looked like he was at a loss for words. Or, that he didn't want to admit something. "It was not … it was me. I lost control."

"You?" I glanced around. He had toppled things over, even nearly broke a gift given to us for our Pompa, the celebration equivalent of a wedding ceremony. "You did this?" I dropped my hands and glared at him. "I thought she came here! I instantly thought it was Dashelle. But no! It was you!"

He started to speak, but this time I didn't want to hear whatever he had to say. I held up my hand, mirroring his prior motion the last time I had seen him. This was no way to treat each other, the way he had been to me, or how I was being at the moment. But that didn't change the fact that I wanted to hear none of this fuckery he had unleashed for the time being. "Nope. I am *done* right now. I don't want to hear it." I had made it barely two steps into our house before I had thought Dashelle had been in there. The belief was enough for me to realize how far in her claws had reached into my brain. At every turn the possibility of her finding her way there had my stress level elevated with hypervigilance. I needed to end her hold on me. It took me all of two seconds before I was out the door and heading down the hall, away from there.

And away from TerraIgni.

CHAPTER 18

Zephyrine was alert as she greeted me in the equus valley, seemingly unsurprised by my visit. Dusk had fallen at last, the misty skies barely had any light left in them. I stroked her neck in greeting, silently asking her if she would permit me a ride so late. I had made no preparations, given no thought to leaving as I started to mount up. I did have one plan in mind, though. I needed information, not a confrontation. Tired of this mental cat and mouse game that was wearing me down, I had finally resolved to go visit the Maeder Tree to find out firsthand why I kept dreaming of her. I would take to the skies and fly myself out of TerraIgni to resolve this bullshit.

I gripped Zephyrine's mane, about to swing my leg over her back when it struck me what I was doing. More like slapped me right across my face. Memories flooded my mind of when I had snuck out of our Ignisfae encampment, then rode Zephyrine into the mist, and finally delivered myself on the doorstep of the Umorfae stronghold. My intentions had been to spare the rest of my group—my friends, my family—from harm. In that case I had knowingly gone into enemy territory, with the ultimate intention of demanding the Syrenni's release from their servitude. Granted, it was a totally different situation, but I was doing nearly the same thing again. I was cutting out their choice in the matter, closing them off from helping me or even the knowledge of what I intended to do. Beyond that, I had made zero plans other than going to the Maeder Tree. Food? Nope, I didn't have any with me. I had no weapons, no contingency plan in place in case I did cross paths with anyone dangerous. Aside from the danger I would have put myself in for multiple reasons if I did leave, this was not something a person with responsibilities to more people than just herself would do.

This was not something a princess would do.

A princess would consider who would be affected by her actions. In truth I didn't know exactly what a princess would or should do, but I knew at least a princess probably wouldn't do what I was about to.

I closed my eyes, steadying myself for a moment. What I wanted to do was to flee, to fly into the night. To leave my current troubles behind. But running wouldn't work anyway. Wherever I go, my problems would go with me. I opened my eyes, then released Zeph's mane. "Later, girl. We'll make this flight later." I started to walk away when she nudged at me from behind, demanding attention, rubbing her head which was more than half my height against my back. I almost smiled as she nearly knocked me over with her forcefulness. I may have been conflicted about my current situation, but Zephyrine's unconditional affection and devotion helped me release a bit of the hold it had on me. I relented, and turned back around to spend time with her. While I pet her forehead, I started to hatch a plan—one that would actually be prepared for, and involved more than me running away.

"Lil, let's think about this a little further," Felix said as he paced the war room. "You have no proof that leaving TerraIgni will fix anything. I don't think this will do what you hope it will. I say we stay until we have more information."

I paused, looking at everyone gathered around the large map of Alternis. The last time we had surrounded the great war table, we had been planning our infiltration of Umorfae territory. It was a plan that I didn't stick to, and nearly got myself killed in the process. This time I intended to make a plan with them and follow through on what we eventually, hopefully, agree on. But Felix was making me regret ever bringing it to their attention.

Rannoch leaned over the table, his hands splayed out for support as he surveyed the vast inlaid map in the resined wood surface. "No," he said at last. He stood, then faced Felix. "We should go. Lily has been having relentless dreams of the Maeder Tree. It is true that we do not know what she will find at the Midgard Well, but there must be a reason for it. We will find no answers for it here, that much I'm sure of."

"You're just trying to get in her good graces again," Felix muttered.

Kerenza coughed a laugh. Dhirdre rolled her lips and looked away, while Dhiren seemed to nod his agreement with Felix.

"Whose side are you on?" Rannoch balked at Dhiren. "Whatever my motivations may or may not be, I do believe it should be the next course of action. And, as she has told us, she almost left without us. At least now we can decide how best to help her."

I gave Rannoch a half smile, but kept my link closed to him. I was not over how he had reacted in our quarters, but I did appreciate his effort.

"We do travel to the Midgard Well once a cycle," Kerenza added, "it would simply be earlier than usual. I see no problem with the journey."

"No problem?" Felix butted in. "How about Dashelle? She could be anywhere."

I sighed. "Yes, she could be. I realize you haven't been plagued by the same dreams as I have, Felix, but something tells me there's more to it than that. I don't think I can just hide here in TerraIgni while these visions slowly drive me crazy."

"But what is the likelihood we would even cross paths with her?" Dhirdre asked. She motioned to the table. "Alternis is so vast it takes considerable time to cross it, even by equus—which she does not have. Even if she found out we were there, we could be long gone by the time she arrived."

I tapped my chin. "True, but she and I are both Vale Born. Technically we are connected by way of the Maeder Tree. She could be having dreams just as I am."

"But *I* haven't felt anything, and supposedly I'm connected the same way, right?" Felix countered.

I paused. Why was Felix untouched by the dreams? He would be just as susceptible to them ... if that was where they were originating from. If it was the Maeder Tree, wouldn't he also have them? My stomach turned, it may be proof that it was not the Maeder Tree reaching out, but rather me slowly losing myself to madness.

"Dashelle does not have the same foothold she had before,"

Kerenza offered. "She has lost her Umorfae allies. She is now just one female left to find her way by her own devices."

Dhiren cut in. "She has lost *those* allies, what if she found others? There are dark forces in Alternis, granted some of those are mainly dormant. Left on their own they are nearly benign, but what if she found some of them? The Pythonisamul for instance, she was a known previous ally of Vitus Augustus. And the Kakodaimons, they are tormented spirits who barely seem sentient, but perhaps with a master they could be turned into something more."

I shivered at the mention of both the witch creature and the horrendous clawed spirits of the desert. I shook my head. "Well I sure fucking hope that's not the case. I'd hardly call the Pythonisamul benign. That bitch is terrifying. Also considering the Kakodaimons, Dashelle would need the ability to cross the Hinterdunes to make that a possibility, right? They only appear there as far as I know. Though, I did realize that she only needed to find another Vale Born who had the skill of fire. They wouldn't have known who she was, and would probably be unprepared for the level of depravity Dashelle can sink to. I know of two tears in the Vale, do any of you know of more?"

Dhiren stepped forward, pointing at the map to the west of Umorfae lands. "The Southwest Tear, of course you know of that one because that is where you and Felix came through." He moved around the table and slid his hand to the rim of the world above the Praegra Forest, the massive swath of treed land that covered most of the realm. "The North Aperture, perhaps that is where Dashelle came through?" he asked.

"Not sure. Any others? I don't think there would be anymore Vale Born coming from there if that is where she came from, I'm pretty sure she killed them all already and took their powers … at least that's what she had claimed."

"I have heard of one called the Ita Hua Tear," Dhiren pointed to a region to the east of Limnaer, at the western-most side of the northern Hinterdunes. "Strong, cold winds in the area make the journey nearly impassable. I am pretty sure there is one there, but the Caelifae keep it swept free of all beings. They have for the last fifty cycles or so. I would guess that is something Prince Ser'Ti's faeder enacted, King Ventar Zan Cireclos. So I would doubt she came from that one."

I tapped my chin. "If she's looking for more Vale Born, she will probably be in that direction. Unless there's more tears we don't know about. But, all of this is just conjecture, it's possibilities without any concrete information. That's what we need, information."

Rannoch's posture swelled a little, his eyes sparkling with pride at me. "I take it you have an idea beyond going to the Maeder Tree?"

I relented and smiled at him at last. "I do. One I'm taking from your book, Rannoch, but in my own way. And something from Don'Li, too." Rannoch had been plucking at our link, softly asking me to open up to him. I finally did, and I felt his surge of relief as our connection sparked between us. It wasn't something anyone could see or hear, but as we met in the middle, two arms lengths away from each other and yet bonded by an invisible cord between us, I could practically see the charge it created. Everyone else faded to the background as I focused solely on him. My heart fluttered as we stared at each other.

"Um, hello! What is this idea you have?" Felix threw up his hands in exasperation. "Maybe you can let us in on the plan before you go ogling each other."

"Oh, right." I laughed. "Might as well not drag it out." I smiled at Felix, waiting a moment.

"Really?" He deadpanned. "You're the absolute worst sometimes."

"Okay, okay. Rannoch had taken us to the Amabilis once, they knew of things because they travel the sub-layer of the world. I don't think you've traveled that way, Felix. It's like a microscopic universe that connects every part of the realm. They have knowledge because of their hive mind. I thought we could seek them out and see what they might have heard, any rumblings in the world."

"We can try that," Rannoch said, "but remember they like to remain neutral. They keep themselves set apart from the Fae because they do not want to get involved."

I nodded. "True. Well, I figured, *if* we cross paths with any Amabilis on our way we can ask them if they know anything. And if they know of any other tears to the human world. There's no way to know where the Amabilis would be, correct?"

"A few can usually be found to the north of our nomadic encampment, between Umorfae territory and the Maeder Tree," Kerenza offered. "But, there is no guarantee."

"Okay, well that's only part of my idea. The other plan would be to call Livi."

"Your Faerie friend?" Felix asked.

I nodded. "Don'Li taught me how to send messages by way of the Faeries. I think Livi was the difference between success and failure multiple times. Livi flew all the way to Rannoch in TerraIgni when I was in the Hinterdunes, and Livi flew to the Arbor Elves when we needed help to get the Syrenni out of Umorfae territory and to a new home. Though they be but little, they are fierce. Livi and their Faerie cohorts should never be underestimated."

"Why don't you just call her now, so she can tell you what she might know without you leaving TerraIgni?" Felix asked.

"Them," I corrected. "Faeries are gender fluid. And no, I won't call them now. It's too dangerous for them to cross the Hinterdunes."

"But, you just said Livi crossed the Hinterdunes to tell Rannoch!" Felix objected.

"I did, but it wasn't safe for them to do that. Had I known the first time I had asked I wouldn't have done it. I won't allow it to happen again. Besides, we need to go to the Maeder Tree either way. This plan is to try and get the most information possible."

"I agree with your plan, Lily," Rannoch announced. "We should leave on the next rotation."

"Well I guess that settles that," Felix muttered.

CHAPTER 19

The war room had cleared, leaving Rannoch and I staring at each other from across the thick wood slab table.

When Felix and Dhiren left, Felix was still unhappy with the results of the meeting. He had made it abundantly clear he didn't want me leaving TerraIgni. It was his protective nature stepping in again, that much I was sure of. But maybe he had his own reasons for fearing crossing paths with Dashelle. Felix was one of several I needed to have a private conversation with to clear the air before we left. Another such person was standing right in front of me.

Rannoch eyed me warily, his ears shifting as he tried to ascertain my mood. In milliseconds he went from the stoic, self-assured leader I had first met, to the worried, scorned mate of mine, and back.

"I would like to apologize again," he said at last.

I sighed. "I forgive you, we need to move beyond this and resolve our issues. If we're struggling with things between us, it will distract us from what we might face when we leave TerraIgni. I have my own difficulties which I need to apologize for, too. I'm sorry for not understanding how you felt when I was with Kerenza, for not even thinking about it. I should have recognized. I need to do better."

He closed his eyes and sucked in a breath, then emphatically bobbed his head in agreement. "Yes. We are stronger together, but when we have strife it becomes a weakness. If we are about to face something dangerous we need to have clear heads."

"Hopefully next time it can be without the alphahole behavior," I said in a half-joking manner.

"… Alphahole?"

"Alpha male asshole." He dropped his jaw. "You aren't that," I added quickly, "but when you do stuff like what you did it falls into that category. Not only that, but everything I've been dealing internally with regarding Dashelle made me think that she was there, in our *home*, what should have been my safe space."

He raised his palms. "Okay, fair point."

"What I mean is, we need to smooth things out. I *want* us both to be happy. I wasn't just thinking of impending battle or facing something dangerous. Although, this campaign—if you could even call it that—doesn't feel like it has the same gravity as when we planned the Syrenni coup. Or when we fought the Umorfae outside of the cave. This feels so much smaller."

"So, because this is not a full scale battle you feel it is less important?"

I shrugged in resignation. "I guess so. This isn't about saving anyone else. It's not about planning some big event that could turn the tides in a critical moment like we've done in the past. It feels a little … self-centered. Actually it feels a lot self-centered."

He walked around the table, then took two strides toward me, raising his hand to my cheek. "It does not have to be a massive battle for it to make a difference. Sometimes it is the narrow approach that is the best choice, slip in and slip out, be exacting and precise. Sometimes it is those personal wounds which require a delicate handling, and eventually have a much bigger impact. Look at when we fought the Umorfae at the cave. That was a long lead up which started from micro-maneuvers. Kerenza and I subverting here and there, not large assaults leaving casualties on both sides. And it all started from a personal injury. Kenneder was killed and Emblyn was taken, along with several other children. That was very personal for Kerenza and I."

I searched his eyes, the fire dancing in his pupils, and I felt the truth of his words through our link.

"Speaking of Kerenza, she told me what she has been going through, what you helped her with. I understand now why you wanted her to be the one to tell me. I know you've learned the Fae don't often say thank you. But in this case, I feel you deserve to hear it. Truly, thank you for what you did for her. I did not understand what was going on. It's another example of you being there for those that you love. We are all ready to be there for you for this next mission. And whatever missions may follow."

I nodded, holding myself together by sheer willpower. Still, the edge of guilt chewed at me, that the expedition would be primarily for me and taxing for everyone involved.

"You said the need to go to the Maeder Tree feels self-centered to you," he continued, "but that is not how I see it. I believe the effort will be rewarded with a better understanding. Perhaps we will get answers about Eiulans, the ability to know—rather than guess—where Dashelle is and to find what has been happening lately. We do not know these things out here in TerraIgni, we are split off because of the Hinterdunes. The region is our protector and our isolator. We *have* to leave to gather information, we always have. It is one reason we have gone on expeditions every cycle. We hunt, and trade, and find out what has happened since we last set foot in the Praegra Forest. Your arrival has not changed this. The difference is that this time there are issues tied up with you, and the only way we can unravel them is by seeking out that which might be causing them. The death of Eiulans is more than just you, it is our family, you are the closest to it, but we are all involved because of who he was. The issue of Dashelle can very well impact all in Alternis, it nearly did before, who is to say that could not happen again? She made no secret of her hunt for you at the time, which we have to assume still continues. It is up to us to prevent her rise again."

I hung on to each word he said like a lifeline. They were not sugar coated, easy to swallow words that he tried to feed me, to supplicate me into oblivious comfort. They were straightforward realities of our situation, unfiltered and unskewed. The heartfelt truth that nearly caused me to choke up was that though I was closest to the situation, it was about the many and not the one. The sense I had about it being about me had led me to isolate. I had almost completed that detachment by leaving on Zephyrine, to accomplish the task by myself.

For the first time in I wasn't sure how long, I no longer felt alone.

Felix paced his quarters as Dhiren excused himself.

"Why don't you tell me what you're upset about regarding this decision, rather than trying to wear a hole in the floor," I said as I leaned against the counter where two used capuli cups sat.

"I should think it would be obvious."

"Well, I guess it is, but I'm not entirely sure why. You were okay with going to Limnaer."

He stopped and looked at me for a long, hard moment. "I have a lot to lose. Dashelle nearly beat us before, and now that we essentially no longer have Mom, you're the only family I have left. Limnaer was a dream before we went there, a magically floating city where I could train? Who wouldn't be excited about that? Then she apparently snuck in there, flexed her murderous muscles in secret, then bounced. It could have been you, or me, or Dhiren that she killed. She is cunning and we never seem to see her next move coming. She burned down our family home, neither of us anticipated that. Leaving again … it fills me with dread."

"I understand. I really do, but I can't keep hiding here. I feel her tormenting me from afar, like some psychological warfare bullshit. I have to break the cycle. And I understand if you want to stay here with Dhiren."

He shook his head. "Of course I won't do that. I wouldn't leave you to face her on your own."

"I wouldn't be on my own."

"I know, but I would not … I couldn't do that. I think I'm just still coming around to the decision, because I didn't realize that we'd have to leave to solve this."

I nodded. "I know you didn't cross the Hinterdunes the same way as me and develop the same understanding of the region. Rannoch calls the Hinterdunes both the "protector and the isolator" of TerraIgni, they don't know anything of what is going on in the rest of the world unless they venture out."

"I'm starting to get that."

"This is also Dhiren's way of life; he leaves every cycle with Rannoch to essentially make a pilgrimage, hunt the mutus— the beasts of the hinterdunes, and trade. Has he talked about that at all with you?"

"We did just earlier." He motioned to the empty capuli mugs. "I do understand better now, though this is far from being like their annual trip. I'm still not thrilled about the idea of putting you in harm's way again, but I also want this resolved."

"I think Dashelle is mentally harming me whether I go or stay. I need to go to release her hold on me. I don't know for sure that it will work, but I've got to try. It's hard for me to accept that this expedition is essentially for me, I don't like that one bit, but I'm convinced the Maeder Tree needs something, something big. So maybe it's not all for me like Rannoch has been telling me."

"I didn't mean to make it harder for you. But don't you dare suggest I stay behind again. I'm going whether you like it or not."

I grinned. "I wouldn't dream of it."

I found Kerenza's quarters open with a breeze flowing through from the open terrace to the front door. She and Zia were inside cleaning together. I knocked on the wall to get her attention.

"Why are you knocking? Get your culus in here, you silly

filia!" she called out in her sing-song tone she used when she was in a good mood.

"Glad to see you are feeling well!"

"Yes! Zia and I are preparing to leave. I always like to return to clean quarters."

I gave her a half-smile. "I was hoping to talk to you, if you have time?"

She stopped her dusting and looked me over. "Certainly. Zia, will you do me a favor? I was hoping you would see if Lennaraz was available before we left."

Zia kissed her on the cheek. "Anything for you." She disappeared out the open front door.

"Come, let us sit on the terrace and take a break. Percala juice? Or capuli?" Kerenza asked as she motioned for me to follow her further into her home.

"Capuli! I could use a drop right now."

She brewed us a fresh pot, using her Ignisphaera to light the flame. I realized she had donned the glass bauble necklace that carried the living fire after our meeting in the war room. The last time she had worn the gift given by her mother, was when we were battling the Umorfae to free the Syrenni. I also thought back on how she had used it to kill the Daemalum, creating a river of flame that engulfed the creature. She never went into a fight without it.

She poured us both a hearty mug full, then set out frothed cream to add.

"So, I take it you intend to join the expedition?" I asked, motioning with my chin to her necklace. She had said as much when I arrived, but wearing the necklace was a sign to me that she intended to be prepared to fight.

She curled her fingers around it, with the same hand that still bore the ring given to her by Kenneder. Her expression went as dark as the bezel-set gem in its center, its fire having died out at the same time his own light withered. "Of course I am. I would not miss it. Plus, I think you might need me, do you not think so?"

"It isn't that," I said after taking my first sip, then setting my cup down. "I wanted to make sure you felt up to it. You've been through a huge change and the recovery seemed physically taxing for you. I wasn't sure if you needed more rest. I didn't want you to feel pressured to go."

"I think it will be the best thing for me, actually. Maybe the Maeder Tree will finish the last of my physical healing, just like I had mentioned to you many rotations ago. Of course, I did not foresee the coming changes, but the truth is I may need to replenish in the Well either way. Not only that, I want to be there to help you, if I can. Going will give me something I very much need, purpose."

"And what about Emblyn?"

"You always ask the hard questions." She smiled in jest, but then her face fell. "Yes, it is true. Emblyn is also my purpose, but she is well cared for with my maeder, and I am not yet ready to face her. I am becoming a better version of myself, she deserves that much. I will give her the best version I can be. I have the luxury and the privilege of having my maeder to help with her. And because she had missed out on Emblyn's early cycles, this is good for them both. I have spoken with my maeder, she knows of my struggles and what efforts I am making now. I am lucky to have her support."

She spoke with self-assured belief, but worry creased her brow. I could tell she felt conflicted over the need to have Queen Deniza shoulder so much of the mothering duties lately. I reached forward and squeezed her hand. "Asking others for help isn't easy, I know I wrestle with the guilt of reaching out."

She nodded and looked down. 'Yes, that is exactly it. The guilt of it all. The logic is sound, I need to get better and my maeder is willing, plus they are building a relationship. But the guilt … the guilt is strong regardless of how much sense the choice makes. Having a young one is not easy, but it is worth it, as you may find out in the future."

My whole body stiffened. I really didn't want to once again discuss the prospect of Rannoch and I having a baby.

"Perhaps you will choose that path, long from now when you are ready," she added, and I visibly relaxed at her words.

It felt like it had finally gotten through to everyone that someday, after my mate and I had spent a lot of time together and were actually settled in our lives, I might consider the possibility of having a child. But I wasn't going to allow anyone to pressure me into it.

Kerenza blew out a breath and closed her eyes for a beat, when she reopened them she seemed to have swept away her momentary slide into unsettled thoughts regarding her guilt. "I wanted to ask you if you would consider doing a rite with me."

"A rite? Like what?"

"A colormaking ceremony. I always saved space on my arm, in case Rannoch ever found a mate." She pointed to the one bare section on her inner forearm, just below the elbow. It was the only spot she had on that arm that wasn't emblazoned with colorful tattoos. "It is a way to bond us, by us both getting the same colormark, it would commemorate our sisterhood."

I had always admired her tattoos, and Rannoch's, for that matter, but I had never really considered getting one myself. Mostly because I wasn't sure what I would choose. It took me less than a second to decide. "Let's do it!"

She smiled. "First, we have to collect what is needed."

CHAPTER 20

Kerenza led me on a winding path away from the fortress. We had passed through the equus valley, Zephyrine stopped nuzzling Rannoch's equus, Steren, to watch me walk by without greeting her. I shrugged apologetically as she whinnied. Kerenza kept walking straight ahead toward a narrow opening at the end of the canyon. I rushed to keep up.

The trail banked steeply up to the right, winding and climbing at an odd angle. I had to brace myself on the craggy wall for support. Fortunately, Kerenza still wore the Ignisphaera, the light it emitted was just bright enough to cast a warm glow on the rugged path. When we had entered the opening that was only a little wider than shoulder width, the walls had towered over us by at least two hundred feet. As we continued down the path they shrunk to half that height. We had climbed so quickly we were already halfway to the top. It wasn't long before we reached the plateau, my knees were shaking from the exertion. The lingering effects of her withdrawals meant even Kerenza was winded.

"Where are we going?" I asked between gulps of air. My eyes were still adjusting to the darkness of the desert at night. The faint glow coming from the fortress center far off in the canyon below the plateau, and Kerenza's Ignisphaera, were the only sources of light.

"To collect the colormark blooms." She pointed to a region in the distance, further away from the center of TerraIgni.

At first there was nothing I could pick out, not even the shape of land against the sky. But then, I saw it. Flickers of light and color started to filter through. They were the faintest, tiniest specks of light against an inky black backdrop. From a distance they looked like fireflies or Faeries floating in the night air.

"Those are flowers?" I had only seen glowing flowers once in Alternis, in the Praegra Forest near where I had slipped through the Vale. Opius had braided the stems together of a few he had plucked, then placed them in my hair.

I grinned at Kerenza. Something about making a new memory to replace ones he had soured filled me with an intangible sense that missteps could be righted one day. A rebalancing of what went wrong. He had left micro-wounds along with the obvious ones with his treachery, any good memory there had been was tainted by his duplicitous ways. Ever so slowly, I was chipping away at my mistakes from when I had first arrived in this mystical land. The flowers may not have had any impact or changed anything that had been in progress, but they represented a moment for me in which I had become charmed by Opius. My previous hesitations about him had been swept away by the gesture of putting flowers behind my ear, and now, standing on the sacred desert above TerraIgni, I was picking up the last shreds of his wrongdoings. I was taking back my memories into my own hands.

"Let's go!" I called out as I launched into a run.

She laughed and caught up with me quickly. We ran the whole

way there, I was beaming from ear to ear by the time we reached the glowing field. Soft oranges and purples lit up the bobbing petals of the knee high flowers. Thousands of them scattered out in a circle around us. Their presence seemed to defy nature itself, surviving in an arid region with little to no moisture. I spun, looking at the blooms which splayed out wider than my hand. "How is it that they live here?"

"Their roots grow through to the sublayer, that is also what makes them glow. They do not need water to survive." Kerenza slipped her hand under the head of an especially large bloom, admiring it for a moment.

I gasped when I noticed her arm. "Your tattoos are glowing too!"

"Tattoos? Oh," she laughed, looking at her arm, "yes, the colormarks glow when they are near the blooms that they were made from. Pick at least ten blooms, the ones that you are meant to pick will appear brighter to you. We will take them to the colormark artifex, Lennaraz. She will ink our skin with them."

"Do we have time to do this before leaving for the Maeder Tree?"

Kerenza nodded. "I did inform Rannoch that I intended to ask you to join me in the rite before we left. He agreed that it was an auspicious time to do it. He did not seem concerned about the time it would take."

I nearly squealed with glee, I was actually *excited* about something. For that alone I was thankful for Kerenza, but much larger than that was the appreciation I felt for the friendship and sisterhood she had shared with me.

We waded further out into the flowers. As I looked around, I realized one or two turned toward me, and became brighter, bolder. Their petals unfurled more, calling me closer.

"When you find one that you feel is meant for you, lift the bloom off like this," she said as she demonstrated, placing the stem between her fingers with her hand cupped gently around the head of the plant. She popped it off with one motion. "Removing the blooms like this doesn't hurt them, it will simply grow another." Kerenza placed it in a thin fabric bag she had tucked into her linteum, then handed me another one she had stowed with it to put my own flowers in.

There was a calm that settled over me as we began collecting the flowers, something about the comfortable night air amongst the glowing blooms soothed my soul. Every time I set my hand in place around a stem to collect a flower, I felt a surge through me, a connection to the sublayer. The pulses that I had witnessed when I traveled the network with the Amabilis flowed through the flower petals just the same. It reminded me that the whole world was connected, for every cause there was an effect.

It wasn't long before we had collected all that we needed, and were heading back to the winding canyon which led to the city. The purple and orange light emanating from the flowers seeped through our bags, as we wound down the dark path. I was careful not to crush the petals as I anchored myself into the rough wall, leveraging my weight against the surface to keep from slipping. In spite of having to carefully navigate, it was thankfully much easier to make it to the bottom than it was to climb to the top.

After passing the equus, Kerenza walked past where we would have turned to head into the fortress proper—where each of our quarters were—and instead went toward a less traveled portion of TerraIgni. We entered the opposite corner of the city from the bazaar, the eastern-most reaches. It seemed most of the darkened doorways were residences, their wall sconces snuffed out while they rested. I followed Kerenza through a dimly lit narrow street, until we came to a courtyard. A fountain stood in the middle, with a small flourish of water bubbling from the top of the smooth, slowly rotating stone sphere. I nearly stopped walking, its design wasn't like anything else I had seen in TerraIgni. Detailed etchings were patterned around the base which held the perfect sphere.

"Come, she is waiting for us." Kerenza angled her chin toward the partially open door. The light spilled out of the folded back fabric, pooling on the red earthen tiles laid in concentric rings around the fountain. Someone played music from within, filling the tall rotunda walled garden with the gentle plucking of a stringed instrument.

I stepped into a room to find the circular design continued throughout, stone sculptures bordered the compact entryway. The music that drifted down a short hallway stopped, then a figure moved toward us. The overhead brazier cast brilliant highlights in her coppery hair which reached her waist, as she stepped closer to greet us.

"I am honored to have you here," she said, her silken tone as enchanting as her tawny skin.

Kerenza smiled and hugged her in greeting, then formally introduced the two of us.

Lennaraz ushered us into a room past the foyer. Lighting a stick from a candle, she lit each wall torch one by one.

"I could have helped you with that," Kerenza said, holding the Ignisphaera toward her.

Lennaraz waved a hand. "No need. I am used to doing it this way."

I paused, realizing that she had not simply lit them by funneling flame from one source to another like most Ignisfae would. She finished lighting the wicks, then snuffed out the flame with her fingers.

"Ah," she said, turning toward me, "I see you have already noticed. I am not like most Ignisfae. I am only half, and half Petrafae. I am able to command rock, but not flame. Even my ability with stone is not like most Petrafae, I can do things which take more time, shaping stone to my will, but sudden bursts of energy to move mountains is not something I can do."

"The fountain, you made that," I stated.

"Yes," she said as she smiled. "As I have less brute force with my skill, I use it to make things, delicate and finely crafted things. Please, sit." She opened her arm to the low table with backless seats around it. An arm-length brass cylinder sat on the floor, its woven hose which attached into the side was wrapped around a thin hooped handle.

I took the closest chair, Kerenza sat next to me, then she set her bag of flowers on the table. I copied her, and placed my bag beside hers.

"Magna, it will take me a little time to prepare the dye," Lennaraz said, as she seated herself across from us. She picked up the brass cylinder, then set it on the table and lifted off the top. Inside were various fittings and chambers. It looked familiar in a way. She dropped in Kerenza's flowers one by one, placing them in different compartments depending on their color. Once they were all inside, she tightened the lid on, then clicked the whole apparatus counter-clockwise from the joint at the midsection. I realized as I watched the fittings adjust, that it reminded me of the Starcrest telescope.

"Did Yantz make this?" I asked.

"He did! I learned to colormark from him, back when he used to do it."

"Figures," I chuckled, "that guy has done everything."

Lennaraz glanced at Kerenza curiously, probably trying to get a read on my way of speaking.

"So," I said, "was your maeder or faeder Petrafae?" I had never met a mixed Fae before, and hadn't heard that it was possible for the different races of Fae to have children together.

She nodded, checking the machine as it clicked. "My maeder. My faeder is a guard for King Ashwan. He met her on a trade expedition long ago. They petitioned their rulers to be together, then they had me." She looked up at me, studying my expression. "There are not many like me, it is not easy for the Fae to mate with others not of their kind. Most cannot survive mating with an Ignisfae, and their offspring cannot produce younglings. So, we are a limited number. Umorfae and Caelifae can have more success, but no one wants to mix with an Umorfae."

I blurted out a laugh. "Well that doesn't surprise me. So, mating between the different Fae factions is more about whether it's possible, rather than whether it's accepted or not?"

"Yes, because of the risk, and because any youngling would then not be able to carry on the line, it does not happen often. But, fortunately it is not looked down upon. I have made a life for myself here, the fact that I will not have a filia or filio to call my own does not lessen the richness of my existence. There are many full-blooded Fae that never have younglings, and it does not define them. Why should it define me?"

"Well put." I smiled. The machine clicked, pulling my gaze down to it.

Lennaraz pulled out another smaller brass fitting, one that funneled down to a fine needle. "Kerenza, if you would," she said, holding it toward her.

Kerenza twisted open the Ignisphaera, then funneled a flame to superheat the tip of the needle. Once it was sanitized from the fire, Lennaraz attached it to the hose, tightening down the clamps to ensure the connection was solid.

"So," Lennaraz said as she motioned for Kerenza to lay her arm flat, "what is the inspiration for the colormark? Zia told me a little, and I know that it is one that you and Lily will share, but what do you both feel for this occasion?"

Kerenza smiled softly. "Something that indicates the bond of family, of sisterhood. As always I want you to ink what inspires you, but I feel this should signify our trust."

"And the belief in each other's strength," I added.

Kerenza looked over at me, then reached her hand to grip mine. "Yes, something that will be a reminder to the other, if either of us has ended up on a dark path alone, or the feeling that the weight of the world is too great, to be able to look at the colormark and remember our strength."

"Strength through sisterhood," I agreed.

Lennaraz smiled, and got to work. I watched as she laid down beautiful, graceful curving lines. The colormark bloom ink glowed for a moment before the illumination seeped fully into the skin. Kerenza would wince every so often as the needle continued its path, but she never flinched or retracted her arm. Before long, Lennaraz was ready to start on mine. She placed my blooms in the canister, and while they were transmuted into a gorgeous glowing ink, she undid the needle from the hose to prepare it for my skin.

"Lily, perhaps you would like the honors," Lennaraz said.

I grinned, so often I was a little uncomfortable Fire Bringing around Ignisfae that didn't know me. Even though fire was a normal part of their lives, they usually reacted with such surprise that I tended to keep it under wraps. I unfurled my hand and let go of the damper which was always barely resting in place, like a kettle lid with pressurized steam underneath making it jitter and dance. The flame erupted and grew to envelop the tip quickly.

She held the apparatus in place and didn't shrink in the slightest at the tumult of flame which sprung from my palm. "Does fire not affect you?" I asked.

She used her chin and a flick of her eyes to indicate for me to cap the flame. I clenched my fist, ending the release of my fire.

"No," she said as she put the needle portion back onto the hose end. "I have no skill with fire, but it also does not hurt me. Though I did not receive the direct gift of fire from my faeder, I was born with the ability to resist it. That is normal for a mestisius, a half-breed. Whatever skill they are not born with but their bloodline carries, they carry the ability to not be affected negatively by it."

I stopped myself from adding some uninspired single-word response as I marveled at this world. Of course there were lots of people that were born of more than one heritage back home, but it was a factor I hadn't really thought much about regarding Alternis, whether or not mixed races were common. I decided not to mention anything about the only mestisius I knew of, which was the first known child of a Syrenni and an Umorfae. Naiya and Locrien's baby, Sereia, was now in the care of Naiya's sister Neila. Hopefully Sereia was growing well, surrounded by the recently freed Syrenni in their new home.

Lennaraz started working, and it quickly snapped me out of my thoughts. The pain that seared into my skin was a slow, dull, burning sensation. The delicate interior of my forearm instantly ached, but in a subtle, bearable way.

"Are you all right?"

"Yes." I laughed a little. "I've never gotten a tattoo, I mean colormark. I wasn't sure what to expect. It kind of feels like a sunburn."

"What is a sunburn?" Kerenza and Lennaraz asked in unison.

I chuckled. "Right, I forgot." I explained the sun and sunburns, as well as the meaning of jinx—which they both thought was hilarious—as Lennaraz worked.

I was entranced as I watched her skim my arm, the pattern grew as she continued. Kerenza's arm stayed near mine, Lennaraz using it as reference to get every detail to match.

Before long she finished up the last of it, the darker blues and purples added shading to the brighter oranges and reds. Lennaraz coated both of our inner arms with a clear soothing jelly, which helped lessen the burning sensation. I admired the design, it reminded me of a Celtic knot spliced with a complicated mandala, yet it was entirely different from anything I had seen. Kerenza put her arm up close to mine, and I gasped. "They connect!" The lines glowed again for a brief moment as they met. The final result was stunning, it was a complete pattern on its own, yet when it was placed next to Kerenza's it formed a larger interwoven design.

"Strong on your own, and strong together," Lennaraz said as she put away the equipment. "You are connected in your lives, and each of you are a reminder to the other of what you can accomplish."

I looked at Kerenza, who held out her hand to clasp mine. "I never knew how much I needed you in my life," she said. "I am forever grateful to have you as a sister."

My lip wobbled as I looked at her. I had lost Maris, then Josie was there to help with that loss. Then I lost Josie. I couldn't say Kerenza filled that void that both Maris and Josie left, because Kerenza made that vacant space all her own. She filled it beyond brimming. I would always miss and honor the first sisters of my heart, and I would always treasure what Kerenza was to me. She was the sister that I looked up to, that one that led by example, that comforted, that taught me, that acknowledged her own issues and worked to move through life with grace and dignity. I squeezed her hand tighter. "I will always appreciate everything you are to me. I am stronger in part because of you. We are stronger together."

She smiled as tiny tears gleamed in the corners of her eyes. "Stronger together," she affirmed. "And now, on to our next adventure."

I nodded, wiping the back of my hand below my dampened eyes. "Let's get to it."

CHAPTER 21

I was surprised to see Zia after saying our goodbyes to Lennaraz. Waiting by the stone fountain which I now had a new appreciation for, Zia's smile split her face as she saw Kerenza step out of the doorway behind me.

"I thought I would walk back with you both. Lily, Rannoch is waiting for you in your quarters. Everyone will take a quarter rotation rest, then meet in the dining hall for Mane Fare and capuli, before heading out."

"Will you be joining us for the trip?" I asked. In truth, I had hoped she would join us. It would be good for Kerenza to have Zia there for support. Plus I had grown fond of her.

"Yes, I will help with supplies. We will not be traveling to any of the caches in the Hinterdunes to collect food stores, so all food will need to be brought with us."

I had to admit I hadn't thought of the logistics and planning. I was tempted to break Fae tradition and thank her for her foresight and organizational skills. The two of them had already started walking, so I followed behind. I watched them chatter happily back and forth. Grinning at them, I realized how happy Kerenza seemed. She had been through so much, and she could still find moments of peace, a respite from the trauma and heartache. It was a blessing and a miracle.

My pace slowed as it dawned on me that I had had my own relief from my troubled thoughts. Neither Dashelle, Eiulans, or the Maeder Tree had crossed my mind once during the entire time Kerenza and I had ventured out to pick flowers, nor during our colormark session. Not once did I mentally slide into the abyss of tortured wondering. Thinking through problems was one thing, but being abused by one's own mind was quite another. My colormark session turned out to be a wonderful form of therapy.

Kerenza beamed at Zia again, and time seemed to slow for a moment as I watched them. We were *allowed* to be happy again, and if happiness was elusive, we needed to fight for it. I would fight for it.

Kerenza noticed that I had fallen behind, and stopped to half-turn toward me. "Lily? Are you coming?"

I smiled and nodded. "Definitely."

"Damnatus, Kerenza," Rannoch cursed, again. "Always with the bacon! *My* bacon! Will you ever get your own plate?" He used his muscular arms and hulking form to shield his haul from the banquet table, to prevent her from getting more of his precious food. When it didn't work, he shifted his plate further out of reach, and twisted in his seat to angle away from her.

"Not likely," she said as she swiped another piece. She sat back in her seat with a grin, triumphantly crunching the pilfered bacon.

I chuckled as I ate my tortam. Felix, Dhirdre, and Dhiren laughed as they watched the siblings exchange taunts. Zia walked back over to our table with a loaded plate and sat down next to Kerenza.

"At least Zia has enough on her plate now to tempt Kerenza away from mine," Rannoch said as he swatted at his sister again.

"I can see how you might think that," Zia said around her first bite, then swallowed. "But this is all for me."

Kerenza stared at her and dropped her jaw. "You will not share with me either?"

Zia shook her head slowly, then took another bite. "No, it means too much to me."

Kerenza let out an exasperated sound and everyone burst out laughing. Zia giggled then slid her plate to share with Kerenza.

I smiled at Rannoch. He and I had a good night before our breakfast. He had admired my new colormark, then told me stories of how he got his own. I had dreamt of the Maeder Tree again, but it was restful sleep nonetheless. Overall it was a peaceful, comforting night before we would launch ourselves into the skies, to ride our equus over the Hinterdunes all the way to the Praegra Forest. I was surprised I wasn't nervous. Spending time with him, with everyone and getting our fill of food before we left was exactly what my heart needed. It was going to be a long, tiring flight, and we all needed every bit of relaxation we could soak up before we left.

When the last strip of bacon was stolen, and the last of my capuli cup was drained, we all headed out from the banquet hall, going straight to the equus valley.

It had already been a long time since we took to the air. Zephyrine never complained once, her wings beat through the mist in an unending rhythm. I adjusted my woven linteum, trying to get a little more coverage on my shoulders. It had been a comfortable temperature in TerraIgni, but now that we were way up in the mist that shrouded Alternis, it was a little too chilly. Fortunately the golden-hued fabric stretched and adjusted easily, I managed to pull the sides down of what was previously a halter top, it transformed into a shawl-style wrap without undoing the tie. Kerenza was right, her description of linteums being the most superior garments anywhere was spot on, she had done her best to convince me of that the first time she dressed me in one. A person could fight in one, or be comfortable enough to lounge on a sofa. There was nothing more versatile. It was case in point for how quickly I had changed the top. The bottom half of it though was another story, that would require dismounting, and we wouldn't be stopping for another rotation. I squirmed, trying to get it to cover my legs a little more.

Look in your bag, Zia packed you an extra wrap.

I shot my glance at Rannoch, who merely pointed to the leather satchel slung over Zephyrine's back. I undid the flap, then rooted around for something soft. I found it at the bottom, under several layers of snacks and provisions, rolled in a compact cylinder. I smiled at him and gave him an appreciative nod as I unfurled it. It was a heavenly warm weave of variegated purples and muted blues, reminiscent of the mist in a way. The color seemed similar to the blooms used for colormarking. I had never given thought to how they dyed their distinctive fabrics, but it made sense they would use the flowers for their weaving process as well. I thought about their various skills as I wrapped tightly around my waist, ensuring that it wouldn't flap or fly off in the wind. I settled in for the ride, adjusting my position on Zephyrine's bare back to take a short rest.

My mind wandered for hours on end, trying to get through the seemingly endless flight with no landscape to even look at as we flew. One thing that did change was the temperature, and sometimes the density of the mist. Strangely, it felt drier over TerraIgni. We were heading southwest to cut across the Hinterdunes where the desert was the narrowest. Flying due west would mean a straighter path to the Praegra Forest, but it also meant less ability to land easily should the need arise. I knew where we were flying to, we had used it as a rest point when we had gone to collect Felix at the border of the Hinterdunes. I smiled sadly as I thought of that time, of all the things Don'Li had done to help us, to help me. It felt like a lifetime ago that we had met up to pick up my brother, so much had happened in those short few months. I supposed to my human sense of what the time passage felt like it was quite a few months, but we had not yet crossed past the summer season as far as I could tell, as one day-to-night cycle back in my former home equaled twenty-eight rotations in Alternis. When I had first arrived in Alternis, Opius had explained it as a different frequency resonance, existing at a slower rate than the human realm, allowing the two places to exist overlaid on each other.

My chaotic shifting thoughts were halted as we started to descend. I breathed a sigh of relief, I was beyond appreciative for the impending ability to jump off of my equus and stretch my legs, not to mention use the bathroom.

After everyone had done what I had been needing to do, we met at the familiar camp area: a flat, sandy nook nestled next to a partial ring of rocky cliffs. I had peered over them as we had come in for a landing, it seemed like the edge of the earth. The mist dropped below the horizon on the side, like the strange, continent-sized biodome it created terminated somewhere off in the distance to the south. Zia unrolled a few blankets, which had been bundled behind her and Kerenza on their equus. She smoothed them out on the ground for us all to rest on.

A few minutes later, everyone was laughing and enjoying some snacks. I realized with dread that this was the point the vinirubrum usually came out, inside a waterskin, sometimes accompanied by sativa to smoke. I tried to hide my concern that this may be triggering for Kerenza.

We only brought water.

I exhaled as I looked at Rannoch. *Bless the Gods, I didn't think of how we usually had something to drink at this point until this very moment.*

He smiled at me, then reached forward to take my hand. *It's a small thing, but hearing you say that makes me think you now think of Alternis as your home. And I adore how you watch out for my sister.*

I was confused for a moment, and then realized he was

referring to how I used their phrase "bless the Gods", rather than my former human habit. I squeezed his hand in return. *My home is wherever you are.*

He wrapped an arm around me, scooting me closer to him and nuzzling his nose into my neck. We had gotten more used to being apart during the long equus rides, but reuniting was always a relief. I looked around at everyone, our small group off on another adventure. It would be another six rotations of flying at least, then we would find out how the rest of the realm fared since we had ventured out last. I thought of my Faerie friend, Livi. I hadn't called them in a long time. I had intended on doing it when I went to Limnaer, but our return trip home was so rushed and overshadowed by Eiulans's murder that I hadn't thought of doing it until it was too late. Hopefully the Faeries had good information to share, or some hint as to what we may expect to find. Maybe Livi could even help us locate the Amabilis, which could end up being a considerable shortcut, so as not to need to hunt through the Praegra Forest to find one.

"Well," Dhirdre said, "I think it is finally time for a game."

"No," Dhiren stated. "Absolutely not." He chopped his hand through the air in an emphatic gesture.

I steepled my fingers under my chin. "But just think, Dhiren. Maybe for once you might actually win. Winner's choice for the prize, remember?"

He groaned.

Felix perked up, instantly less sleepy. "No, we're *definitely* playing. Ludens palas, right? That game is awesome. Besides, I need to kick my sister's ass at this. Deal me in."

I mock-gasped at him, feigning offense.

I looked at Kerenza, who looked a little worried. Ludens palas was typically a drinking game. Zia rubbed her shoulder and whispered something in her ear. Kerenza breathed a sigh and smiled softly, nodding to her. "Yes, a game sounds magna! I could always use another favor notch on my card, Rannoch."

He glowered at her. "We'll see."

Dhirdre laid out the leather-bound game board, then dealt out the various etched cards to each player. We played three rounds, building up the tower and watching it eventually topple until everyone was howling with laughter. In the end, Dhiren had won his first hand in what he claimed was ten cycles. He was more animated than I had ever seen him as he hooted and danced around. Kerenza won also, then Rannoch took the last win, canceling out Kerenza's favor demand she had won only the prior round.

After a quarter rotation rest, we were back to our flight through the misty skies of Alternis.

To answers, I hope, and not to our doom.

CHAPTER 22

The tents of the Ignisfae camp were a welcome sight. We made quick work of settling in after the journey, getting the equus to their paddock on the eastern side, then headed to the central hub where the leather-covered shelters and cooking chimineas sat waiting for us. I was surprised they remained untouched after such a long absence. I imagined at least some animals would move in and make it their home. I also thought about the fact that its location was known to other Fae, namely Umorfae. Kerenza had told me that Umorfae had destroyed it before, several times in fact. But it would only be a nuisance at most if they did it again while we were away, as long as it wasn't an ambush like when Opius's henchmen had attacked them and stolen their children, they would simply rebuild. Tents could be replaced, lives could not.

Given the last time we had seen their previously pristine castle, I would have figured the disgruntled Umorfae would lash out in any way they could. But, Lacausia Palace was a long way from where we were. The castle was to the far west of Alternis, and the Ignisfae camp was what seemed like a month's march east from there, or whatever the equivalent was called in rotations. The Umorfae would need supplies to make such a journey. Maybe their lack of resources after our coup and their lack of servants now that the Syrenni were free, meant that all of their energy was being spent on surviving with what they had left. Perhaps that was why the tents remained standing.

Whatever the reason they had not made the effort to venture to the Ignisfae camp and disturb it, I was grateful. It meant we all had tents to rest in, and most likely didn't have to worry about them showing up. My skill with water was only enough to protect myself against an Umorfae attack, I'd possibly be able to help one or two Ignisfae near me, but other than that I didn't have enough control to defend with it. I looked at the tent I would share with Rannoch, the same tent he used to share with Kerenza when his sister needed someone nearby, next door to the smaller tent where I had stayed when I first met them.

Thinking about anything and everything again?

I spun to Rannoch, and lightly smacked his shoulder. "Reading my thoughts through the link again?"

He dodged too late and flashed his brilliant smile at me. "I was not, I swear. It was a guess. You were just standing there looking around."

I chuckled. "It's true. I was lost in thought. Remember when I first came here?"

He cringed. "I'd rather not."

I huffed a laugh. "Feeling guilty about our rocky start?"

He shrugged. "I think you would call it 'alphahole behavior.' It was not my finest moment."

"At least you know that now." I put my arm around his back and looked up at him. "I'd say we both grew from who we were, and at the time were also both reacting to our situations. But, yes, alphahole about covers how you were then." Looking in his eyes, I thought back on how I had ended up there in that sandy canyon wall where he and Kerenza found me. I had run from the Pythonisamul after she tried to inhale me, then eventually took shelter in a nook to get some sleep. In a way I had started running long before then, before I even left Black Oak Grove. Exhaustion overcame me.

"Come on," he said, smiling with that suggestive twinkle in his eye. "Time to stop thinking about so much for a while." He pulled me toward the tent, which Zia had made sure had fresh blankets and a wash bin ready to go.

The Praegra Forest was even more lush than I remembered. Subtle chirps and the low humming of unseen insects and creatures created a sense of the forest feeling alive. It always felt like there was a presence there, like the forest knew all, saw all.

We had arrived to the south of the Well, after departing the Ignisfae camp. After an eighth rotation rest to recover from the flight, we departed and ran through the winding canyons for as long as we could. As soon as I had fallen asleep, the Maeder Tree greeted me in my dreams. She knew I was close, and though her words were still hard to understand, one thing was perfectly clear; she wanted no more delays and wanted me there as soon as possible. She was becoming somewhat easier to understand the closer we got, but I realized she now sounded weak and lethargic.

We were finally at the border where the forest would become denser. A little further in we would encounter the prehensile carnivorous vines, the same ones which had caught me once. We'd have to move carefully to get through their maze untouched. Everyone took a water break, so I decided it was a good time to finally call Livi, and find out what the Faeries had heard lately.

I started the call the way Don'Li had taught me, with a rolling sound that emanated from the back of my throat, building in intensity as it spread outward. The wait was longer than I expected, the sense that I was heard by them was also delayed. When I finally felt the ping, I also felt the dread. There was something, some elusive sensation of panic that rippled through from Livi. They were still a ways off, and I paced back and forth while I waited. It took ages, my nerves ratcheted up a notch as I watched expectantly in the direction I could feel them flying from.

"What is it?" Rannoch asked, after he came over to see what I was wringing my hands about.

"It's Livi, or the Faeries in general. Something is not right."

Livi finally arrived, and the tinkling song which should have been joyous was filled with frantic bursts of barely understandable emotions. After several tries, the message eventually clarified enough for me to grab the gist of what had them so worried. "Livi says the Faeries have been divided," I said to Rannoch. "Dashelle befriended one, and turned their heart dark, even their body became that of shadow. That Faerie convinced others to join. They have become Dashelle's sentinels, watching the various parts of Alternis and reporting back to her."

"That is definitely not good."

"Dashelle sends them into the known tears, looking for other

Vale Born. And she is searching for more tears. She hasn't stopped her insane quest for more power. How did she even learn how to call the Faeries?" I paused, looking around. "She must know we're here, or that we've left TerraIgni, at least."

My stomach clenched as Livi confirmed that the Faeries did know. If they knew, Dashelle knew. I reiterated that to Rannoch, who frowned.

"We need to make quick work of getting to the Maeder Tree," he said, "and keep our time there short."

I nodded, trying not to panic at the thought that informants of Dashelle could be anywhere now. "Wait, if she has been using the Faeries, maybe she knew we were in Limnaer because of them, and that's how she knew to go there." I turned, connecting with Livi to ask, but the answer was vague. "Seems like no, or that Livi doesn't know for sure. Dammit, it's always more mystery with what happened in Limnaer."

"Does that even matter at this moment?"

"I suppose not, but it's still part of the reason for our quest."

"True, but right now, we need to focus on getting to the Maeder Tree. Then, we can determine our next move."

"I agree." *And, for critical information we don't want out in the open for prying ears to hear, use the link.*

He nodded once. *Agreed.*

After a unanimous group decision to limit discussions, we were off and running toward the dense middle of the Praegra Forest. Livi decided to join us, zipping alongside me as we headed further to the north.

Felix funneled a draft which sped our pace through the tangled forest; it took extra effort to avoid obstacles as we raced through the trees. The vines were always a moment too late trying to catch us thanks to Felix's push, the sound of snapping vines trailed behind as the wind sped us safely through their gauntlet. Before long we were past the section where they lived and hunted.

When Felix was nearly spent and we were all panting from exertion after an entire rotation run, we at last came over the rise which opened up to the lush valley where the Maeder Tree lived. Her luminous lake glowed like a breathtaking azure gem, but as my eyes traveled further up to where she stood my heart stopped.

"Oh my Gods," Kerenza breathed.

"What has happened?" Dhiren asked.

Felix and I looked at each other, and I knew he could feel it too. I shifted my gaze back to the Maeder Tree, our creator. My heart cracked as I looked at her drooping form. "She's dying."

CHAPTER 23

The sight of her severely weakened state shot me like a harpoon through the chest. I berated myself that I had not gotten there sooner. Her vast branches, which normally lifted high in the air holding millions of leaf-like fibers aloft, now swayed low, nearly dipping into the Well. Her trunk bent over at an odd angle, and her previously supple, dewy bark now appeared dried and ashen. I raced down the hill toward her, pushing my legs to carry me as fast as they could.

"Maybe you can heal her!" Felix shouted from my rear left, keeping pace with me.

"How?"

"You can do … the thing! The gold thread thing from your hand! I don't know!"

Felix and I dove into the Well before I could answer him. The truth was, I seriously doubted I could heal her. When I had tried to heal the leader of the Arbor Elves, Aurelian, it hadn't worked. My healing ability had little effect on anything other than the water within Aurelian. I wasn't really sure of what the Maeder Tree's biology was, but I surmised she was probably closer to flora than fauna.

I surfaced, and heard Rannoch, Dhiren, Kerenza, Zia, and Dhirdre dive in as well. I might have been relieved to have them all there were I not so worried. I plunged my head down as I pulled arm over arm, swimming with all my might to the far side of the Well where she stood anchored in place. The viscous fluid of the Well slipped around me, hugging me in a welcome, familiar embrace. My magical reserve inside of me settled, quieting the ever-present bubbling of energy just below the surface of my skin, an anxious entity that existed within me. That too would have been a comfort. She was sick, and there would be no peace for me until she was better … if it was even possible for her to heal. I had to wonder what would happen to the Well if she were to perish.

I wasted no time placing a palm on her trunk. The tiny hairs on the surface which had danced and shimmered the first time I had interacted with her remained inert. Taking a chance, I unthreaded a gold filament, testing to see if I could seek out something within her to heal. I tunneled my power into her gently, searching. But it was merely a mass of bound cords, nothing that I could pinpoint as an area that I could focus on. I couldn't heal her, but I could sense that those cords now lacked the pulse I had felt from them the first time I had touched her. I released the thread, then snapped back to regular vision. As my eyes adjusted, I noticed my colormark emitted some kind of aura, an imprint, perhaps from my connection to her.

I clasped Felix's outstretched hand, completing the circuit. The others encircled us, forming a ring around the Maeder Tree. I felt the strength and support of our group, with all of them surrounding me their faith and hope swelled to bolster me for what might happen next. It took a long moment before I heard her, the soft humming of her song was more wail-like now, but it was at least clearer than when I had heard her in my dreams.

"Hommmmme. Bring them hommme." She sang the melody again and again. Understanding dawned, and with it came the knowledge of what would happen if "they" didn't come home. She flooded my mind with mental pictures, laying out why she is so sick, what needed to be done, and how it happened before. In the visions, Vitus Augustus looked like a dark lord of death, swelled with power while she began to weaken. The more he took, the sicker the Maeder Tree had become. Now, Dashelle was doing the same, and unless we acted quickly it would not be able to be reversed.

"Do you hear her?" Felix asked the others. "Do you see what she's showing us?"

Dhirdre shook her head. "I sense something, but hear and see nothing."

He nodded, then looked at me. I wasn't sure if we should be quiet about what he and I now knew, then try to find a way to convey the news to the others so that Dashelle's informants did not hear us. But, I could only express it to Rannoch, and the others would be left wondering. I decided not to stop Felix as he proceeded to speak.

"She wants the other Vale Born back. The ones Dashelle killed. She *needs* them back. They must be returned to the source."

My heart panged. One of those souls was Josie. I had wanted to return her to the source like I had returned Maris. The thought of her spirit being bound in Dashelle's wicked body tormented me.

"This is why she ails?" Zia asked.

I slowly bobbed my head. "Dashlle holding onto the other Vale Born spirits has created an imbalance. Without it being corrected, the Maeder Tree will not be able to create life, and eventually will wither and die."

"Life? Not just Vale Born. All life?" Rannoch asked.

"All life," I affirmed. "Even the Fae. There will be no new Fae in Alternis. The Maeder Tree has no descendants like her and no way to carry on. It must be corrected or—"

"Or it all ends, when the last Fae dies," Dhiren finished.

"This is the second time it has happened," I continued. "When Vitus Augustus did this, murdered other Vale Born for their power, the Maeder Tree nearly died. Until he eventually died she was not able to create more Vale Born, that is why there were none for so long, why they were so rare. He created an imbalance which was corrected after he died hundreds of cycles later. She didn't die then because she was much younger, but still it dramatically weakened her. She was only able to create life within Alternis for a long time after that, so Fae, Faeries, Syrenni, and not in great numbers."

"She told you all of that?" Dhirdre asked.

"She showed us, more than told us," Felix answered. "With images in our minds."

Kerenza looked dismayed. "It does make sense, young ones have been incredibly hard to create for eons it seems, but history before then tells otherwise. How do we help her?"

"The only way I know to return the other Vale Born that were killed, is by pulling them out of Dashelle."

"And how do we do that?" Kerenza asked.

"By dragging that bitch's ass back here, and forcing her to touch the Maeder Tree. The connection that will form will allow them to leave the prison she is for them, finally returning them to their source. The balance should then be restored." I spoke with confidence, though I felt anything but that. Marching Dashelle from wherever she currently was scheming her next plan was certainly easier said than done. Even bound and surrounded by guards she would be a threat. We could never underestimate her, especially if we had to endure a lengthy journey with her.

"I have a question," Dhiren spoke up. "Why is the imbalance created only by Vale Born killing each other? Fae have been killing each other in droves for countless cycles, why does that not cause an issue?"

"I guess because you can't absorb each other," Felix answered.

"The Fading?" I added. "Maybe it has something to do with that. We don't Fade, as far as I know anyway, our energy transmutes into another like us."

"Whatever the reason, we may not find an answer for that soon," Rannoch said, "but we have the information we came here for. We know what we need to do now." He stopped for a moment, paddling in place and looking at each of us. Then lastly to me. *Time to find the Amabilis.*

I nodded. *To the Amabilis.*

CHAPTER 24

After exiting the Well, we clustered in a circle away from any trees or rocks. Livi decided to stay with us longer, checking the area first so that Rannoch and I could share our next move with everyone else. Livi had told me that Faeries could easily blend themselves into the bark of a tree, or the pebbles of a rock. But out in the open it was more difficult for them to hide. Rannoch quickly laid out our plan, which didn't consist of anything more than finding the Amabilis. As to what we would do after that, we weren't sure.

There was a noticeable feeling of desperation that had grown amongst all of us. I had to wonder, if the Maeder Tree died, what would become of us? Aside from the fact that no new Vale Born or Fae—or anything else in Alternis—would be created, what would happen to those that already lived? Would our powers disappear? Would that drastic change result in chaos, or in war should a new struggle to rule begin? Her death could mean the beginning of the end for us all. I kept all of these thoughts to myself, though Rannoch watched me in his sharp, knowing way. Our gazes met, and I could feel similar thoughts coming from him. This could all end very, *very* badly. I did not need to voice aloud that the end of the Maeder Tree may mean the end of the world as we knew it.

We departed, running through the forest in search of the hive-minded Amabilis. If one of them knew something, they all did. Since we had gotten all the answers we could from Livi and the Maeder Tree, we needed to widen our search and find the Amabilis fast.

It always stunned me how vast the Praegra Forest actually was. It had been several rotations of searching, and we still had not located the winged creatures. Every time I had encountered them they had been in their smaller, rodent-like form. I figured it would make them harder to find, but not impossible. The first two times I crossed paths with them I had been lucky, extremely lucky. The first time Rannoch had guided us nearly straight to one, after about a rotation of searching. The second I had run straight into one, when Silvanis was pursuing me through the western side of Alternis. They had facilitated my escape from him, then whisked me to the safety of the Arbor Elves.

Now, we trudged through the forest, passing trees which I swear I had seen before. My anxiety was through the roof, though I tried to maintain my patience, trying to simply focus on the task at hand. It didn't help that some of our time had to be spent foraging for food, we had run out already and only had our water skins which we kept refilling.

My well simmered and grumbled at me from below my skin, which only increased the anxiousness I felt from the fruitless search. I was tempted to spout fire, but it very well could have been a beacon which could be seen from a distance by any Faeries Dashelle had turned. Livi had advised me to keep a lid on it, to all of us. We wanted to be the ones to find her, not the other way around. The element of surprise could make the difference in our success.

We took another rest, but my legs wouldn't obey. Everyone else flopped down on the mossy ground, while I paced in circles.

"Lily, *sit*," Kerenza ordered. "Your constant moving is agitating me!" She smirked in her usual joking manner, but there was an undertone that added a slight bite to her words.

"I can't, I'm going to walk a bit."

"Stay close!" Felix said, trying not to shout it.

I walked a short distance away, looking at a grouping of softly glowing flowers. We had made it further west, I could tell by the flora. We still hadn't reached the center of Alternis, but we were nearing it. I bent down, and brushed my hand over the ethereal petals.

A rush went through me as I did, and my colormark bloomed at the same time. "Whoa! What was that?" For half a moment, I felt an undercurrent which reminded me of touching the Maeder Tree. A pulse of energy that branched and split along pathways.

Kerenza picked herself up off the ground, then sauntered over. "What?"

"I saw my colormark glow when I touched the flowers! Just like the ones it was made from. And I felt something, too."

"Oh, that is normal. Because their roots connect to the sublayer, they channel the energy through them. That is why they glow. The colormark retains a small imprint of it."

I looked at the flowers, picturing their roots somehow reaching into that nebulous, mysterious region that interconnects everything. "That's why my colormark was glowing when I touched the Maeder tree, she is connected in that way. Wait … the Amabilis. They travel the sublayer, "like no other can" they had said once. Can their presence be felt there? Through the flowers?"

Kerenza's mouth opened in surprise. "I had never thought of it! Could they?"

"Maybe not by me, I only have the one colormark, I barely felt a tremor. But you, your arm is filled! Maybe you can *feel* where they are to find them."

She looked at the designs inked in her skin, turning her outstretched hand palm up to palm down, debating. "I suppose, I have never considered it." She reached down, touching her hand to the tallest bloom. It glowed stronger, and her arm lit up at the contact. "I can feel the flower, the energy of it. But I do not know if I feel more than that." Pulling back, she looked at me and shook her head.

I thought for a moment, recalling how I would leave my regular vision when I would heal someone. "Try pushing in. Close your eyes and *push* your sight into the flower, into the roots that reach into the sublayer."

She closed her eyes and adjusted her shoulders, then reached her hand forward to try again. Her brows furrowed.

I held my breath, waiting. Watching. Willing it to work. We *had* to find them. Without the Amabilis, we'd be relegated to wandering the Praegra Forest looking for clues to Dashelle's whereabouts. That could waste precious time, of which we had little to spare.

"I feel something," she said.

"What is it?" I tried my hardest to reign in my excitement

and my nerves, I didn't want to distract her and pull her out of whatever altered state she might have reached.

"I feel the roots, the pulses that pass. I feel but do not see. I—" she gasped. "I do see! I think if I …"

Kerenza stopped talking for a long minute, her face was expressionless as she stood with her hand on the flower, frozen in time. She didn't breathe, not even the subtlest movement shifted her body as I stood watching her.

I started to worry it had been too long since she took a breath, when she suddenly inhaled, back into her body and back to the present.

"I found one! He is waiting for us. He saw me there, or felt me, and guided me to where he will be."

I could have shrieked with relief, but I kept it in and excitedly grabbed her hand, beaming at her.

"It was a good thing I joined the journey." She smiled.

"It was a *magna* thing," I said. "I was glad from the beginning, and this is yet more proof of the difference you make." I gave her hand one last squeeze. "See? Stronger together."

We ran to the others, motioning to leave rather than divulge any words out loud. Rannoch looked at me quizzically. *Kerenza found the Amabilis!*

He nodded and blew out a breath, smiling at his sister.

It was farther than I had hoped. I don't know if it was misplaced assumptions, but I had figured we would be near the Amabilis as they knew to expect us. They knew Kerenza had sought them, why would it not exit the sublayer close to us? I reeled in my frustrations as we ran further, and further still. We didn't have the luxury of time to traipse deeper into the forest.

Lily, quiet your mind. We will get there.

I didn't bother slowing down to glower at my mate. I knew it was usually on me when I shouted thoughts, not him pulling them out against my will, and I was not good at hiding when I was irritated.

Kerenza turned toward me, toward us all who followed her, with a big grin and waved us further, indicating we were almost there.

I nearly smacked into Kerenza's back as she ground to a halt in front of a massive, glossy-leafed tree.

Everyone stacked up behind me, pressing forward to peer into the branches. There, on the smooth bark of a narrow limb, sat the deceptively small rodent creature that represented our potential salvation.

CHAPTER 25

The squirrel-like Amabilis never tore his large, beady black eyes from us once as he charged forward, then leapt off of the branch. He swelled in size rapidly, the speed of it creating a temporal echo as he grew, grew, grew. His arms flung out to the sides, the thin membranes that ran along his sides caught the air and ballooned open, slowing his descent.

With a graceful final step onto the ground, he peered down at Kerenza, the mental conversation with her appeared to begin. It was mere moments before the Amabilis entered my mind, flipping through recent memories like sorting photos on a table. I steadied myself when he was done, feeling a little disoriented as he began with the others in our group. Satisfied with what he found in our thoughts, he angled his triangular face up to the mist, sending out a call to ask more Amabilis to join. "We will take you."

"Wait!" I yelled out with my mind. "I have questions! We need information! And where will you take us?"

Six more Amabilis arrived, each growing in size to accommodate our height. "We will commune in the sublayer, it is hard to give knowledge easily outside of it."

One by one, we were enveloped in their strange embrace.

Felix's eyes were wide with uncertainty. I nodded to him, trying to give what reassurance I could. In truth there was little I could say to prepare him for what was about to happen, for what traveling the sublayer was like. He had made the crossing through the Tear three times now, he could handle this way of moving through the world. The pain of the Tear was absent in the sublayer, likely warded off by the diaphanous wings that would hold us in place, but the bright, overwhelming fractures that crackled through the atmosphere were brutal. Even burying my face into the chest of an Amabilis did little to shield from the chaos. But, Felix didn't suffer from the same afflictions of post traumatic stress disorder and anxiety that I did. He was a bracer for me against such things. The fear of the unknown may have been troubling him, however it would be a momentary discomfort.

I should have mentioned to him that they could easily read his mind during transport. We shrunk and spun into near nothingness before I had a chance to tell him.

Light and energy blasted my eyeballs as we went subatomic. To avoid thinking about the nearly indescribable feeling of hurtling along an electrified pathway while being held firm by skinny rodent arms, I instead asked my questions to them. Here, in this strange place, their thoughts were instantly transmitted to each other. For better or worse, all was communicated and unfiltered.

I dumped all of my questions at them, in one mangled, run-on, stream of consciousness sentence.

"Does anyone ever tell you to calm your thoughts?" Their harmonic voices rang in my head.

"You're the mind readers, you tell me. Or was that an attempt at a joke?" Rannoch would be amused to hear they made a comment about my mental ramblings. Part of me did hope it was a joke, it wasn't funny, but the thought of introducing humor into their collective mind did please me. I may not have been willing to foster technological advancements in Alternis like Ser'Ti had hoped, but dammit they could all use a dose of funny in this realm.

"It was meant to be in jest. Now you can vibrate," they said.

"Vibrate? What the … you mean laugh?" That time I actually did laugh. "Okay, I'm laughing. Now, do you have any answers for us?"

"Yes, to your first question, we do know of Dashelle and where she is. She is near the Ita Hua Tear."

"So there is a tear there?"

"It had been blockaded many cycles ago by the Caelifae."

"I had heard that, but it was unclear if it was still there or was a myth, I wasn't sure," I said.

"Yes, it is there and she is actively attempting to access it."

"Oh … shit. She is trying to catch more Vale Born."

"A likely explanation. To your question of the Maeder Tree, of what might happen if she dies. We do not know what the result could be. It may be that without her to create, more of the dark forces of the world will propagate."

"Such as?" I asked.

"The Kakodaimons for one. They have spread to encompass the sublayer of the Hinterdunes. What if they could expand into the Praegra Forest? Our brethren could become stronger without the Maeder Tree."

"Your … brethren? The Kakodaimons?"

There was a pause before they answered. "Yes. They were once like us, they once *were* us. The Pythonisamul turned them, whether by accident or by design, they were created. So to call them brethren is perhaps not accurate. They are mutated versions of what we were. Forces like them could gain a foothold where they previously had none."

I thought back on the last time I had traveled with the Amabilis, when I wanted them to help find Rannoch. "They are why you don't use the sublayer that runs through—under, whatever—the Hinterdunes. I know it exists there, my colormark is proof of that."

"Correct. We have sentinels that guard those pathways, the few connections that are there. We do not cross them and we do not let the Kakodaimons enter. Once they were banished there, we prevented them from returning."

"But they don't look anything like you! They're monsters, with fangs and claws, and one eye—"

"Yes. They have been hideously disfigured over eons. But they were once just as we are."

My mind reeled as I thought about not just a war above, but a war below as well. "So when you said to me long ago that you travel the sublayer like no other can, it included them, because they're essentially related to you. And now, if they gain strength, they could rival you."

"Yes. And now perhaps the weight of this will be truly felt. They are a danger to any, should they gain access to the Praegra Forest. We are not merely traveling the sublayer when we pass, we are scouts. We patrol as we have for the many cycles since the split happened. While we prefer to remain neutral, not usually involving ourselves in the political machinations of the Fae, this is beyond that. What Dashelle has done, is doing, affects us all."

I mulled their words as the thick clouds crashed around us, the resulting thunder and bright purple lightning could be felt even though their protective wings. "So you would fight with us, if it came to it?"

"We would not fight, but we would aid. Yes, we would join."

I looked out at the pathways of the sublayer, at the branching forks and the pulses that traveled along it, like neurons sending electrical signals. While sometimes this world made sense, and a connection between things could be seen in a way that didn't exist where I came from, sometimes it was all too much to process. Wondrous sights, adventure, love, and things I hadn't experienced where I grew up, though I still occasionally longed for the safety of my birthplace. Perhaps my town wasn't as safe as it seemed, being on the fringes of civilization, threatened by dangerous firestorms every season, and too close to the border of this world, but the sense of safety with my mother had been there. It was times like this, where I teetered on the edge of an anxiety riddled meltdown, when I missed my mom. The thought of a multidimensional war in this world had me tasked with finding that difficult balance on my own, without her to hug me and tell me that everything would be okay.

"Take heart, young one. You are not alone here. You have your devoted family, your mate, you have found a rare thing. A sense of commitment resides in each of you that we do not always see. Do not forget, we looked into each of you, and that is something you all share. The bond of belief in each other is strong."

I nodded. "I guess I'm looking inward right now, trying to find my bravery. I have to confront someone who wants to kill me, has tried to kill me before. I have to find that unwavering stance, but instead of simply fighting her, I have to subdue her and take her back to the Maeder Tree in order to fix this. It would be easier to fight to kill her."

"You could do that, if it came to it."

I caught my breath. I *could* do that. I could kill her if it came down to it. If it came down to defending the people I loved, I would do it. But if I did …

"You would then carry all of them," the Amabilis finished, "and could then return them to the Maeder Tree yourself."

"But if I did that, I would also contain her. I would contain the power of four *other* Vale Born, plus mine, so five. How many did Vitus Augustus have? No, if I did that, I think I would go mad with power. I would be uncontrollable."

I would then become *her.*

My ultimate fear, the thing that terrified me beyond anything else. The fear that I would lose myself, my one shred of humanity that still remained, and become her. Her malevolence was so powerful, what if she then managed to push aside what little of me was left, and take over from within me? This wondrous world that left me awed, also had the space for such a thing to be possible. If it were anywhere else it would sound insane, but here, in Alternis it could happen.

"No," I stated. "There is no situation where I would be willing to do that. Containing the other Vale Born alone would be too much to handle, I believe. On top of that would also be her, who is the most evil being I have ever encountered. And I have crossed paths with both the Pythonisamul *and* Kakodaimons. When I find her I will *subdue* her, and bring her back to the Maeder Tree. Dashelle can then have the other Vale Born forcibly removed, and be judged for her crimes. I will not be the one to mete out her punishment. I will do as the Maeder Tree instructed. And her instruction did not include me killing Dashelle."

Saying it aloud solidified my resolve in my mind, in my spirit. In whatever it was that added together to make me who I was. I was still learning who that was, what various parts created a sum to add up to me, but I knew what I would not allow myself to be. To prevent that, I had to face her without hurting her to the point of death.

"And in that endeavor, we will help you. When you catch her, we will bring her in the passage to help you return her to the Maeder Tree. This one time we will forgo our usual demand for one of pure heart to travel with us. We know what is in her heart, and will make the crossing to restore balance to the world."

A bolt struck at that moment, lighting up everything around me as I looked up to the Amabilis that carried me safely through the erratic sublayer. In that moment I felt their truth, their resolve to see this end.

"Now we just have to get to her," I commented, both to them and to myself.

"I do not know if you will be relieved to know: we have arrived."

CHAPTER 26

We spun out of the sublayer to an icy blast of wind. I tried to look around, but the haze of my eyes still adjusting left me blinded. Standing, the world tilted, and I saw a long-fingered hand reach for me a moment too late. A flat stone area rushed up into my vision before he could catch me. I reflexively shot out my hands to lessen the impact. My face hit the ground, knocking my forehead against the rock. I rolled to the side, dazed, and my sight line passed the others. Everyone was on the ground, some sitting, most of them lay awkwardly. Even knowing what comes after exiting the sublayer wasn't enough to get my feet properly under me in time to regain my stability. Shrinking to a microscopic size and then instantly regrowing left my entire body trying to figure out what the hell just happened.

"Lily," Rannoch croaked from the ground.

I pushed myself up to look at him. "I'm all right."

"You're bleeding."

I cursed, then sat forward, unspooling a healing thread. I could feel the scrape on my face. I finished quickly, but realized that I should have saved my strength as I remembered what the Amabilis had said last. We were here. Wherever here was. To where Dashelle was. *She* was nearby and I very quickly may have to be in fighting form. I chastised myself for fixing a superficial cut unnecessarily. It was a nuisance at most.

I glanced around, trying to ascertain if she was in fact close. Maybe she was, but I couldn't see her. "Everyone okay?" After some unconvincing responses, but responses in the positive nonetheless, I said quietly, "We have to move quickly. Dashelle is here somewhere. We have to find her."

In moments everyone was on their feet, the Amabilis closest said in their telepathic way that they would wait for us, and be ready to take her with us when we had succeeded. He pointed north. "North we go."

Rannoch had been carrying my sword for me, it had been nestled in tight next to his. He unhooked the baldric and fitted it to me. It had been so long since I had even used my selwaer, the blade like an old friend. Having it close lent an additional layer of confidence, like having the support of a trusty companion. "Be safe, and remember your training. Alternate sword attacks with kicks, and using your power. Do not use the same pattern more than once. You are a *force*. Burn brightly. And—" he leaned forward, then pressed his lips against mine. The saying that everything else faded away was such a cliche, but it was a saying borne from truth. When he kissed me, nothing else mattered. His belief in me rang through our link, his knowing of my capabilities. He did not give me reminders on how to fight because of doubt. It was out of love, and his own worries. It was his way of reminding me, I was more than his princess.

I was his queen.

His queen that was about to restore the fate of this world.

He broke off the kiss, regarding me for a moment.

The corner of my mouth tipped up as I said, "Let's go find our prey."

I was the predator, and I was coming for her. Straightening my back, I leveled my gaze directly ahead, to a narrow passageway through a split in the rocks. I could hear the wind howling louder through the crevice.

Our group lined up behind me as I charged forward.

"The Ita Hua Tear," Dhiren breathed. "I have only heard of it."

I merely nodded, the mythical Tear was real, or Dashelle must have believed it to be real. I turned my shoulders sideways, shimmying through the gap in between the stones. Rannoch had a more difficult time, but made it through, earning a few scuffs to his broad shoulders in the process. As I exited the other side, I realized we were high up in the air, on some sort of platform. A narrow stone ledge the width of my foot stretched across an impossibly wide chasm, the bottom of which was obscured in mist. The extremely slim thickness, as well as the unnerving length it spanned made me realize with dread it could not hold much weight safely.

"What kind of Indiana Jones bullshit is this?" Felix muttered from behind me. "You'd think the Amabilis could have dropped us off on the *other* side of certain death. I thought the idea was to survive?"

"Quiet," I snapped. Quips were not helping the situation. "We go one at a time. Felix, you stand ready to assist with an air lift or push if anyone slips or falters. Be *ready*."

I had no time for his remarks. Give me a deadline, and I became a fucking menace. Sure I may deliberate in my head an awful lot, more than most maybe. But when it comes down to it and it's time to make something happen, that is when I rise. I moved a step closer, putting my foot out to test the surface.

It felt solid enough, and I had no time to waste. Waiting, or worrying about crossing would do me no good. I looked straight ahead at my goal, keeping my sight firmly on where I was going, then walked forward. Step by slow step was the pace I had to take when overcoming a panic attack, step by step was how I would get through this.

I inhaled deeply, and foot by foot I moved across. Breathe out, *one,* step, breathe in, lift my next foot. Breath out, *two,* step. After sixty agonizing, counted steps paced with my breathing, I made it across, never once looking down at the perilous drop.

One by one each companion started across, Kerenza made it first, Zia was next, then Dhirdre. With each arrival to the safe zone of the tight landing I would feel an invisible weight lift off of my chest again. I was more nervous for them than I was for myself.

Rannoch prepared to start the crossing, when a powerful gust of wind churned through the crevasse and forcibly pushed him back. Felix lifted his hands, combatting the cyclone-strength gale with his power. It knocked his hands aside like it was swatting a fly. All of our group that had made it across held onto the rock face that surrounded the landing, gripping it with all their might. Kerenza looped an arm around my waist, I had not yet tried to find something to latch onto on the wall as I was further out on the lip. We clung to each other, waiting out the sudden wind storm.

After what felt like several minutes, it quieted, then Rannoch moved forward to start anew. He didn't even get one foot on the walkway before the wind restarted. It tunneled through with such ferocity it felt intentional.

"Is someone doing this?" I yelled.

"It does seem to be driven with purpose!" Kerenza answered back.

I looked at my nearby companions, *all* of us females. "Maybe it doesn't want males here."

Dhirdre twisted her lips and nodded, seemingly agreeing. I didn't know if spells were a thing in this world, but maybe it was somehow spelled against letting men cross.

The guys on the other side rearranged themselves, Dhiren moved into position to try instead. Again, just as before, the wind picked back up and pushed all three of them to the fissure opening away from the ledge. Felix was fairly strong with his wind skill, but he seemed to have little effect against it.

"Looks like it's just us." I motioned at the guys to stop trying. *Stand down, Rannoch, you'll have to wait for me.* I felt his pain, his fear, his worry through the link. His heart cried out that he couldn't be there to help, to try and protect me. *I will be okay.*

I had to believe it, with every ounce of my being. The realm needed me to do my job, the Maeder Tree tasked me with one goal, and I would see it done.

The wind all but abated as I looked at Kerenza, then held my colormarked arm up to hers. "Stronger together."

Her face held the same firm resolve I now felt in my heart. "Stronger together," she affirmed. She touched her colormark to mine, their lines illuminated for a moment, before the glow retreated.

I glanced back at Rannoch one last time, at my brother, at Dhiren. They stood watching as I said my silent farewell. I didn't want to say any parting words that could cheapen the moment, or that could incur misfortune. This was Dashelle we were hunting, there was no world where this would be a fast or easy task.

I love you, he said through the link across the expanse.

And I love you. I will break through the very mist to return to you.

I turned to head through the crack in the stones, a near mirror to the other side where the males all stood. Slipping through the cold, rough passage, I faced ahead to whatever lay before us.

Once through to the other side, I blinked at the brightness. The wind howled but it seemed to rush around the vast, barren platform, rather than across it. Ice crystals fanned out from each step I took, fracturing and spreading like the cracking of a frozen lake. Far ahead was a familiar sight that made my heart halt. Twisted brambles fanned in a spiral pattern from a central point, and Dashelle stood with her bloodied hands on the wall which was covered in dry, impenetrable vines. The tear was nearly identical to the one I had come through. She had hurt herself trying to open the aperture in the same way I had when I first tried to get back through.

The memory of being ripped from one world to another haunted me, but I couldn't lose myself to recounting that. Here, in what must have been the most northern reaches of the world, was the person whom I sought. There would be no reasoning with her. This was the precipice before a battle, once she realized I was here.

My gaze darted around, checking the area for what I might use to my advantage, or what she might use for that matter. The large stone passages were particularly concerning, what if she was strong enough to pick them up? I realized that was probably unlikely, the towering rocks seemed to be all one piece, reaching far, far down to the ground. She would have to use considerable strength to tear a chunk off.

I would use my flames, that was my strong suit; there was no water nearby. I lifted my hands, palms forward, then moved back one foot readying myself to run full speed. I would trap her where she stood with a V of fire.

A blast of freezing wind knocked me down, then pinned me to the icy ground.

"Dashelle! She is here," a female voice called out from above.

My heart raced as I tried to move, my skin flattened from the forces of wind adhering me to the ground. I gritted my teeth, then managed to slip one elbow up. I wedged my hand under my shoulder, then pushed with all of my might to flip myself skyward.

"No," I tried to say as my vision took in a picturesque silhouette which stood on top of the rock. She smirked at me from above, her long, powder-blue robes licked in the wind. The wind *she* controlled. The mark of Caelifae royalty was unmistakable.

CHAPTER 27

Calria stood with a defiant stance as she basked in her victory. Calria, Prince Ser'Ti's trusted governess, his guardian after his parents had Faded, now flashed a brazen smile at me. She had ruled in Ser'Ti's stead until he came of age. But the question burning in my mind: was she there on his behalf, or for her own designs?

My thoughts spun as I lay facing her, my body immobile against the ground. It dawned on me, that was how Dashelle must have accessed Limnaer. Calria was her person on the inside.

The wind subsided at the same time that I was dragged to my feet from unseen hands under my armpits. In a rush, I was thrust forward on a rippling wave from below, the rock became a rolling surface which propelled me into the wall which had previously been ten strides away.

My face met stone for the second time since reaching the great precipice of the Ita Hua Tear. Seeing stars was the same in any realm it seemed, and I shook my head to try and clear my vision. Dashelle spun me around. I didn't even see her wind up to punch me hard in the cheekbone. I heard the crack of my face before the back of my head echoed the sound, ricocheting off of the wall I was pressed up against.

This was not how this was supposed to go. We were supposed to surprise *her*. I had known she would likely seek out more alliances after the Umorfae deal had fizzled for her, but I didn't expect it to be Calria.

Kerenza and Dhirdre started climbing the wall to reach Calria. "We will deal with her!" Kerenza shouted down to me.

I needed to get up, and fight. Another punch sailed in as I realized I was still standing. This time it was my jaw, and the strike was hard enough to nearly unhinge it. She was likely trying to knock me out. If I was hit hard enough, a punch to the jaw could pinch a nerve that would cause unconsciousness.

I struggled out of her reach, along the wall. "Dashelle," I forced out, "you can't do this. You could kill us all."

I didn't manage to say anything further. Another hit came to my temple. I fell to one knee, swaying. She lunged forward to hit me at a downward angle, twisting her hips to put force behind the punch.

Just like Kerenza had taught me. I had learned to read those familiar movements whether I was doing them myself or watching another execute them.

My head cleared enough that I could see the direction she was already turning, the motion started and where her body could continue to rotate if it were deflected. I raised my right forearm, her strike skittered off to the side, then I jabbed with my left fist at her outer thigh. Her leg went dead and her knee bent in, sending her further in the direction she had already been headed. I pushed her shoulder away then pummeled my knuckles into her lower back as her turned body offered a clear shot.

She gasped and stumbled forward.

A blast of heat came from above, flames shot out in arcs from the peak of the rock where Calria had stood. She was out of our sightline since Dashelle had pushed me back to the wall's edge under the rock, she would be unable to intervene if things went awry in Dashelle's fight with me. Now it seemed a fight had come to Calria as well, fire shooting out would most definitely mean Kerenza made it up there. I smiled through a split lip, Calria would have a major issue to deal with. Armed with her Ignisphaera and limitless offensive moves, there was no doubt Kerenza would kick her ass.

I jumped up back to my feet, then charged forward to strike Dashelle before she recovered. I put both of my hands on her shoulder, then brought her down into my knee repeatedly. The last blow sent her collapsing in a heap. I danced away to get a look up at the rock, checking on the progress Kerenza was making. We didn't need Calria, we just needed her out of the way. Dhirdre, Zia, and Kerenza lashed her with rapid kicks from both sides, it was looking pretty grim for Calria.

Calria crouched, twisting one arm forward and the other back, she spun on one foot, unleashing dual snaking wind currents. Kerenza was thrown off the face of the rock, and landed not far from me. Zia fell backward onto the ledge on the opposite side of the narrow passage we had come through. Dhirdre was tossed over the edge on the other side.

My blood went colder than the icy air, colder than the shards of splintering crystals that surrounded each footstep. My ears hummed and I shrieked along with Dhirdre as she fell, over the edge which had no lip to cling to. It was the sheer chasm wall. I cried out and felt Rannoch yell through the link. He had stayed and stood guard, and had seen her fall.

I crushed my eyes shut for a moment, my heart ached for Dhirdre. For Dhiren, who likely just saw his sister fall. For Rannoch and Kerenza, she had been like a sister to them, having been raised together since they were younglings. All that was left of her now was her cries echoing off the icy walls.

Calria lowered herself on a gust of wind to the ground, gracefully touching down near where Kerenza fell.

I panted, looking at Dashelle who was still laid out on the ground. I was about to find a way to bind her when I looked back at Calria approaching Kerenza. Calria withdrew a long, rectangular sword, raising it horizontally by her face, then took two creeping steps forward, ready to slash Kerenza to finish her with a warrior's death.

I saw red, and I became a raging bull. I made no sound, no war cry, as I hurtled myself toward them. I had my selwaer drawn by my second pace, as Calria unleashed her swift strike to Kerenza's neck. I slashed upward at the same time I arrived, deflecting her blade with a clang. I kept the same motion, the same rotation, spinning quickly on one foot, doubling my speed and slashed across her midsection. My selwaer sang, its ringing through the air the only sound, followed by Calria's single, sudden exhale. Red bloomed on her immaculate blue satin, spreading outward in feathered stripes. Her wispy white hair slowed its movement, it no longer billowed like it had only moments before. The wind stilled as she collapsed, and the world went quiet.

Red. Her blood was red, like a human's. Red like fire. Not cerulean like the Umorfae, not amber like the Ignisfae. The brightest ruby red, making her spilled blood that much more visceral. More real. I was a killer, and I would kill again if I had to.

But I couldn't kill Dashelle. I needed to deal with her. I had to finish disabling her, I had to finish this for Dhirdre so her death wasn't in vain. I turned, then a foot planted in my chest, rocketing me backward.

I landed on my back, fortunately the kick didn't daze me. I kept the momentum and let it flip me over, rolling and popping into a crouching position with one hand touching down in front of me for balance.

"Okay, Spider-Fae, let's do this," Dashelle said as she approached with her fists raised.

"Spider-Fae?" I questioned, trying to waste time while I evaluated my next move. I could have beat myself up for allowing Dashelle to get back up, but Kerenza would have been killed, and I couldn't live with myself if that happened.

"You're from the States, don't act like you don't know what spider powers are." She made a series of pulling motions, which funneled a long strip of rock into her hand, the tip of it terminating in a deadly-sharp point. She smirked at me, at my stunned expressions. "Yeah," she drawled, "I've gotten better at making my own weapons, don't you think? And the difference between mine and yours is: mine are limitless, you only have one." She angled it toward me, taunting me to parry with my selwaer.

As she motioned with it, I recognized the shape of the rough sword. It was the same diameter and shape as the one that killed Eiulans. "How did you like Limnaer?"

"I imagine I had a better time than you." She ran her heavy weapon along my raised sword, causing sparks along the edge, like flint to start a fire. I smirked. I needed no spark for a flame.

In a flash Dashelle unleashed a series of strikes with her hard blade. Her muscles contracted and bulged, showing just what she had done with her time since I had last seen her. I blocked each strike as best I could, but each block was a barrier that was nearly broken through. It was clear Dashelle had put herself through grueling training. Every sinew was visible, every step she took precise. I instantly regretted all my time relaxing on my balcony, reading. But, in that time, I had not let my mind rest. I had studied, I had learned. I reevaluated that regret, then realized how much more I understood now, and I had also spent that time forming real connections, true loyalties. Loyalties of the heart. Who did Dashelle have? Her new ally was now dead, and she was back to square one.

I pushed my sword in an arc, causing her to lose her grip slightly as it swung around. The weight of the stone now worked against her. It slipped out of her hand and bounced away with a thud.

She lunged at me like a cat pouncing, and though I already held the gleaming tip of my sword aloft, she did not hesitate or hold back. Both of her hands pressed into the depressions below my clavicles, forcing me down, down, down.

I stabbed my selwaer into her shoulder, but she barely paid any heed. She held me firm against the freezing stone, and I held her back with my sword stuck in her and my other hand pushing her arm. Dashelle screamed at me, funneling her fury into the downward motion. Wind rushed around us, and I felt my stomach flip from a rapid descent. She was pushing the rock we were on into the earth far below. I had thought she wouldn't be able to separate the piece, that it would be too big and unwieldy. Clearly I was wrong. I now realized when she had thrown me backward, I had landed on a disc that jutted out from the main rock, a ledge with nothing below it that she now caused to race downward.

She lifted a hand, gave one quick jab to my face. It was enough to startle me which she used to her advantage, wrestling the pommel from me, then she tossed my sword over the edge without looking away from me once. Our plummet picked up speed. The blood from her wound that should have dripped down onto me instead streamed backward, floating for a moment before disappearing.

The tops of trees rushed past in a blur, the massive trunks of the Praegra Forest sped by next, followed by dirt. It became darker, and darker. Cracks began to form below us, and the glow of magma started to creep through.

We slammed to a stop, the heat from below seeped into the cavern she had created. The tall, vertical dirt walls caught the faint glimmer of orange light from the pulsing lava. I could feel its warmth beneath us.

I threw her off of me, then rolled away. Once again I was trapped in a prison of her making, like the first time I had encountered her, surrounded by earth and stone. She stalked forward, drawing up shards out of the ground as she approached, creating two weapons where she previously had one. And now, I had none.

"Poor Lily. Poor altruistic, naive, foolishly optimistic Lily. Why did you think this was a good idea?"

"It was a necessary one, Dashelle. The Maeder Tree is dying. She's dying because of you. We have to return the Vale Born to her, the ones that you killed. If we don't, she dies, then no new life will be created in Alternis." I stood my ground, tightening my fists and my resolve.

She paused for a moment, then clicked her tongue. "Whatever that means. I plan on getting more, what do I care if this tree dies? If only you knew the power it gives you, what it *feels* like when you get more. It doesn't matter what I didn't win back where we're from. I can have it all here. I won't be giving that up."

"What you didn't win? What does that mean? Destroying a realm isn't *winning*. You do realize what would eventually happen if you took over don't you? You'd be the queen of *nothing*. And you'd be utterly alone, as you are now. Your list of allies grows thin. First Opius, then Silvanis, and now Calria."

She advanced toward me, the tips of her stone blades dragged on the ground, making a horrendous grating sound, sharpening them along the top length as she walked closer. She offered no comments, no taunts, no further information as she drew the two weapons in front of her, the sharp edges of them crossing at an angle. All it would take was one quick slice, the uncrossing of that lethal formation to remove my head. I had no defense other than my own magic.

I spouted fire at her, which worked to force her to back away from me. I unleashed more attacks, rivers of flame, one after the other. Each time she would easily dodge, leap out of the way, somersault over them. I felt my well depleting. I had been careful to conserve my magic, only using physical attacks and defenses. Holding as much in as I could until I really needed it. And yet, it dwindled. She was bleeding me dry, and she knew it. I threw my hands down to end the flames, sick of her games. *Time for a change of pace.*

I planted my feet and held up my right hand, gritting my teeth as I reached my power *into* her. Like when I went beyond sight for healing, I could go beyond matter when I probed with my water power. I felt the mass of volume inside her body, all the water her blood contained. I slammed my hand forward more, gripping my fingers in the air to squeeze her insides. All of her motion arrested, her only movement was her eyebrows tensing. She pushed against me, against an invisible force. Dashelle was frozen in time, even her heart was unable to beat.

Veins started to pop out on her neck, tiny capillaries around her forehead became apparent, some of them burst under the skin. Her lips had started to turn slightly blue, when I felt my hold on her falter. Her foot broke free first, then her other foot. She took one step closer, then broke free completely and lunged with her closed fist to my gut.

I doubled over, and while my face was low, she backhanded me hard.

I fell back as I lost my balance. Dashelle's chuckle was dark as she neared. "I'm surprised you waited so long to try something like that. Don't forget how deep my well is, I can outlast you for days."

Rotations, I corrected her in my head. I was tempted to suck in breaths as I tried to recover from exertion, but I didn't want her to know. I closed my mouth, pretending I wasn't winded. I didn't want to give her that satisfaction.

"Why use that skill on me at all?" she asked. "It's clearly not your strong suit. I still say it will have a better home with me. I will know what to do with it."

I scooted away from her. She was right about one thing, it wasn't my greatest skill. Maybe my greatest skill wasn't any magic I possessed, or Vale given abilities, it was the parts of me that survived the transition through the tear. The loyalty I had engendered with more than one person of this world that I earned by being myself, and by being true to them. Loyalty wasn't going to win a fight with her right now, if she killed me that would be that. I needed to get up off of this ground, and find the strength to face her head on. I stood up, ready to fight again.

I felt a pulse in my colormarked arm, then I heard a metallic sound from high above us.

CHAPTER 28

My colormark lit from within, surging with power. I looked up, past Dashelle, all the way up to the lip of the opening that had been ripped into the ground. Kerenza stood on the edge of it, and I knew she had sent what message she could. *Stronger together, and strong on your own.* The design Lennaraz had inked into our skin was spelled for strength, for the clarity to break through when you needed it most. My will solidified, I *would* beat her. My well had not yet regenerated, but determination fueled me from within.

Kerenza opened her hand over the crevasse, then a silver glint caught my eye, dropping like a pin. Ricocheting once, it bounced off the wall, then landed closer to Dashelle than to me.

"What is this?" Dashelle asked, taking several steps toward it. She bent over and picked up a metal dagger I knew all too well.

My dagger. The one I forged myself with Rannoch. Seeing it in her hands made me instantly angry. How did Zia even manage to pack that without my knowledge?

"This has got to be the ugliest knife I've ever seen."

I was fuming, but I kept my fists clenched to avoid any unnecessary spill of power. When I let it out, I wanted to direct it to have the most effect.

Her sharp gaze missed nothing. "Oh, does that make you mad, dear Lily?"

Mad didn't even begin to cover it. I was having a hard time reigning in the fact that I couldn't kill her. For all that she had done, this was the last straw. Dashelle had murdered without mercy, thrown this world off balance and to the brink of annihilation. She deserved justice. And those she killed deserved to have that justice served. All this time Josie had been bound up inside of her, Josie's power taken from her and used for evil. Josie not only deserved justice, she deserved to be free.

Dashelle smirked and twirled the tip of the dagger into her open palm, evaluating me from a short distance. "It is *sharp* though, I'll give it that. It wouldn't win in a pageant, but it doesn't have to be pretty to get the job done, I suppose."

Oh hell no. The subtext was utterly clear, she intended to have the dagger be my undoing at last. My own damn dagger. Fury rippled through me. The air charged, and for a moment I felt everything around me. Dashelle, her blood, me, the ground below us. The lava below that. The molten-hot liquid moved and sang beneath my feet, calling to me. For the first time, I *felt* it. The only other time I had been anywhere near magma in this world was with Rannoch, in the forge. But I hadn't sensed it then. I could only feel its heat. Now I felt its strength, its churning, unpredictable force. It hummed a quiet promise to me, that if I asked it would answer and it wouldn't take too much of my well to command it.

I ignored her blood, the water in her that also called. That *did* take too much, it was draining and harder to control. But the lava, it offered a power all its own and only needed to be coaxed. There was another sound I heard as I listened and watched Dashelle move toward me. It was that of my dagger itself. Maybe it wasn't a sound, but yet another sensation. A connection. It reminded me of how the selwaer would greet me, a near-silent song of acknowledgment. The dagger sensed me as its maker, as the one who had forged it and given it strength. I had used my skill of fire to craft it, and that was the basis of the bonds.

My lip curled into a smile as I tugged on that invisible thread to the dagger. I clenched my fist and sent a quick jolt through the thread. Dashelle shrieked and dropped it, its hilt superheating in a brilliant flash. She screamed as she gripped her wrist with her other hand, looking in horror at her burned palm.

Her face switched from pain to rage. It was the second time I had burned her, the first still left its scar up her leg beneath her leather pants, no doubt. She unleashed a wild yell as she charged the remaining distance between us, her uninjured hand outstretched.

Dashelle plowed into me, knocking me to the ground yet again, but this time, the lava swirled just below us in a whirlpool. I closed my eyes, not caring about Dashelle for the moment, as my sight went below the ground, to the massive volume that churned. I now knew its depth even more, the thin crust of earth she had tackled me on was barely a shell above the liquid storm. Perhaps that was why she had not pulled up flakes of rock to hurl at me, there was little separating us from the unruly pit of fire below. With her skill she could no doubt feel the lack of substantial material to use, but I would bet she couldn't comprehend what we were suspended over.

Dashelle's uninjured hand closed around my neck, after all of the tricks and weapons, she was going to resort to using brute force. She was going to try, anyway.

I asked the lava to bend to my will, and as it had promised, it only sipped a little off of my well. The tap into using it was like a fine straw, which was then magnified to direct the mass of roiling power. With a flick of my fingers like a conductor at the helm of an orchestra, the lava began to push upward. I felt the surge, the power at my beck and call.

I didn't struggle against her, even though my breath had gone out, and her vice grip against my flesh dug in with ferocity. I had entered a state of calm, of euphoria that was set apart from my physical being. I was a watcher who couldn't feel any of the pent up anger Dashelle funneled into her fingers to choke me, I was disconnected from the fierce moment. A sense of knowing was greater than any of her attempts to kill me.

I opened my eyes to watch Dashelle react. The ground started to break apart, and blasts of lava shot high around us. Her eyes went wild with surprise, with desperation as she tried to finish the job of finally ending my life.

But she wasn't powerful enough. She couldn't possibly contend with what I had become. I felt like fire itself. My gaze heated, and my body burned. She gasped and flung herself off of me, scrambling back away from me as I stood. I lifted my hands, the lava responded to the motion. The remaining platform began to lift higher, and higher, and higher.

She yelled as she looked around, realizing that her efforts to push us down out of reach from the others had failed. Throwing her hands down, she tried to push the ground below again, but it wouldn't work. There wasn't enough of it to command, the ascent slowed, but nothing more. The molten magma was too powerful and rose higher still, thwarting any of her useless attempts.

I stalked towards her, and I had truly become fire itself, it radiated from each footstep and from every visible surface of my skin. For the first time ever, I saw her cower in fear. She backed all the way to the platform edge and held her hands up in terror. I had to wonder, did her victims respond the same way? Did they try to shield themselves from her in their last moments, did they know what she was about to do to them? Knowing her, she relished their fear. She most likely encouraged it and dragged out their demise so that she could bask in her power over them, that she would *take* and enjoy it.

The lava responded to my thoughts, putting more force behind me, fueling even further strength should I need it, ready to allow me the ultimate power to be her executioner. I rose up above her, looking down with disappointment in her choices, with a lack of apathy of what must be done. My own anger, hurt, loss, resentment, fear … it was all somewhere far away. I had no emotions of my own, I was a judge, the pointed end of a power greater than myself, prepared to dole out justice.

And she deserved what was to come.

I reached a flaming hand toward her, ready to clasp her neck and mete out the punishment she was owed.

The platform returned to where it had been pushed down from at last. Kerenza stood there, waiting. "Lily." It was the only word she said: my name. It felt like an ill-fitting label, something that I had known and yet wasn't anymore. I was not sure it could fit again. I had changed, transmuted to something else. I swung my eyes to her, but she didn't look away and her expression didn't change in the slightest. "Lily," she said again, her voice a lifeline back to the person I had been.

I blinked, and it all receded. The fire dimmed from my sight and the lava subsided. Kerenza grabbed Dashelle by the collar and ripped her from the platform. I took two strides forward, scooping up my dagger from the ground as I passed it, then leapt off of the platform before it lowered away from the rock. Dashelle let out an unhinged laugh, her madness finally overtaking her honed physical ability. With another stride, I struck Dashelle in the temple with the butt of my blade. She slumped, Kerenza let her crumple to the hard rock below.

I looked at Kerenza and my spirit cracked and healed all at the same time. I flung my arms around her, she had brought me back. It was the span of minutes that I had invited the spirit of the lava to flow through me, it allowed me to not need my well, I was a vessel for the force itself instead. But coming back to myself was painful, it was hard. For the few breaths I had existed as a near-omnipotent being my core self had softened and had the ragged emotions swept away, along with my sense of identity. I was merely a channel at that point. But I was ready to end her, and it was not what the Maeder Tree needed or wanted.

With a look and a word, Kerenza had stood steadfast to call me back. I didn't know if she had ever seen or encountered that state herself before, but something told me she knew to tether me. I hugged her again, then let out a long, shaky sigh. "We did it," I said. We had Dashelle unconscious, and were ready to transport her to the Maeder Tree to finally return the Vale Born. We had accomplished it, with a very heavy loss.

My lip wobbled as I looked at her, she gripped my arms and I knew we were both thinking about Dhirdre.

I felt a tug through the link, Rannoch called to me. When I

opened to him I felt his reassurance first, that it would all be okay. I found it hard to believe and started to formulate a response.

No, he insisted, *it is going to be okay! She's alive.*

CHAPTER 29

My mouth popped open. "She's alive!" I exclaimed.

"Who?" She put a hand to her chest, backing up a step as realization dawned. "Truly?" she whispered.

For half a moment I was worried I misunderstood Rannoch, that perhaps he meant someone else. It could have been Calria. He repeated more resolutely when I asked him through the link that Dhirdre had indeed miraculously survived.

"Yes! Dhirdre is alive!"

Kerenza's eyes welled up. "Thank the Gods!"

I could have run to the ledge to greet her, but we had to pick up Dashelle to bring her with us. We each grabbed an arm, then dragged her toward the split in the rock face to make our way through. I was almost giddy as we approached, relieved beyond belief that Dhirdre had somehow survived the fall. The depthless chasm reminded me of the unstable and impossibly narrow bridge. "Wait," I said, "how will we get Dashelle across?" *Rannoch, we won't be able to cross the bridge with Dashelle. Will the Amabilis come here to get us?"*

"Oh no, I did not even think of having to pull her across the walkway, it barely held one of us at a time."

I nodded, my mind running through the what-ifs. The Amabilis wouldn't take us directly to where Dashelle was at the opening to the tear when we had arrived, was there any reason beyond not wanting to be in the middle of a fire fight with her? They had agreed to take her before, but didn't indicate where we needed to be for them to begin the journey back.

He didn't respond right away, but eventually answered after an uncomfortably long wait.

"The Amabilis will come get her, then hold her in the sublayer until we are all ready to travel back to the Maeder Tree," I told Kerenza.

She didn't even have a chance to respond, before a pinprick of shimmering light appeared near us, then one of our squirrel-like friends flew out of it. He inflated to full size, then enveloped Dashelle into his embrace before disappearing. I managed to project a thought to the Amabilis before they retreated completely, alerting them to be sure she was properly restrained the entire time. The last thing we needed was Dashelle loose in the sublayer. That would have been some feat though. Knowing her however, she'd try to find some way to take over there, too.

I blew out a breath. "That's it. We have her. I almost can't believe it." So quickly she was ushered into the realm between, I barely had time to process she had been taken.

"It is not over yet, we still have to get her to the Maeder Tree, but yes, we did it. *You* did it."

I slung an arm around Kerenza's shoulders and beamed at her. "*We* did it," I affirmed. I walked us toward the fissure in the rock, realizing that Calria still lay where I had cut her down. "Oh, I almost forgot." I stopped, looking at the narrow river of red that ran to a slim channel, then funneled toward the open side which faced the chasm. I frowned at how easily my killing her had fled my mind. Granted, I had been in a heated battle—literally—with Dashelle. But the fact that I had promptly forgotten I had killed someone filled me with dismay. Not only that, I'd most likely have to return to Limnaer to deliver the news. "I guess I'll have to tell Prince Ser'Ti." Once again I would be an emissary of death.

Kerenza nodded. "Yes, later."

Her eyes said the additional words that she withheld, as my colormark warmed. I felt—rather than heard—her "thank you." It wasn't their way to voice thanks, she had done it through other means which struck that much deeper than empty words would have. Like when saying "I love you" doesn't cut it, when the words themselves don't convey enough. I had paused my fight with Dashelle to save Kerenza, and I *always* would. It was the saving grace of dispatching a person, I had done it to protect another.

"Leave her body for now, we have a job to do," Kerenza added.

I agreed, then turned toward the fissure in the rock, to make my way toward our awaiting family.

I had to prevent myself from running across the spindly bridge when I saw Dhirdre. Her brilliant smile flashed at us, and I could have melted with relief. Of course I had known sooner because of Rannoch, but seeing her made it that much more real. I barely registered that I was already halfway across the chasm. Slowing considerably, I took the last thirty paces more carefully, but I practically jumped the last few steps to get to her. Kerenza was across shortly after, all of us hugging and crying. Zia swooped in, looping her arms around us and kissing Kerenza on the cheek.

"What happened?" I asked when we finally released our joyful embrace.

"An Amabilis appeared below me when I was halfway down the fall. At least I think it was halfway, I still could not see the bottom. But a moment later, I was in the sublayer, and then I was on the platform where we all first arrived. After I regained my balance I went through the passage to the ledge where Dhiren, Rannoch, and Felix were. You should have seen all of their faces when I suddenly walked out of the crack from behind them!"

She laughed, but none of the guys looked too amused. Dhiren must have been an absolute mess before knowing she was okay.

"Yeah, real funny, Dhirdre," Felix said. "And by the way, once again the Amabilis made you cross the Terrifying Bridge of Nothing?" He motioned to me with an emphatic gesture. "Why didn't they just take you both when they grabbed Dashelle?"

I dropped my jaw. "What the hell! You're right!" I laughed. "I'm not mad about it, it's actually pretty funny now. Especially since we are already across and we are definitely finished with that. I'm so done with that damn bridge."

Further thoughts about any of the events muted as I felt Rannoch pluck the link. I smiled through water-rimmed eyes as he took one stride toward me, then scooped me up. I buried my face in his neck as he slowly spun. He had waited, rooting for me from a distance but unable to help. I felt his frustration abate as the truth of our success settled, we had done it, and survived. I lifted my head and looked in his eyes, the corners of his eyelids crinkled in a subtle display of elation.

We had overcome so much, endured so many trials. To be at the descent of the tipping point, with Dashelle captured and under guard. We were finally ready to make the trip to the Maeder Tree to heal her, to heal *the realm*. Josie would be returned. All of the things that needed to come to pass finally would. I pressed my forehead to his, savoring the moment.

My mate.

Life could be hard, and messy sometimes. I had thought it before and it was true once again. It always would be. And yet, life was beautiful. Life gives you scars, but they are not wounds to hide, they are ones to be proud of. They are proof of a life lived, because they show that we can heal. It was a lesson I would probably be perpetually learning. Some of my scars were from my mistakes. The massive scar on my thigh where I was shot by an Umorfae archer, when I went alone to deliver myself to barter for the Syrenni's freedom. The way I went about it was a mistake, my scar would forever be a reminder to trust in those I loved, which was proven in what followed during the battle at Lacausia Palace. The scars on my heart from when I lost my father and sister, which was no one's fault, but the scar would forever be a reminder to cherish those I love.

And I loved Rannoch deeply. He had proven himself to be someone who would fight for me, with me, support me, listen to me. It had taken missteps and learning, and it would take more for sure. Because we shared a life *together*.

I pulled my head back to gaze at him, as he swept a lock of my hair out of my face. I must have looked a mess, having been subjected to all the windstorms and fighting. There was no braid that could have stayed true through all of that, no way my face wasn't dirt streaked and blood spattered. But he didn't care. He looked at me like I was nothing short of perfect.

I heard the others shuffle by, heading back through the fissure to the area where we had been dropped off by the Amabilis. In truth I had forgotten they were there, as it usually happened when Rannoch and I focused solely on each other. I didn't glance away from him as they left, I barely waited for them to slip through the narrow crack before I kissed him.

With my lips against his, I felt something that I hadn't noticed before, something far greater than ourselves. The dial of the unseen turned and a spoke of the supernatural clicked into place. I never thought of fate as being real. In fact I kind of despised the idea of it, that we were somehow out of control of our own destinies and subjected to the whims of some blind force. The sense of the rotating dial of the world didn't signify fate exactly, but I also couldn't quite identify what it was. Perhaps it was the sense of us cycling toward being righted, toward good winning and evil getting what it deserved. It wasn't the kiss that had done it, it was all of the steps we had taken to get there, every little step along that circular path which helped it all turn to where it needed to be. It wasn't fate, we were in control of our destinies, the more I thought about it the more I was sure of it. We could fuck it up or we could win the day depending on our choices and actions. But I knew for certain that I was meant to be with Rannoch. We had each grown, both because of our relationship and because of ourselves. Because of the steps I had taken myself, and they were not always perfect steps. But they were mine. We had taken step after step together, while on our own journeys.

I would choose to walk by his side for thousands more adventures, whether they were trying, dangerous, boring, or exciting. Whatever the nature of the path I would gladly walk it with him. I was honored to. I opened my mouth to him and kissed him more deeply, inviting his soul closer to mine, sharing breath for those moments on that rocky ledge next to a bottomless crevasse. In this wild world with unfathomable places and everything felt upside down from what I had been born into, my home would always be wherever he was. My home was me, being settled in my heart, and not feeling like I needed to run.

That was perhaps the greatest gift I had been given in this world. Peace of the soul.

I pulled back, letting the kiss simmer as I loosened my arms which had been wrapped around him. He lowered me to the rock surface, letting the realness of the world back into our bubble.

We had a task to finish, the sensation of things moving toward completion did not mean we were done. I may have found a slice of respite, but the souls trapped within Dashelle certainly didn't have theirs yet. And the Maeder Tree had likely wilted further since we saw her last. And Dashelle wasn't going to let go of her stolen power easily.

I took his hand, then headed through the gap to reach our friends. Once on the other side, we found them all speaking in hushed tones as the Amabilis appeared.

CHAPTER 30

After a short conference, we each split off one by one with an Amabilis. They bemoaned having to take Dashelle, she had already proven to be a problem in the sublayer, but she was a nuisance at most. She had been unable to fight against the Amabilis that held her after she came to. I tried to not relish the fact that she had been scared, but I couldn't help it. I wanted her to feel discomfort, fear, and have her be the one to bear the burden of anxiety. She deserved it, how much did Josie endure because of her? Yet still, I knew deep down I needed to try and step away from my personal feelings of vengeance. Josie was so close to being freed, I needed to keep my focus on the goal. Dashelle was cunning after all, if anyone could turn someone's personal feelings to her advantage it would be Dashelle.

I needed to be blind justice. I was not the one to mete out what she was owed. I was simply her courier. Saying the words to myself was one thing, putting that into action—or rather non-action by not unleashing on her—was another.

I sucked in a breath to prepare myself, before we shrunk and spun to join her in the space between. As the branching pathway illuminated around me, I tried to look around to see if I could spot

Dashelle. I couldn't see her, but I could *feel* her. After a moment, I realized I could hear her, too.

I could tell she was thrashing around, held in place by the Amabilis that transported her. I rolled my eyes, she was going to go kicking and screaming the whole way. I tempered myself, trying to quiet my mind as we traveled. If I could have rested that would have been ideal, but Dashelle would not shut down her madwoman ramblings. Angered over events in her human life, having been caught by me and thwarted from pillaging more power, she went on and on about all the "unfairness" she had experienced. Images flashed in my mind, shared by her: stages with girls dressed up, sashes, judges, crowns. A mishmash of visual snippets flew through my thoughts as she hollered again and again.

"Can you shut the fuck up?" I mind-shouted at her. "We can all hear this nonsense!" I paused, realizing that I hadn't heard other's thoughts in the sublayer before. No one besides the Amabilis that is. I had to wonder how I could hear her. Were the Amabilis allowing the connection?

"No, she is simply that loud," the Amabilis that carried me said into my mind. "She will not stop about all of this. Her thoughts are aggressive and chaotic, it is difficult to tell what is about this world and what is about the one she came from."

I almost laughed. "I really didn't need a window into her deranged head." I tried to take a slow breath in and count. Breathing was different in the sublayer, or maybe it was that my lungs didn't function the same at subatomic sizes. I must not have needed air while I was so small, I had never noticed that I wasn't breathing naturally. I had to stop the rising panic now that I wanted to take long, slow inhales to practice calming myself. I closed my eyes to help shut down the external stimuli.

I can still count. I did the same motions I always did when working to deescalate an anxiety attack. My airways were not swelling and filling with oxygen, but I counted backward, droning out Dashelle's noise with my rhythmic pacing.

She still managed to break through here and there, but overall I was able to counter her obnoxious distractions.

At long last, we exited the sublayer. The area resolved in detail and I recognized telltale signs that we were near the Maeder Tree. I heaved a sigh, we wouldn't have to make an additional trek through the forest with Dashelle.

I looked over at her, writhing on the ground and struggling against her bonds. Dhiren had quickly restrained her before she could get her feet under her. That didn't stop her from taking a few swipes at him in the process. I shook my head at Dashelle, she was a horrible example of what humans could be. I thought about all of her machinations she shouted from the sublayer, when suddenly her face had some sort of familiarity.

"Holy shit, I know who you are," I said as I stared at her face. Her name was a little different, but something in her expression as she gnashed her teeth looked like someone I had seen before. "Felix, do you know who she is?"

"No I … wait! She's that pageant chick!"

"What's your real name though? It isn't Dashelle," I asked her.

"Danielle," Felix answered. "Danielle Frohler. Frohlan?"

"That's it! Frohlan. So what happened *Danielle*, you weren't crowned queen there so you set your sights on being queen of this world?"

She scowled and thrashed again, but still said nothing. It was the same expression she had worn when she made the headlines, "Beauty Queen's Empire of Lies," it had read.

"What are you talking about?" Kerenza asked.

"She's somewhat notorious in the human realm," Felix answered. "Well, she was for about fifteen minutes. That's all the fame she got."

"Shut up! You don't know anything!"

"You could have made a clean start here," I said. "You're wanted for fraud and money laundering, and then you evaded arrest. You were a small time crook at most. But then you became a murderer, if they know it was you who killed the others from your town. If anyone should hide it would be you, you had a chance at another life here, and yet this is what you did, why?"

"Because I should be queen! I should have been crowned! It was mine! And *they* deserved their deaths for what they took from me. I became the predator after what those boys did to me. They were predators first!"

I shook my head. "I guess it doesn't matter who you were there. Who you are here has proven enough what you're capable of. The Maeder Tree will deal with you." I clenched my fist. There was so little holding me back from absolutely pummeling her, from hitting her until she spat out teeth. She killed Josie, and I desperately wanted to take payment for the injustice. For her selfishness, for her lack of remorse. She didn't seem to feel an ounce of shame for killing Josie, for killing any of them. It sounded like whatever the others had done to her may have deserved some form of punishment. But her actions had stretched far beyond revenge. Maybe the worst part was that she wasn't the least bit sorry. She was only sorry she lost. That was what I had heard in the sublayer, she was sorry for herself for losing the crown, twice.

I reached down and picked her up by the collar. "Time to pay up."

I dragged her toward the ridge which would lead down the slope to the Well. We crested the ridge, and there below us stood the previously majestic source of life, bent over and shriveled. The sight of the tree filled me with foreboding, *this* was the result of selfish actions, this was what recklessness could cause. I gripped Dashelle's collar tighter, more to keep myself from shoving her down the hill to the Well's edge. Felix came up on the other side and grabbed onto her. The ground rumbled, then started rolling and shifting. I spread my feet wider to keep my balance.

"Cut it out," I said through gritted teeth. Dashelle was trying to thwart us by twisting the ground beneath us, but her hands were bound so the effect was minimal.

"Can't blame a girl for trying," she said, trying to toss her dark hair back which was stuck to her face. After an unsuccessful attempt, she used her shoulder instead to push back the errant pieces.

Everyone gathered behind us and we all descended the hill together. At the water's edge, I looked at Felix. I wanted to toss her in, to watch her sink to the bottom as every last air bubble funneled out of her. It played out in my mind as I shifted my gaze to the water.

"Lily," Felix said.

I blinked, coming out of the trance that I had been in, romanticizing ending Dashelle.

"Let's check the knots."

I nodded, testing out each one. She smiled at me, leaning in too close for comfort. Just as quickly, she dropped her smile and looked ahead to the Maeder Tree. I wondered if she even knew what it meant, what we were about to do.

After confirming the bonds were secure with Felix, we both jumped and pulled her with us. We slipped through the silky volume and my own well refilled. The wondrous thing about the Well—aside from its healing effects—was how it not only filled my reserves but also balanced it, it wasn't like there was too much like I sometimes felt. It was full while being at ease. It was a sensation I wished I could maintain while not suspended in its magical fluid.

I glanced at Dashelle. The surprised look on her face told me she had never been to the Well, never seen the Maeder Tree. *Interesting, Opius must have kept that to himself.* She had been in league with him for some time before I even showed up, he must have been careful about sharing information about the Well for her to not have been here yet. I would think any source of power would become fair game to her. Maybe it was a big assumption to think she didn't know about the tree and the wells, there were three in total with the Maeder Tree rooted in the main center well.

Felix and I swam her toward the tree, and she closed her eyes as we dragged her, seeming to bask in the Well's life-giving liquid. Her expression of pure bliss angered me. She didn't deserve to feel the comfort it gave. I reached down to check her bonds, I needed to make sure she wasn't about to rip open the walls of the lake since her power well was now completely topped off. I had to imagine that would be a death blow to the Maeder Tree. Flashing my gaze over my shoulder, I saw that the rest of our group formed a semicircle behind us, creating a protective ring in case Dashelle tried anything.

It wasn't a massive battle with a siege force, there weren't arrows flying and countless warriors hell bent on taking down their enemy with swords clanging. It was our small group, an elite task force with a very personal mission. Rannoch was right, it didn't have to be a large-scale assault for it to matter, for it to make a difference.

Everyone pressed in closer, readying to force Dashelle's hand, literally.

I should have been reassured, but I wasn't. I couldn't assume even for a second that it was all going to go easily. I frowned as I realized another difficulty: we were going to have to free her hand to place it on the Maeder Tree's trunk.

We finally reached the base, after the arduous struggle to find, subdue, then transport Dashelle here, we had finally arrived. Rannoch came in closer and gripped Dashelle from behind while I quickly undid her bindings. I didn't want her to know the plan, to know what we had to do or else she may have been able to formulate a way out. The first hand was freed and she instantly shot her arm out of the water, wrenching at the shoreline to try and break a rock free. Kerenza moved in quickly, her hand covered Dashelle's and crunched down, immobilizing her fingers and arresting any use of her earth skill. Dashelle's other hand came loose, she tried the same thing but Felix caught it. I grabbed onto the arm that Kerenza held, and helped bring it toward the trunk. As we had nearly reached it, I heard the Maeder Tree wail that familiar word, the same one I had heard the first time I had returned to her.

"Hommmme." The Maeder Tree's voice was strained, weak. I realized I hadn't heard her since I had seen her last. Perhaps she was conserving her energy, perhaps she was nearly dead.

Dashelle gasped and tried to bolt. "What was that?"

"That is our maker. Now, put your godsdamned hand on the trunk."

"Why? No! What will it do?"

She struggled against me, and even with the strength of the Vale Born she possessed, it was no match for the might of all of us pressing in around her. Kerenza and I fought her arm to the trunk at last, then uncurled her fingers to flatten her palm on the surface. Felix held onto her other wrist, and I reached over to grab his other free hand. We had to complete the circuit if it was going to work. When Felix and I had first visited, Maris was rejoined once he and I held hands and touched her trunk. In this case I didn't know what the specific formula was, what would create that intrinsic bridge that would allow the Vale Born to exit Dashelle and enter the realm of the Maeder Tree. I had to assume something similar needed to be created for it to work.

I felt the bond start, the pathway opened and the spirit of our Maeder became visible. Dashelle shrieked, trying desperately to pull her hand away. Dhiren, Dhirdre, and Zia pressed forward, each one grabbing an exposed area to hold her in place. The charge was palpable as the first Vale Born left her, I could feel the pressure build just before it happened. Dashelle gritted her teeth and tried to fight against it, trying to close off the invisible, intangible release valve that allowed the souls to pass. But it had already slipped through. It reminded me of the sensation of popping through the

Vale, the first time I had ended up in this realm.

The faint image of a young man with russet hair went first. He turned toward Dashelle as he floated by, and the look of fear in her face was unmistakable. And yet, ultimately he did nothing. His glance looked disappointed in her, but he was now at peace and seemed to not care to attempt any sort of retribution. Perhaps there was none he could give, or perhaps it wasn't important to him anymore. He was moving on with no ill will it seemed.

Another young man went next, slightly older than the last. Dashelle looked pained as she saw him, but then quickly shook her head to wipe away any indication of guilt she may have felt. It was the closest thing to shame I had seen on her. Maybe she was actually capable of more human emotions than she had shown thus far. He joined the Maeder and she caressed him with a loving arm.

The pressure built again and I knew who I'd see next. I choked back tears as I finally saw my dearest friend. I had been waiting for so long, my journey had started in search of her, and when I knew she would not be found alive but where her soul existed, I endeavored to free her from Dashelle. It was finally coming to pass after the difficult, twisting path. Josie smiled at me, at Felix. She was as lovely as ever, her long brown hair had the same silkiness I remembered. She was so much more serene now than she was in life, it soothed my heart to see her content. I wanted to reach out to her, and I almost let go of Dashelle, but Josie made a motion with her hands that we had used through all of our years riding horses together. She held up her hands, then pushed them in a repetitive, circular motion down and forward.

I scrunched my eyebrows, confused about what it might mean. When we were riding, it meant slow, or wait. It was a visual cue so that the other person could see it from a distance without needing any words shouted.

"I don't understand, Josie!" *What do I need to wait for?*

She made the motion again, then pointed to Dashelle. I still didn't understand, but I held tight. I sucked in my tears as Josie joined our Maeder, and the others who had just crossed over. I could see her, but I couldn't touch her or hear her. I had done what I needed to do, but for me it wasn't enough. I wanted to hold her, to give her one last hug. I wrestled with the reality of only partially getting what I wanted. Josie was free, I *had* to be satisfied with that. She was no longer trapped within a monster. I looked at Dashelle, and all over again I wanted to kill her myself, even if I had done what I said I would. *Unfair.* She had complained about the unfairness of life and yet she had committed that which was the *most* unfair, taking another's life. More than once. Anger bubbled in me and my palms heated. I squeezed her arm tighter, and tighter, when I felt another tremor.

Another soul exited Dashelle.

"What the fuck!" Felix hollered. "There's more!"

Oh my Gods, there were more. *That's* what Josie meant. There were more Vale Born. We had to keep her connected to the Maeder Tree until the others had made it out.

This time it was another woman, older than Josie and me but not by much. I frowned, another life cut short by the murderous, selfish Dashelle. The female looked at me appreciatively, probably relieved to have the imprisonment end. Was she killed before Josie, or after? We had only known about the three. Where was she from? What was her name?

I glanced at Josie, who again motioned with her hands to wait.

"Keep your hands on her, there are more," I said to Felix and the Ignisfae. We all held fast, waiting.

The feeling of something pressing up an invisible wall began again, and then a fifth Vale Born passed through. She was a much older woman. The sight of her made my heart halt, for a split second I thought it was my mom. I looked at Felix, who also squinted at her in confusion. It wasn't her, but her appearance did give me pause. The thought that a Vale Born could avoid the call of the Vale for so long surprised me. After a moment I realized if that person had moved away, had a life elsewhere and was removed from the whispers of the Faeries—and the insistent, silent beckon of the gateway they were born near—they might be able to avoid the draw.

Josie nodded and signaled that it was over. We had done it, we had returned all five to their rightful place. No wonder Dashelle had gone mad and the Maeder Tree was so deeply affected, that would seem to be too much for one individual to contain. In a way it made sense that it was possible for Vale Born to absorb each other, should something happen not in the realm of Alternis, the spirit energy could be stored until it could be returned to its source, the ecosystem of the energy flow would be able to retain balance. But clearly it was a flawed system, all it took was one individual with ill intentions and a loose understanding of what having the power of multiples could mean.

"That's it, we've done it."

Could that really be it? After so much effort, it was difficult to fathom that I would not be enduring this trial anymore. But, the Vale Born were returned, and the Maeder Tree had already begun to perk up.

Everyone exhaled in relief, loosening their flexed muscles to allow Dashelle to detach from the tree. She wailed and sobbed, then screamed in anger.

I looked at Josie one last time, who had already receded farther back into the Maeder's branches. That was all I would get, one final look until I myself joined her in the aether in the far future. Someday, I would, and it would be us against the world with Maris at our sides once again.

I kept a hold of Dashelle's wrist, and Felix pulled her other arm.

We dragged her to the shoreline. She didn't even fight, she sagged and let the fluid swell around her defeated form.

We reached the edge, Rannoch and Kerenza jumped out first, then helped haul her onto dry land, leaving her in a crumpled heap as Felix and I got out. Dhiren, Dhirdre and Zia emerged last.

"What do we do with her now?" Felix asked, looking at her. She sat toward us a few paces away with her head hung and back curved.

"Well," I said, "she is wanted for more murders than the Vale Born. She admitted to killing Eiulans." I looked at Rannoch. "Perhaps your faeder would like to dole out his own punishment. We can take her back to TerraIgni." I supposed it wasn't really over until Dashelle was officially imprisoned.

Rannoch nodded, but Kerenza did not look pleased.

Dashelle looked despondent, maybe even catatonic as I spoke. Not the faintest flicker of an expression crossed her face. I was the closest person to her so I leaned down to get a slightly closer look at her. With a defeated, blank stare, she looked about as far away as possible.

I stood and addressed everyone standing nearby. "Let's tie her back up, then get going."

I didn't even see the change in Dashelle's demeanor, before she unleashed an insane, shrill war cry.

CHAPTER 31

Dashelle lunged at me, her face wild and twisted in rage as she leapt with her hands outstretched at my neck. The skin of her one palm looked mangled and angry as she sailed toward me. I lifted my arms to fight her off, when I heard the telltale sing of a sword being unsheathed. There was a swipe and a rushing sound, then most of her hair flew to the side. After a split-second I realized her head had been separated from her body. My jaw dropped as a ribbon of blood splattered my face, her severed head sprayed as it sailed by.

Dashelle's body took a moment to drop, while her head bounced away. Kerenza stood behind as Dashelle's lifeless corpse fell to the ground. My mate's sister heaved heavy breaths, holding my bloodied selwaer in her hand. No, *Kenneder's* selwaer. Her departed mate.

"Kerenza!" I shouted. I was stunned, I had wanted Dashelle dead so many times, and I couldn't deny that I was relieved that she was no longer our problem, or, I would be relieved at some point after my spiked adrenaline had a chance to subside. It all happened so fast, I didn't even expect it, for a moment I didn't process what I had seen.

"It needed to be done," Kerenza said with conviction. "Taking her to TerraIgni could *never* be enough to satisfy the debt she owed to me. Because of her, and her deal with the Umorfae separatists, Kenneder was killed. Emblyn and others were *stolen* from us. Dashelle has owed me this life-debt since then. You may have promised not to kill her, but *I* did not." She flicked the blood off of the sword, punctuating her declaration.

I started to speak, when a surging, invisible wave hit me in the chest.

Stumbling back, I felt everything grow. I turned my face up to the misty sky and opened my mouth in a silent yell. Or maybe it wasn't silent. I felt power flex from me, into me. Reaching my arms wide with my fingers rigid, I gripped at nothing in particular as everything in the vicinity bowed outward, then curved inward toward me.

Me. I was *everything*. I was anything I wanted to be. I could have it all. I swung my eyes down and saw everyone whom I could command. I curled my lip in satisfaction, things were finally right. I was exactly where I wanted to be, finally poised to take control of every last being. They wouldn't kill me, they loved me too much. They would bow to me. They would bow to the queen I was.

"Lily," I heard my brother say. But it didn't sound right, it didn't fit. He would no longer be my brother, I would be his commander, I would steer this realm and everyone under my control.

"Lily," Rannoch said, and I felt something. A tug through me, it reached right in and pulled. I paused, remembering what that feeling was. It was our link.

I gasped and backed up a step. It wasn't only me I sensed inside myself, it was Dashelle puppeteering my mind. She had stepped in and intruded on my thoughts, my goals had shifted. She had taken over for that moment. I had carried Maris for all that time and never once felt any attempt to direct me. But, Maris wasn't an invasive virus like Dashelle. I had worried before we came to the Maeder Tree that killing her would mean an influx of power from her and the several Vale Born she carried, an amount that could drive me as mad as she was. It was one reason I had specifically avoided ending her, to prevent either myself or Felix from absorbing such a disproportionate amount of energy. Apparently she alone was enough to cause that.

I had to release her, to send her back to the Maeder so that balance could be restored and Dashelle would no longer have any means to cause additional trauma to this realm, that realm, or to anyone in either of them.

Felix narrowed his eyes at me, appraising me. "You absorbed her, didn't you?"

I nodded. He visibly tensed, but I was going to handle it, and send her back myself. I only wanted to feel what earth power could do, just once. Then I would go to the Maeder Tree on my own and do it.

I reached out, feeling the layers of earth. I sensed them, like flakes I could pull up, cards I could shuffle. The thought of fraying the ground sounded appealing, like it would feel good to reach in and pull a few pieces out, to ruffle the ground and change the surface to my will.

Felix moved toward me, readying to grab me. I scrawled my fingers and made a quick motion toward myself, hooking into the air with a yank. The land responded with a delightful release of resistance, the section below Felix angled up and shot out, sending him backward. He blasted a quick funnel of air behind, catching himself from falling onto his ass. I drew in a sharp breath, I was right, it *did* feel good. After a moment I laughed, I was only being playful and testing what this skill could do, but he scowled at me nonetheless.

"Release her, Dashelle!" he yelled.

"Oh for fuck's sake, Felix. I'm *fine.*" It was only harmless fun. I looked him over, and suddenly wondered what *his* skill would feel like. It was the only one I didn't have now. If he pressed too much, well, that could change. I advanced a step, my gaze honing in on him. He used to be the better fighter between us, maybe now that wasn't the case.

A pair of arms encircled me from behind. I snapped my head to the right, seeing Dhiren had somehow snuck up on me. "Let me go!" I struggled against him, then I crouched down before exploding upward. A narrow pillar of earth blasted from below one foot, shooting me skyward, causing him to have to let go and fall away. I jumped forward and called another pillar a pace away as my stride met it, then I leapt down.

Zia tried to ensnare me next, but I was too quick for her. Dhirdre and Kerenza teamed up to flank me, but I flicked my hands to both sides, sending wide rock blockades at a diagonal in each direction, creating a protected channel for myself which led away from all of them. I raced forward, then in an instant Rannoch appeared at the other end.

I skidded to a stop. I could fight him, I could use my size to my advantage, just like he taught me. Or I could simply escape and regroup, before I figured out my next move.

I blew out a breath, coming back to myself. Dashelle was *strong.* She had maneuvered her way into my consciousness again.

I closed my eyes, shutting out everyone around me.

Three, two, one. You are safe.

I blinked my eyelids open, then took two long strides over the angled wall toward the Well. I was careful not to use any earth skill that begged to be let out, didn't look at anyone else, and I didn't open the link with Rannoch. Shutting out all external voices, I focused on only one. My own.

Me, Lily. I was going to end this. Dashelle had taken her last shot at wrenching control of this realm, and this time she had attempted it through me. I didn't think or pause as I dove in head first and with as much force as I could muster. I wanted that dive to get me as close to the Maeder Tree as possible. As I started to surface, I didn't allow myself to slow as I pulled hand over hand, alternating strokes. I reached the tree with vitriol burning in my veins. I slapped my hand to the trunk, not waiting for another attempt by Dashelle to avoid her final fate. She was *going home,* even if I had to kick her metaphorical ass there.

I heard the others not far behind, but Felix wasn't close enough, so I didn't wait. Maybe I could complete the circuit myself. I pressed my other hand to the smooth, segmented surface.

"Get. *Out.*" The connection started and I felt the pull from the Maeder Tree working to draw her out. Dashelle fought it, somehow gripping me from the inside. "I said get out!" I closed my eyes, using my healing sight to tunnel inward. I couldn't see anything, I wasn't sure if I expected to see her face, but there was no visual cue that she inhabited my body. Since I had nothing of her to pin my gaze on, I instead focused on my inner self swelling. I pictured myself filled with gold light, with no room for the putrid black taint she tried to inject into me. I forced her further to the edge, where there was nothing substantial for her wicked spirit to cling to.

I opened my eyes just as she exited, her fury shone in her ghostly visage for a moment, before it washed away to a more placid expression. Our Maeder was there, ready to scoop her up and cradle her. Dashelle's expression changed again, looking terrified and trapped. Just as quickly, it shifted. She was no longer hateful, spiteful, vengeful. She looked … remorseful. As I watched her return to our source, I finally got the one thing I wanted since I had learned Josie was gone, I wanted Josie's killer to feel regret and sorrow for her actions.

I didn't get to see if the other Vale Born were there to witness Dashelle's crossing, to get their own resolution of how their lives ended. I had to trust that Dashelle would be served her justice, that she would learn her lesson and pay for her crimes, in whatever way that was possible now that she was moving on.

I pulled my hand away, the warm sensation on my palm tingled, then the Maeder turned back to me after she had ensured Dashelle had completed her transition. She spread her arms to me, her golden, transparent hair flowing once more. "Hommmmme," she sang. Her spirit caressed mine, thanking me, praising me. I had done right by her, and she was grateful. She turned away, and her form looked like it had the first time I had seen her, a beautiful maiden goddess who approved of how everything fell into place in the end.

She wasn't my mom, there was no one who could step in and fill that role, that place was reserved solely for Rachael Brennanfalk. But seeing the Maeder Tree happy, healthy and approving of my effort, it filled me with pride that filled the void of parental approval

I could no longer get.

I turned, wanting to share that feeling with my family. Pangs of guilt washed over me as I looked at all of them, swimming in place in a semicircle around me, ready to help if I had needed it. I had acted against them, but none of them wore any expression that made me think they held it against me. The moments that Dashelle had taken over were already forgotten. She had crossed over, and finally, at long last, we were safe.

Felix reached forward, and I hugged him with all my might. It was finally *over*. After we all exchanged hugs, we lounged in the Well for some time, laughing and enjoying the moment of victory. I smiled at Rannoch, it was both a large and a small win at the same time. It hadn't been a huge battle to turn the tides in a great war, it had been an intimate, re-righting of the world as we knew it. The Maeder Tree's healing process had already begun, she visibly looked younger and more vibrant. Life would go on, children would be born, and good things could be possible once again. Perhaps that would be my path with Rannoch one day, but for now, I was content in the fact that we had prevailed, and our lives could proceed.

We swam toward the edge to finally exit the luminous lake, when Livi rushed to me.

"What is it?" Felix asked.

"Livi is trying to tell me something about the Ita Hua Tear." I leaned in closer, listening to their distinctive tinkling voice. I gasped after I realized what the message was. "There are two Vale Born coming through!"

CHAPTER 32

I couldn't believe it, Dashelle had been right. There were more Vale Born there, but she had miscalculated and they came through later than she anticipated. I smirked, *switching from days to rotations really is a bitch, huh?* If Dashelle had spent more time learning about the realm, maybe she would have mastered the time-shift difference better. I shook my head, coming back to the pressing reality that there would be two brand new Vale Born in this world. Having them know who we were would be best, before they went wandering through the realm unguided.

"We've got to get there," I stated.

"Right," Felix agreed. "For sure." He huffed a laugh, then covered his forehead with his palm. "I think we're fated to constantly rush all over the place. I mean, we were literally there like a rotation ago."

I shrugged. "Hopefully this will be the last sprint. No use complaining about it now, let's find the Amabilis again." Livi flew up to my ear to tell me further information. "Wait," I said to everyone, "the Amabilis are gone. They have retreated to the sublayer, all of our requests may have tired them out."

"Dammit!" Felix exclaimed. "We have to take the long way?"

"Nope." I grinned. "I mean, probably not. The Faeries spotted an Arbor Elf contingent not far to the north, they just exited portals." I interwove my fingers as I thought about it, we'd have to find them before they left through their next fenestram, their folding doorways they used to move about the realm. "We should hurry, Livi says they're that way," I said, as I pointed to the northwest tree line. At that moment, a figure emerged from the trees.

I beamed as I recognized an old friend immediately. Dendris twitched a smile at me, always reserved with her outward displays of emotion, I knew that the subtle expression conveyed a lot more than it showed. Her gaze flicked to the blood on me, then around our group, then finally, to the headless body on the ground. She motioned to unseen Arbor Elves behind her, who then stepped forward into the clearing to join her. Aurelian, their leader, was the second one to become visible. Still with a cane in her hand, but walking with much more surety than I had seen her last, she looked every bit the fearless leader I remembered. They walked toward us in formation.

I moved to meet them halfway, saluting with a fist across my chest. Rannoch and Kerenza joined me. "Aurelian, Dendris, it is so good to see you all," I said, dropping my head in a respectful bow.

"Lily," Aurelian said as she stepped closer, "what happened here?"

"Dashelle happened. We captured her and were returning the Vale Born she had taken, afterward, she tried to kill me again. Kerenza finished her once and for all, she is dead. She is no longer a problem."

"And the Maeder Tree, I see she is healthy again. We had heard she was ailing, so we came to see what could be done."

"It *is* done. She is healthy once more and the realm is safe from Dashelle." The weight of the world released from me further, saying the words out loud resounded through me that it was in fact done, even if we had another mission to complete. "However, we have another issue. There are two unknown Vale Born coming through the Ita Hua Tear, the Faeries just told us about them. Dashelle had been trying to lure them here before we caught her. We need to get there right away."

"Ita Hua? Are you sure?" Dendris asked. "The Caelifae had made that location impossible to reach, and caused relentless winds. No living creature has been seen there in at least fifty cycles. I went there myself last cycle, there is no way."

"Perhaps the deal Dashelle made with one of the Caelifae is what changed that. I don't want to say too much, as I have not been able to notify their leader yet. But, we were there. I think they did something to reopen it."

Aurelian held up a hand. "No need to say more, we will take you as close as we can."

I blew out a breath and nodded my thanks. "It seems we are always asking something of your people. At some point, we should host a celebration to show our appreciation for all you have done."

"It would be welcome," Aurelian said, "and perhaps, a celebration will finally be warranted." Her eyes cast over Dashelle's lifeless body. I stopped myself from clenching my fists, I had come so close to losing myself to Dashelle, to not only becoming like her, but becoming *her*. A person whose death Aurelian subtly suggested we celebrate.

A few more Arbor Elves made their way from the cover of

the foliage, averting my prior thoughts. They stepped forward to Aurelian, who gave them quick instructions. They fanned out, motioning to each of us to join them. I went to Dendris, who held up her outstretched arms, then pulled back one hand like she was drawing an invisible bow taut. The fenestram started, their portals which began as sizzling, bright sparks edged in a prismatic rainbow enlarged to doorways wide enough to step through. She looped her arm around my waist, then guided me through in a spin reminiscent of a waltz.

By the time we had completed the turn, we were through. The icy air of the high peaks blasted my face, but it wasn't anything like when we had tried to cross the needle-like bridge across the chasm. It seemed more like wind you'd encounter at high altitudes, rather than something created by Caelifae to keep people away. Dendris looked around, checking the area.

"This has definitely changed. There were fierce winds that blew me back the last time. It is quieter now."

I glanced behind us as other portals opened. Everyone stepped through in short order. We were further away than where the Amabilis had brought us before, but not by much. I could see the rocky outcropping where the split in the rock was. "The actual tear is ahead a little ways, through a crack in a rock, across a narrow bridge, then through another crack."

"We will wait here for you," she stated. Aurelian walked over to hear what we were discussing.

"Actually," I said as I thought about it further, "can one of you come with us to cross the bridge? These will be new Vale Born, at least I think they are. Passing through the tear is a big physical change, it's painful and a person comes through the other side completely altered. The pathway to cross over the chasm is harrowing, one mistake and it's a long, long way down. Plus, I frankly don't want to have to cross it more times than is necessary." I scoffed as I thought about how I had commented the last time we were here that I was done with the bridge. It had been wishful thinking. "If you come, we can fenestram them back here."

"That is considerate for you to think of them," Aurelian said. "Dendris, you shall accompany Lily across."

"It's personally motivated," I admitted. "I crossed it twice already. I don't especially want to do it again. Although, it's kind of poetic that it will be you and I again, Dendris. Ferrying people from a difficult location after we put ourselves through danger to get there. Reminds me of us swimming through the cave to get to the children."

She shuddered. "I could do without the swelling from too much water this time around."

I silently agreed, then motioned to Felix to join us. "I think Felix needs to come as well, we should both be there to talk to the new arrivals, so that we can explain what we can. It will help having more than one Vale Born that has been through the transition. Dendris, can you come back to get him once we have crossed? I think it won't be an issue this time around, last time none of the males were allowed to cross. I believe it was the Caelifae that was blocking the path for them, but we might as well just be on the safe side."

She dipped her chin in acknowledgment, then we all hiked up to where the larger boulder blocked the path forward. I hung back for a moment to catch Rannoch.

He took both of my hands in his, and for a long moment he

said nothing. The air was heavy between us as I waited. "You know what I will say," he said.

"Be careful, I love you, call if you need us?"

"Exactly. I know it is unlikely these new Vale Born are anything like Dashelle, but, be on your guard just the same. We will be here for you."

I smiled, then stood on my tiptoes to brush a kiss to his cheek. "We will."

I turned, then headed toward the massive boulder with Dendris. I was a mix of emotions as we wriggled through the passageway. Excitement sent a thrill through me, the chance to meet new Vale Born was momentous. Opius had said we were a rarity, even rarer now that Dashelle had killed five. And now Dashelle was dead, so six gone, leaving just Felix and myself. It was entirely possible there were more, and that there would be more in the future was now a possibility since the Maeder Tree had been healed. But, how many more might there be? This could very well be it for many cycles.

Nerves plagued me, what would I even say to these people? *Hi, welcome. Everything you know just changed.* What would be the best way to tell them what they needed to know, without overwhelming them and coming off like a complete weirdo?

The other emotion churning through me was one of dread and foreboding. If these two *were* like Dashelle, rather than more like Felix and I, we would have a whole new set of problems on our hands. *Not to be selfish, but I need a godsdamned break from all of that.* I shook my head, spending energy pre-living the situation would do me no good. I led Dendris through to the other side of the cramped, twisting pathway, then stood on the ledge before the bridge. She gasped behind me as she looked over my shoulder.

"I understand why you wanted to limit how many times you crossed it." Dendris pushed her mossy hair out of the way of her face, seeming to ready herself to cross the dangerous path. "How do I always end up in these situations with you, Lily?"

"I know, I really am the worst." I lifted the corner of my lips in a lopsided grin as I looked at her over my shoulder, and she laughed. I dropped my jaw, I had never once heard her so much as chuckle, and I had tried multiple times in the past to get a reaction out of her. "A laugh! A real laugh from you! It only took us going to the ends of the realm and crossing a bridge that couldn't be more treacherous."

"It could be crumbling as well, that would be more treacherous."

"Was that a joke now, too? Someone needs to write down this momentous occasion. Okay, all joking aside, I found it's best if you look at where you want to get to, and take your time. Slow and steady, there's no need to rush. We go one at a time, the bridge can't hold the weight of more than one."

She nodded, then stretched her fingers outward, her radices growing out in little root-like extensions. I glanced at them quizzically, I knew they used them to drink water and broth, it was how I had helped Aurelian recover when she was shot. I had forced water into her radices to help her heal.

She noticed my curious glance. "I am testing the area, my radices can sense things that my eyes cannot see. I feel nothing of note, let us proceed."

I settled my shoulders, then moved forward, foot after foot until I was across. Perhaps it was having done it several times, and the knowledge that Dashelle was not on the other side, but the way across was remarkably easier. I turned around, then motioned to

Dendris.

She looked down, then shook her head at the chasm. With a quick motion, she opened a portal then stepped through next to me. I dropped my mouth, unsure of what to even say. "You have to be kidding me! I just unnecessarily crossed that bridge *again?*"

"I am sorry, I was so caught up thinking of walking across that I did not consider opening a portal, I realized I could easily see where it ended and so would not end up stepping through into a rock."

I pinched the bridge of my nose. "Okay, well that was *definitely* the last time! Let's get going." We made our way through the next split in the boulder. I peered around the edge of the opening, looking ahead at the twisted, dry brambles that radiated from a central point. The rocky plateau was barren, and there was no activity that I could see.

I moved away from the cold rock face, Dendris came out next to me to look around as well. "So, what do we do now?"

"We wait." I wished I had an idea of how long it might be. Who knew how long Opius had stood waiting for me at the bottom of that wall that I had descended after I came through. He had been the one to orchestrate the entire event. He sent the Faeries to whisper to me, he beckoned me from the other side, then was there to swoop in at the right time, to guide me along the path like a lamb being shepherded. I frowned, I had been so manipulated, then cultivated to be what he wanted. This time, for whoever these Vale Born were, I would endeavor to be a guide to only help them, that they could pick their path. Hopefully, they would be there with honorable intentions.

"I think it's a good time for you to get Felix," I said to her, realizing it may be awhile. She tipped her head in one quick nod, then opened a fenestram and departed. I blew out my breath, watching the visible puffs from the cold float before being whisked away by the wind. It wasn't nearly as windy as it had been the first time, when Calria had been thwarting us with her cyclones. I twisted my head as I remembered her, looking far to the right where I had cut her down. She lay forgotten there, her body now frozen on the rock surface. The blood had iced over and formed crystals which faded from bright red, to pink, to bluish white where it melded with the stone. With her blood drained her body now matched the blue of her robes. I debated if I should plan to collect her and return her to her people, but then decided it was a problem to deal with later. The fenestram reopened next to me, then Dendris stepped through with Felix.

"Any sign yet?" he asked, rubbing his bare arms to ward off the cold.

"Nothing. I should have asked Livi how long they thought it would be, if they even knew," I said, as I released some fire above my palm to help warm my brother.

"You could call, right?"

"And make Livi race all the way here just so I knew how long we'd stand around? I'm okay with waiting and letting my thoughts settle for awhile."

"I hate waiting."

I let out a laugh. "You're just like Dad! He never could wait anywhere. Remember when we went to that restaurant for dinner and the wait was going to be over an hour? He couldn't handle it and we drove to three other restaurants looking for a better wait time."

Felix chuckled. "Yeah, I do. And in the end we ended up waiting over an hour and a half anyway."

"What is a restaurant?" Dendris asked.

I explained it, then wondered if there were any restaurants in Alternis. There were carts in the TerraIgni bazaar where you could buy skewered meats, tortams, and citrus drinks. But so far I hadn't seen an actual sit-down restaurant. Perhaps it was another thing from my former home that simply wasn't a part of this realm. It would be nice to surprise Rannoch with something like that, a restaurant-like experience, something of the human world that I could share with him. I loved my home with Rannoch, and was looking forward to settling back in once we were back in TerraIgni and could move forward, but I couldn't deny there would always be things I would miss. Small things like restaurants, big things like people I loved.

I shifted on my feet, my thoughts moved to how far away we were from the Maeder Tree, and the speck of life I had witnessed once near the tear I had come from. It was a great distance to get from the tree to the aperture, and then further still to make it through the passage, then to a human host. It started to make sense why there were not many Vale Born, it was a long journey for such a small fleck of light to make its way. I imagined it being like sea turtles heading to the ocean after hatching in the sand, and the perilous passage to reach the water and the possibility of growing. Whoever these two Vale Born were, they must have been resilient, to have made it all that way to then get through the tear, and everything that came after that. I dropped my hands that had been crossed and tucked under each arm, finally realizing something that hadn't quite added up.

"This tear has been closed for a long time, right?"

"Supposedly," Felix answered.

"Like many cycles, long before you and I were born."

"Right, and?"

"I'm thinking these Vale Born are not young like us. How could they be? The Caelifae shut this area down for the last fifty cycles or something. Even if the Maeder Tree sent whatever they are called, Vale Born seeds or I don't know what, they wouldn't have been able to get out. The wind would blow them away, dash them to bits. The closure would go both ways, no one out or in. No Faeries, nothing."

"Makes sense. I suppose we'll see when they come through. But, do you think that means anything?"

I chewed on my lip. There was *something*, something I couldn't put my finger on. Perhaps it had to do with that great dial of life I had sensed, the clicking of another spoke into place. We were edging toward another event like that, and there was a reason that it mattered that the tear had been closed for so long, for *that* long. But whatever the answer was, it was not clear to me, it was like it was obscured by the mist of the realm, hidden just out of view and about to step through, to clarify and tell me how it was all connected.

"I'm overthinking things again," I said at last.

"I don't think you are," Felix said in all seriousness.

Dendris held up a hand, quieting the both of us. I snapped my head to the brambles, my sight zeroing in on the central point where they twisted into an impassable knot.

The knot loosened.

I gasped and flung my hand out to grab Felix's. We watched

as it released its powerful vise and widened. Sparks shot out of it, bright, electrified currents crackled in the air with thunderous claps and made all the hair on my arms and neck stand on end. A maelstrom of energy sizzled from it, I could see two indistinct forms, but the bright lights were so intense they burned patterns into my eyes.

I was still blinking, trying to get my vision to cooperate when the tear closed. For the first time in however many long cycles, the Ita Hua Tear opened and let someone in. Two someones, who were on the ground in heaps, shrieking.

I cringed, remembering the pain of the first crossing. The changes in the body happen so fast it makes childhood growing pains seem comfortable. I felt for them and what they were currently experiencing. I gripped Felix's hand tighter, waiting. I had to stop myself from running to help them, there was little I could offer at the moment. Their shrieking subsided a little, but they still hadn't been able to get their feet under themselves. It was two females, that much I could tell for sure. Beautiful auburn gold hair fell forward, covering their faces and sweeping the ground.

They started to attempt to stand, and I knew we had waited long enough. "Let's go, Felix. Time to introduce ourselves."

They stood and turned toward us, and I gasped. Or maybe screamed. Any sense of self fled for a moment while I looked at them. I flashed my gaze to Felix, who looked wild with excitement.

"Looks like there's no need for introductions!" he yelled at me as he ran toward the newcomers.

CHAPTER 33

I nearly fell to my knees three times trying to get to them, praising whatever Gods there were in this realm.

"How?" It was the only word that escaped my mouth as I looked at the two of them. Still shaky from the transition, but also equally stunned to see us, our mom and Aunt Maureen opened their arms as we neared.

They cried, we cried, everyone cried. They were the happiest tears that had ever flowed from me, they were tears I gladly allowed. My mom was *here*, our little family unit was complete. Just as quickly, my happy tears turned to laughs as I hugged them, checking to make sure my eyes didn't deceive me. It was really them, changed from the transition, but it was *them.* My mom looked as beautiful as she always did, taller now and with more angular features, but it was her. The same slight corner crinkle that was stronger on her left eye, the same lopsided smile that I sometimes had, too.

She cupped my face, looking up to me. I was still taller than she was, but not by as much as the last time I had seen her. "Lily Mae, Felix, I have missed you both so much, my sweets." She finally looked around. "Where are we? I guess this is what you were trying to tell me before. Only, what does this mean? Why are we here? And what the hell was that back there?" She massaged her arms, clearly still feeling the effects of the change.

"It can only mean one thing, you and Aunt Maureen were born near a tear. It's like a thin spot that connects the realms, this realm and the one you knew, it means you're of both worlds. The transition changed you." I took my mom's hand and showed her.

She inhaled sharply, then looked at the rest of what she could see of herself, then glanced at her sister. "Look at you! You're … you're …"

"I'm hot is what I am!" Aunt Maureen exclaimed, admiring her body. "Look at my tits! The girls haven't looked this good in twenty years!"

Felix covered his face and I groaned. This world was not ready for Maureen O'Shea. Her raunchy brand of humor would undoubtedly cause a ruckus. I cringed, picturing royal functions with my unruly aunt trying to shock Rannoch's parents with inappropriate jokes. *Rannoch, his family, oh man there is so much to tell my mom and aunt.* I realized he had no idea what was going on, so I sent him a message through the link to let him know the incredible news.

"We should get going," I said, glancing over my shoulder. I realized Dendris had hid herself from view. "Dendris, can you join us?" *This ought to be interesting.*

Unsurprisingly, both my mom and aunt loudly gasped. Dendris's face didn't show a hint of emotion, she simply waited for them to take in her appearance, before walking closer to us.

"This is our friend, Dendris. She's an Arbor Elf and has helped us many times. I trust her, you can, too. She's going to help us transport you. There is a dangerous bridge over a bottomless pit on the other side of that rock. Instead of crossing it she will make it so we don't have to, but, this is going to be startling for you both. They are portal-walkers, they open doors called fenestrams to other locations. We are moving to a spot that is on the other side of these boulders where the rest of our group is waiting. We have some … people to introduce you to."

Felix's eyes widened a fraction, and I realized he had his own introductions to make. He never told me if he told our mom, so he very well might have been introducing Dhiren *and* telling our mom and aunt his very personal news at the same time. I reached forward and squeezed his hand, silently telling him it would be okay. I had no idea how that would feel, to have that moment suddenly thrust upon you where it was necessary to tell something so intrinsic to who you were but hard to say.

"I'll go first," he blurted out.

I nodded, he probably needed a moment to prepare Dhiren. Dendris opened the doorway, then spun through with Felix. The fenestram closed, but my mom and aunt's mouths remained open.

"Pretty incredible, isn't it?" They merely looked at me, stunned. "I still can't believe you both are here." I suddenly thought of the things still tying my mom to the human realm. I had told her when I felt the Pull that I wouldn't be able to stay in Black Oak. Now the same would be true for her. She wouldn't be able to go back, not for long anyway. "Mom, about the horses …"

She gulped. "Yes, well, I wanted to talk to you about that. You had said you couldn't ride Apollo anymore. I gave him to Holly, the Richter's daughter. She's fourteen now and desperately wants to ride. She'll be a good match for him. And the others, they're with the Phillips. I told them I didn't know when I'd be back from Ithaca, they said they could stay as long as needed."

I didn't want to mention that it probably meant for the rest of their lives, but kept it to myself. At least they were taken care of and she hadn't decided to move them across the country to be with her.

The portal reopened, then Dendris stepped through. "Aunt Maureen, you go next. It's as simple as a dance, you take one easy spin and you're on the other side of it. There is no pain and it's instantaneous."

She adjusted her too-tight top, ill fitting on her now elongated body. "I bet it won't be the strangest thing that happens today," she said as she readied herself.

A moment later, she was gone.

"Just like that?" my mom asked as she looked at where her sister had previously been standing. "Is it far to walk instead? I think I'd rather walk."

"No, Mom, trust me. You do not want the alternative, it's a terrifying bridge. This isn't like the human realm where there's usually safety measures in place. This world is beautiful, but also wild. This way is better." I thought of the other alternative, which was traveling with the Amabilis, so really this was by far the most gentle and least jarring way to be transported. I took a slow breath through my nose, there was *so much* to explain to her. "Mom, I need to tell you, these people you're about to meet, one of them is—"

"—Your boyfriend. You had said you fell in love when I saw you last."

I broke out in a cold sweat thinking of having to describe our relationship. Boyfriend didn't accurately describe who he was to me. *Lover. Mate. Everything. He is my everything.* I had to remind myself that to her I had not been gone all that long, a few weeks at most, certainly not the months and months I had lived in Alternis for. I started to speak, to try and explain how he and I were bound to each other, when the portal appeared. I urged her to go through with Dendris.

She obliged with no complaints, and within a few heartbeats I was by myself. I looked around at the desolate area, at the tear my mom and aunt had come through. In a weird twist of fate, somehow Ithaca must have been where the tear connected to. That nebulous unseen wheel of life felt stronger to me now. I had disliked the idea of fate before, but if this was somehow destiny, I was now grateful for it. I had the rest of my living family back, I wasn't going to fight that.

The Ita Hua Tear. The name echoed in my mind again, and I remembered something from long ago. When I had reunited with Rannoch in the Hinterdunes, he had said the place my mom was from sounded *familiar.* Ithaca. All this time the clues were right in front of me.

Dendris reappeared, and I gladly accepted as she held out her hand to ferry me across. I stepped through to everyone waiting expectantly for me. Dendris rejoined the Arbor Elves, who stood aside conferring until we were ready to depart. I blinked, looking between my mom and Rannoch. I walked closer to my mom and finally introduced her to my mate. The ability to have them meet face to face was something I never thought would happen, seeing them both together filled me with a sense of everything in the world finally being set in place.

After hugging him warmly, she asked, "Mate? Not boyfriend?"

Her eyes darted between the two of us, taking in every detail.

My hand instinctively went to my mating marks, to the physical identifier that showed we were indeed promised to each other. "Yes. There are other terms here than what you're used to. We do not say boyfriend, or husband. Rannoch is my conniunx, which is comparable to spouse."

My mom looked shocked, and then overcome with joy. "Lily! You have become … you have grown so much."

She threw her arms around me. I didn't even have time to lift my arms to reciprocate the hug. I didn't know what I expected her to say, but it wasn't that.

"I must say this happened too fast," she added as she backed up to look at Rannoch and me, " but we can talk more on that later."

"I realize it seems fast to you, and even still yes I agree it is somewhat fast. But, you are not only in a different place, but a different time frequency. Time passes differently here. For every day that passes in the human world, twenty eight pass here."

Her eyebrows shot up. "Twenty eight? A month to a day? How does …"

Felix stepped forward. "There is a lot more to explain, but first I want to introduce you to," he turned and motioned for Dhiren to join him, "Dhiren." Felix took Dhiren's hand as he stood beside him. "Mom," he started, then paused. He stood taller. "This is my conniunx."

A smile split her face. She didn't miss a beat as she squeezed them both in a huge hug, then leaned back to look at Dhiren. "This makes me so happy! I have wanted him to find someone he could be himself with for so long. I'm so glad to meet you, Dhiren."

Felix looked surprised.

"What?" our mom asked. "I knew, honey. You're my son, I know your heart. I knew for a long time. I never wanted to press it because I figured you would talk about it when you were ready. I love and accept you for all that you are."

"We *both* accept you, Felix, my love," Aunt Maureen chimed in. "And I mean, please, *look* at Dhiren. He's delicious. Who wouldn't go for him?"

I shrieked, while Dhirdre and Kerenza burst out laughing. Felix's cheeks reddened, then he and Dhiren finally laughed, too.

I laughed as well until little tears collected at the corners of my eyes. "Leave it to Aunt Maureen to shake things up. Buckle up, everyone, expect a lot more comments like that in the future."

"Oh you know me, I'll be on my best behavior!"

I nodded dubiously. "Sure you will." I laughed again, then it faded as I looked at our group, my found family and my family by blood. I realized I had finally been blessed with the ability to be grateful. Perhaps I was too consumed before by the bad things that happened, and those events had overshadowed any good in my life. But now, I glanced around and was beyond grateful for everything I had.

Time to go home, I said to Rannoch through the link. He smiled and nodded, the embers in his eyes lighting up as our gazes met.

I turned to the Arbor Elves. "It's time for us to head out, will you return us to the Praegra Forest?"

"Indeed," Aurelian said.

"Before we do, I wanted to introduce you all to my maeder, Rachael, and her sister, Maureen, the two new Vale Born that have entered Alternis. Mom, this is Aurelian, the Venitor of the Arbor

Elves, and her contingent of skilled warriors."

"Rachael, I owe your filia my life, she saved it once. She is brave, you should be proud." Aurelian bowed with a fist across her chest.

"Filia?" my mom whispered to me.

"It means daughter, or girl, there's a lot of things to teach you about this world."

She nodded and bowed back to Aurelian after a moment.

I smiled at my mother, I had to hand it to her. For everything that had happened in a very short period of time, she sailed in like she could handle *anything*. She took Felix's news with such heartfelt love, and welcomed Rannoch easily. I supposed with what she had already endured in life, having overcome many painful trials, these were the moments where she was rewarded. Her children were back with her. Even if it was not in a way she was familiar with, it was a gift that she most likely did not expect. I recognized that familiar feeling emanating from her which I was only recently learning: gratitude.

The Arbor Elves paired up with each of us, then whisked us back to the edge of the Well.

I watched as our elders stared at our dramatically different surroundings. The stark, icy mountains were replaced by the towering trees of the Praegra Forest, and the glowing Well cast a bluish light on the nearby area. I motioned to Felix to talk privately for a moment. "We should take them to the Maeder Tree and connect to her with them. It will be hard to understand, but maybe …"

"Who knows what will happen, but yeah I agree. We shouldn't tell them much, just in case."

We walked back over to everyone. I quickly asked Aurelian to wait until after we were done in the Well, then take us further south to the Ignisfae encampment. We would have to get there soon, the equus were there and it would be a necessary stop before we could return to TerraIgni. But, we were at the Well with two brand new Vale Born who needed to be shown how we were created, and perhaps, they would know and see more. There was time for something so important first.

We brought my mom and aunt to the edge of the Well, then convinced them to dive in with us. The cool fluid slipped over my skin, soothing any aches and calming my whole being. I watched them delight in the sensation, and suddenly I wondered, what skill did they come through with? I hadn't mentioned anything about what I could do, what Felix could do. And we had been right there when they exited the aperture, they may have been distracted and not felt the surge of awakened power. Yet another aspect to help them learn and explore.

We swam to the tree, and instructed our elders on what to do. This time, we had them touch the trunk's surface, while Felix and I held their hands from the center of our ring. It was a different sensation, being the conduit, I felt the charge pass through, but didn't feel the pull of the power which anchored in place from the palm. My mom opened her mouth in a silent yell, but then shut it as the image of the Maeder appeared. She sang to us, cradled us, imparted her soothing embrace and knowledge of creation. I was glad it was something we could give to them so soon after arriving, that they didn't have to wander the realm before being given that understanding.

Then, another form appeared near the Maeder. Both my mom

and aunt instantly cried out in stifled sobs. I looked at Felix and lifted a sad, but fulfilled, tearful smile. Maris had appeared, then Josie appeared next to her. They came, as I hoped they would. To see them again was such a blessing, to feel their content presence. And to give that to Mom and Aunt Maureen, it hurt and healed at the same time. The pain that Maris and Josie were gone was back in the forefront as we looked at their transparent faces. But they still *existed*, they were still them. They still loved us. The pain was heartening, the pain was a sobering reminder, and a catalyst for healing.

Maris and Josie retreated, then the Maeder Tree gently closed our connection to her. We all hugged as it ended, holding each other for those precious moments. I closed my eyes, sending a silent thank you that Maris had come this time. We hadn't seen her when Felix and I ferried the Vale Born spirits to the other side.

We swam back to where everyone else stood. After a few moments of silence, the questions started. I had expected it, but it was difficult to both limit my response for speed and resist the urge to unload and tell them everything. In the end, I promised a thorough discussion after we had reached the Ignisfae camp, there would be food, water, and a change of clothes for them, plus a rest while we got ready to fly to TerraIgni.

Finally, they agreed and we stepped through portals with the Arbor Elves, before long we were around the familiar campfires of the Ignisfae tents, where Felix and I told them all we could. Rannoch worked with everyone else to prepare things, while the four of us sat and talked for hours. Seeing my mom's face light up with understanding and belief was something I didn't realize I needed. When I had seen her in Black Oak Grove and Felix and I told her all we could in that short time, she had never believed the story. Now, she was living it.

We all had tortams around the fire. Rannoch and Kerenza told my mom and aunt about the first time I had been there, and about how Rannoch and I didn't get along, how I was *always* testing him and pushing his buttons.

"They were both smitten with each other, though neither wanted to admit it at first," Kerenza said as she elbowed me in jest.

My mom smiled and cocked her head at us. "So, Rannoch, what do you do in TerraIgni? I take it that it's like a city?"

I should have known this was coming, that she would inevitably ask for more details about who he was.

"I enjoy working in the forge," he answered truthfully.

That's not what she's asking, this is a human custom to find out who, exactly, you are, I said to him through the link.

Are you ready to tell her?

"So you're a blacksmith?" she probed further.

I decided to take answering her upon myself and sat up straighter. "I should have been more … forthcoming with my introductions. But, at the time there was a lot to process, and I didn't want to overwhelm you." I sucked in a breath. "Rachael Marie Brennanfalk, I'd like to formally introduce you to Prince Rannoch Ashwani Albericus, leader of the Ignisfae warrior regiment, and son of King Ashwan and Queen Deniza Albericus of TerraIgni."

Everyone went quiet. Aunt Maureen looked beside herself with excitement as her surprised glance darted back and forth between my mom and me.

My mom carefully set her cup down, then motioned to me. "So … wow, that makes you—"

"Princess Lily Mae Brennanfalk," Rannoch finished for her.

"Holy shit!" Aunt Maureen exclaimed.

"She was crowned for her service to the Ignisfae," Kerenza added, "for the heroism she displayed when she rescued our children. She has more than earned her title, aside from the fact that she is Rannoch's mate. And, because of her, our maeder was rescued from imprisonment. The list of her accomplishments is long."

Aunt Maureen laughed maniacally. "Hot damn, Lily!"

My mom opened and closed her mouth a few times, seeming to try and formulate words, connecting all the dots. "So you are a princess as well?" she asked Kerenza.

Kerenza nodded once.

My mom turned to Dhiren. "And you?"

"I am Rannoch's first in command. Not royalty but bound to the throne. As is my sister, Dhirdre. We were raised with them since birth."

My eyes widened. When he said "since birth" I realized there was yet another fact my mother would come to learn. Their incredibly long lifespans and current age would be something for her to grapple with, namely because I was now with someone who would be long dead in the human world based on how old he was. A certain unsavory term came to mind, even though Rannoch looked like he was no older than twenty-eight. I pushed it from my mind, that subject could be broached another time.

"It's not as intense as it sounds, Mom," Felix offered. "Rannoch, Kerenza, and Lily prefer not to use their titles. It's much more easy-going than you might think."

I was relieved for the slight shift in subject, in case our mom's next line of thinking led her to ask how old they were. I gave Felix an appreciative look.

"It is good to know before we go back to TerraIgni, though, so you aren't surprised," I said. "We're going to rest here for some time, because it's a long flight there."

"Flight?" Mom and Aunt Maureen asked in unison.

I nodded as a knowing smirk crept over my face. "Yep, flight."

CHAPTER 34

We soared down to TerraIgni out of the mist, with Aunt Maureen hooting as we descended. I smiled as I thought back on when they had first seen the equus. Both my mom and aunt had been shocked and excited to see actual winged horses. The excitement over the equus had definitely worn off early on during the long passage. The long trip was good for some things. When we had arrived at the rest point, Felix and I showed our mom and aunt our skills, then helped encourage them to discover what they could do. Though there was little in the area she could try it on, my mom found she had the gift of controlling water. Aunt Maureen had the skill of air, like Felix. They were at the beginning on a long road to learn to control their abilities.

The second half of the trip proved to be physically uncomfortable, for all of us and the equus. With almost every equus carrying two, we were all sore and ready for a break. I was beyond relieved to see the south facade of the fortress as we came through the mist, and the massive statues of Ignisfae holding the braziers of living flame. The beacons were lit as we came into view, sending their plumes high in the air to announce our arrival.

I spotted King Ashwan and Queen Deniza on their expansive

balcony, they watched our approach, then headed toward the doorway. I knew they would most likely meet us in the equus valley. Rannoch led the way past the fortress, then to the north where the stables and pastures were. After we landed, they arrived just as I expected.

"Well, Mom, you're about to meet a king and queen," I said as Rannoch's parents approached.

She adjusted her linteum, which had been wrapped carefully by Zia. Fortunately, we had enough with us to be able to swap out their old clothes which no longer fit, to something more appropriate for the realm.

The introductions went far smoother than I would have expected, King Ashwan was downright welcoming to my family. I was glad I hadn't said anything disparaging about him first, in fact I had been careful not to. I didn't want to cause further stress to my mom, having to worry that he was going to say something rude. I could have hugged him, he was clearly still working to make amends.

Rannoch ensured my mom and aunt were given their own quarters quickly, it was not long before everyone disbanded and went their separate ways to rest.

My mom didn't emerge from her new room for a whole rotation, at which point she discovered her appetite had reached ravenous levels. Felix and I dined with her and Aunt Maureen in the main dining hall, having time to enjoy her company, talk, and eat. Knowing that this was the beginning of a new life together made my heart happy.

Aunt Maureen wasted no time in finding someone who was interested in her, they walked by our table together in the hall when I realized I knew who it was. Rovan smiled at her in a way that even gave me butterflies.

"Who is that?" Felix asked.

"You haven't met Rovan? He's the animedicus, their version of a horse vet."

My mom perked up. "I bet you were excited to meet him! Did you tell him you studied veterinary medicine as well?" Mom asked.

I recounted the story of when he and I had saved Steren together, Rannoch's equus, and how the event was what had turned a previously sour relationship with Rannoch into a kernel of something more. The look of pride on my mom's face made me swell with emotions. I honestly never thought I'd have the opportunity to tell her that story, and have her believe it for that matter.

Every time we met up, she learned more about our adventures, more about the world that she was now a part of. Felix and I took my mom and aunt on tours of the city, took them to the bazaar and to meet Yantz. I treasured every moment with them, getting to show them the place I now called home. Some rotations weren't easy, especially for my mom. Though the chance to see Maris again was something she was grateful for, it was understandably difficult for her. It opened wounds, but, we were there together to feel those feelings as a family unit. We found a beautiful burbling fountain in a courtyard on the outskirts of the fortress, it became the meeting spot for my mom, Felix, and I to sit down and have quiet talks. We spent several rotations together, sometimes all four of us, sometimes a larger group where they got to know everyone a little better. Sometimes it was only us three, just a mom and her kids spending time together like families do.

After quite a few rotations of rest, Rannoch, Dhirdre and I departed for Limnaer. Much to my mother's chagrin, we needed to make a trip there. I had also decided that a trip with Rannoch would be good for us, since the last time I had gone there I had left TerraIgni upset, with unfinished business between the two of us. Going to Limnaer was a chance to put those issues further behind us. Dhirdre came along as our guard and to assist where she could. I needed to tell Ser'Ti in person what had happened with Calria, and where she could be found. Since the Ita Hua Tear was part of their domain, I had decided allowing them to recover her body if they wanted to would be the best choice. As a peace offering, we were extending an invitation to the Caelifae to visit TerraIgni, to the celebration that King Ashwan and Queen Deniza had recently announced. There was also the matter of Yantzen J'Dun, Prince Ser'Ti was still hoping to have him come to Limnaer and invent things, but as of yet Yantz hadn't taken the offer. Perhaps if Ser'Ti came and spoke to him in person, he could convince him to go.

The trip was at first uncomfortable, with having to tell Ser'Ti the unfortunate news of Calria's betrayal and subsequent demise, but he was not surprised. He had grown suspicious of her after we had departed the first time I had visited. He figured her misdeeds had caught up with her after she disappeared without a trace. He was glad to know the truth, though it wasn't easy for him to hear I had been the one to kill her. After all, she had been his caretaker for many cycles, that was a betrayal that stung deep. In the end, he accepted the offer to come to TerraIgni as a way to cement the evolving relationship between the Caelifae and Ignisfae.

Rannoch and I prepared to return home, while I chattered on about all the planning that would need to happen. "We'll have to send enough equus to carry them all to TerraIgni, since they can't cross the Hinterdunes. Who will lead them?"

Dhirdre stepped up. "Do not worry, Lily. Dhiren and I will return and escort them."

"We should invite the Arbor Elves, too!"

"That's a magna idea, we should invite them," Rannoch mused.

"I'll call Livi, maybe the Faeries can deliver the message."

I focused the sound wave, then sent it out to Livi. It took some time, but Livi arrived eventually, bringing news as well. "The Faeries are okay!" I blurted out to Rannoch and Dhirdre. "Livi says sometime after Dashelle died, the darkness that permeated some of their kind dissipated, they have all returned to how they were before." I breathed a sigh, the damage Dashelle had done was slowly being corrected. The lives she took could never be replaced, however. I thought about the Ignisfae that had died in the first battle with her, in the massive mountain where she had first trapped Rannoch and I so long ago. I hadn't known any of the warriors that fell in that fight. I decided I should visit each of their families, and honor them for their brave service. Livi left with the message to the Arbor Elves, it would probably be a little while longer before they returned, then it would be time for us to head back to TerraIgni. "We'll need to make arrangements if they accept. Perhaps a second run for the equus because the Arbor Elves won't be able to open fenestrams across the Hinterdunes, they'll have to travel by equus as well."

"Dhirdre, will you give Lily and I a moment?" Rannoch asked.

Dhirdre nodded, then stepped away to handle more preparations.

He took my hands in his. "We'll need to leave some of this planning for others to take care of. I debated about surprising you with this, but thought better of it. The celebration will not only be to welcome your family, it will also be our Joining ceremony."

"What does that mean?"

"It is the time when our lives are tied by a ring, each of us would wear one, it connects our lifeline to the rings and the rings to each other. Usually it is done directly after the Pompa, but with everything that had been happening, and because suitable rings were not ready, it was postponed."

I thought of Kerenza's ring, and how it had gone dark when Kenneder died. But the one connected to Emblyn still burned fiercely.

"Traditionally I would not ask if you wanted to do it," he continued, "it is simply the next step, however I learned from Felix that asking is a custom where you're from. Lily, will you accept the Joining with me?"

I looked at him wide-eyed, surprised but also overjoyed. I didn't know they had something akin to a wedding ceremony, but it seemed perfectly fitting. And now that my mom and Aunt Maureen were with us, it was the perfect time. I felt it again, that intangible sense of a wheel of life, when things felt right, it rotated forward. I sensed it move once again. "Yes, Rannoch. I would love to."

He picked me up and spun me around, trying to kiss me while he smiled ear to ear. "We should get back to TerraIgni then! We have so much to do."

I laughed. "But the Arbor Elves!"

He chuckled. "All right, we'll wait for Livi, then make plans. But then, home to TerraIgni."

I smiled and affirmed, "Home."

CHAPTER 35

I sat and smoothed the layers of my cream satin skirt as Tanzara carefully wove my hair into intricate braids. The fabric felt like the silkiest weave I had ever touched. The Ignisfae were renowned for their skills with weaving, but this was not like what we had made during Praetexia. The holiday, which encouraged everyone to work together to create hundreds of yards of beautiful fabrics, hadn't yielded anything quite this fine. The fabrics we had made were indeed beautiful, but they were more functional, designed for daily use. This was something special, a fabric which masters had created. I looked at myself in the mirror as Tanzara worked, the drape of the dress's neckline caught the light, before it twisted and cascaded from both shoulders in a long, flowing cape. Firestar rubies were encrusted along the waistline, which descended to a point down the center.

When she had finished, the top half of my hair was braided, leaving the bottom loose and curled. She had even carefully shaped the curls around the upper bodice of my dress, creating a stunning silhouette. My mom and Aunt Maureen were dressed in gorgeous yellow-gold wrap dresses, their auburn hair looked enchanting with the rich color. I couldn't stop staring at them as they arrived to escort me to the event. Their eyes looked bright with tears held back as they gazed at me.

"Oh, honey, you look so beautiful. The most beautiful bride." My mom was overcome with emotion as she held out her hands to me. The moment was something I would always remember, I took in every detail, from the look in her eyes to how her hands felt holding mine. To feel their warmth right before this incomparable event was a gift I would treasure forever.

I took a breath and flashed a giddy smile at them. "It's time, everyone else should be arriving now."

We walked with arms linked to the main square. They had seen the area in passing, but had never seen it when it was adorned for something special. Everything of note happened in the wide space. We had celebrated Pratexia there, held the pompa for our first union celebration, I had been crowned on that stage, had Eiulans's funeral pyre there, and now we would perform the Joining ceremony together with the masses in attendance. Prince Ser'Ti and a group of his attendants would be there, as well as Aurelian, Tenaeran, Dendris, and more Arbor Elves. Even Livi and a few other Faeries made the journey, taking advantage of the equus ride with Dendris as their companion. It was an occasion marked with the first ever visitors from other provinces of Alternis. Livi had managed to bring a message from the Syrenni, who we also invited. They decided against coming but sent their best wishes, as well as the news that the Syrenni were thriving and little Sereia was growing well in their new home.

We arrived at our appointed location, a wide hallway with draped fabric closing off the main square. Rannoch and Kerenza would come from another hallway adjacent to ours. I still hadn't seen him since I had woken up, both my mom and aunt had insisted on that. Rannoch found it a curious custom, but easily obliged. I peeked carefully out from the curtain to see the decorations. The square was filled with Ignisfae, every available spot along the battlements was already occupied. There were rows of seats lined up facing toward the elevated platform, most of them already filled, the ones closer to the front would be reserved for the Caelifae and Arbor Elf guests. I couldn't see anything beyond the first set of chairs. Bunches of fresh flowers lined the walkway, the larger center blooms were a rich, deep red, then ringed in flowers that looked a lot like lilies, with pointed oblong petals which graduated from brilliant orange to a vibrant purple. Aunt Maureen had helped with the flowers, she was the one that had proclaimed the need for flowers on both sides of the aisle.

"Lily! Someone will see you!" my mom hissed a whisper from my side.

"All right all right!" I dropped the curtain, even though it was only opened enough to look through with one eye.

"We really should have had a rehearsal," Aunt Maureen muttered, "how will we know when to go?"

The music started up, which was a slow, pulsing melodic drum beat, then ropes started to pull the curtain open.

"That's how we'll know," I said with a smirk.

Aunt Maureen laughed a little. "You definitely got your snarkiness from me."

I was about to make a follow up comment, when the entire square came into full view. Any lighthearted jokes retreated from thought as all eyes were upon us, and the majesty of the beautifully decorated space overwhelmed me with emotion. Musicians drew their bows across their stringed instruments in long, driving notes which built in a slow moving crescendo. The sound gathered around us, propelling me forward, when Rannoch appeared from the other hallway.

My breath went out of me as I looked at him, his regal fitted suit was made from the same light-catching fabric as my dress, but was sewn into a structured jacket with a collar which flared out at the neck, then curved down his chest and reached his mid-thighs. His black hair with ruby highlights was half braided back, keeping the lower part swept behind his shoulders. His eyes were alight with fire in his pupils as he looked at me, and he didn't take his eyes off of me once as we slowly marched toward each other. Kerenza—dressed in the same yellow-gold as my mom and aunt—was close behind him, carrying a small box.

Felix stepped forward from my right, dressed in a similar suit to Rannoch's, but matching the yellow hue instead. I nearly paused, realizing I had told Rannoch multiple times that I loved that color, anytime we saw an item that shade in the bazaar I would mention it. He smiled at me, he watched my expression as my gaze darted between their custom-made clothing.

That was your idea, wasn't it? The color.

He grinned and nodded as he took another step toward me. Felix guided me the rest of the way. We met at the entrance to the aisle, then Felix passed my hand to Rannoch. Rannoch's hand took mine, and we walked forward together.

Together, the same that we would proceed with a great many things in our lives. Marching toward a future that we had rescued, because when we had stepped in and fought for the realm, we were also fighting for ourselves, for our very existence. For the chance for our love to endure.

We reached the stairs to the dais, my mom and aunt seated themselves in the open seats at the front. I saw Rannoch's parents stand from their seats with the Firestar Crowns in their hands. Taking a few steps toward us, King Ashwan placed the larger one on Rannoch's head, then Queen Deniza set the other on mine. They bowed to us, then sat back down. We dipped lightly to them, acknowledging them. I hadn't known they wouldn't be on the stage with us. I looked past them and saw the friends and allies we made along the way. Prince Ser'Ti sat with Yantz, Tanzara had settled in with Zia and Lennaraz. Tenaeran couldn't hide her gigantic smile and she whispered something to Aurelian. Even Dendris smiled. I nodded to them all before we proceeded hand in hand up the steps to the platform, with Kerenza and Felix behind us. I finally noticed the backdrop up on the stage that would frame us for all of the guests. It was a massive threadpainting, depicting Rannoch and I flying over TerraIgni on our equus, with an expansive view of the incredible fortress in the rocky canyon which we called home. I glanced over at Yantz, remembering him hiding something large at his outdoor workshop. He beamed at me, I shook my head and smiled at yet another thoughtful surprise.

Within a few moments, we were at the front, then Rannoch turned to me. There was no priest there, no person that would perform the rite. It was just him and me. Our siblings were nearby, as a silent affirmation of their support.

Rannoch motioned to Kerenza, who stepped forward with the box. She opened it for him, holding it so he could reach in to pick up the ring. He turned toward me, holding my hand and about to place it on my middle finger. "I have been working on these for a long time, it is what I was always going to the forge for, I was learning the skills necessary to craft them myself. The work needed to create them is a symbol for what I will always do for us. I will work for us, I will always try. I will always do my best to be who you need."

I almost dropped my jaw, I hadn't known that was what he was doing when he went to the forge. I looked into his eyes, and smiled with elation as he slipped it onto my finger. I glanced down and saw the incredible detail which Rannoch had painstakingly etched into the lustrous gold, and the bezel-set dark ruby in the center which matched our crowns.

Kerenza came to my side with the box that contained the other ring. I reached in and felt its warm weight, then looked at the matching gold ring he had spent so much time and effort on. We had both worked for our love, and though life is a learning process with rarely a straight path, we would walk it together. I picked up his hand, then held the ring poised over his waiting fingertip. "I will always endeavor to do my best, to work for us and our success. I will always work for our future, by your side." I slid the ring into place, then wove my fingers into his.

The braziers of the Ignisfae statues surrounding the square lit up in a brilliant display, sending their flames high, as something awoke in our link. The ring on my hand warmed, and a bright red light illuminated for a moment from each of our hands. I smiled at him as our bond deepened. The rings now both flared to life with a vibrant red flash.

I pulled him closer to me as the crowd cheered, and our family clapped.

To our future, whatever it may hold. It will be together.

The End

Lily and Rannoch's story may have come to a close,
however there are more stories of the Vale to come!
Follow the author to find out when Sereia's story
and the fate of the Syrenni will release,
a duology spinoff set in the future when Sereia is grown.

www.lorinpetrazilka.com

Pronunciation Guide & Index

Lily lil-EE
Main Character and general badass woman, Vale Born

Felix FEE-licks
Lily's brother, Vale Born

Rannoch ran-NUCK
Lily's mate, Prince of the Ignisfae

Kerenza keh-ren-ZAH
Rannoch's sister, Princess of the Ignisfae

Dhiren DEER-ren
Ignisfae, Rannoch's first in command, Dhirdre's twin brother

Dhirdre DEER-drah
Ignisfae, Kerenza's first in command, Dhiren's twin sister

Deniza den-ih-ZA
Rannoch and Kerenza's mother, Queen of the Ignisfae

Ashwan ash-WAHN
Rannoch and Kerenza's father, King of the Ignisfae

Eiulans EW-lens
Ignisfae, Hand of the King, King Ashwan's advisor

Aurelian ar-RIL-ee-an
Arbor Elf, Venitor (leader) of the Arbor Elves

Tenaeran Ten-AIR-an
Arbor Elf, mate of Aurelian

Don'Li Calbaeric Don-LEE kal-BEAR-ick
Caelifae, former flame of Queen Deniza

Ser'Ti Zan Circelos ser-TEE zan SERK-el-os
Prince of the Caelifae

Calria cal-REE-ah
Caelifae, Regent of Caelifae royalty

Yantzen J'Dun Yant-ZEN jah-DUNE
Ignisfae, oldest known living Fae, inventor and artist

Tanzara Tan-ZAR-a
Ignisfae, Lily's trusted attendant

Lennaraz len-NAR-az
mestisius (mixed Ignisfae/Petrafae) friend of Kerenza and artist

RACES
Umorfae -oo-MORE-fay
Water wielding Fae

Ignisfae - Ig-NIS-fay
Fire wielding Fae

Petrafae - Pe-TRA-fay
Stone wielding Fae

Caelifae - kal-E-fay
Wind wielding Fae

Syrenni sir-REN-ee
amphibious mermaid-like creatures, former servants of the Umorfae

Amabilis a-mah-BIL-is
flying squirrel-like creatures that traverse the sublayer of the realm

Kaikodaimons KAY-ko-day-mons
monsters that terrorize the Hinterdunes

Pythonissamul pie-THON-iss-ah-mool
witch creature that hunts in the Praegra Forest

Vitus Augustus VI-tus og-GUS-tus
First Vale Born to amass power (historical figure only)

Opius OH-p-us
Generalis (leader) of the Umorfae army, nephew of Empress Celestine

Rachael Brennenfalk RAY-chel BREN-an-fallK
Lily and Felix's mom

Maureen O'Shea MORE-een O-shay
Lily and Felix's aunt, Rachael's sister

PLACES

Praegra Forest pray-GRAH fore-EST
the majority of Alternis, the entire central portion

Midgard Well mid-GARD well
center of the Praegra Forest where the Maeder Tree is rooted

Hinterdunes HINT-er-DOONS
Nearly impassable desert area between the Praegra Forest and TerraIgni

TerraIgni TARE-ah-IG-nee
Ignisfae fortress and city at the eastern-most reaches of Alternis

Limnaer LIM-nare
Caelifae city and stronghold to the north

Lacausia lah-COW-zee-ah
Umorfae territory and palace

Adrilan add-RIL-ahn
Petrafae stone city to the northwest of Alternis

WORDS

capuli cah-PULL-ee meaning: coffee

vinirubrum vin-eh-roo-BRUM meaning: red wine

vocafortis voke-AH-four-tis meaning: clear alcohol (like vodka)

stultus - stuhl-TUS meaning: dumbass, idiot

faex - Fay meaning: shit

culus - KUL-us meaning: asshole

cunne -QUEnh -one syllable meaning: bitch, cunt

ACKNOWLEDGEMENTS

First, let me thank my coffee. I'm four cups deep as I write this, because damn, Nespresso can make some great coffee. You can imagine with writing a whole series, there were a lot of very late nights or very early mornings. Coffee was a silent friend throughout the entire process.

Huge thanks go to you, the readers. I dedicated this book to you all for a very good reason, having people that loved this series helped me push through to finish it when things were tough. I would read reviews, emails, comments online … they all helped me to remember that there were people out there that got something from the story. Truly, thank you for reading and for letting me know what mattered to you.

Thank you to my husband, Kirt, and to our kids Amy, Donovan, and Liam. We have a busy life that I am so thankful for, thank you all for being my family and for sharing this adventure with me. Life can be absolutely nuts sometimes, but it's really amazing see us all do our different things, reaching for goals and celebrating the wins in between all the glorg (our word for mundane tasks) we have to get through. I love you all so, so much.

Laura L Hohman, you dang talented and wonderful writer/human/artist/FRIEND! I'm so grateful for having you as my bestie, and writing with you is the most fulfilling process. Thank you for everything you do. I could fill up this page with all the reasons I'm thankful for you.

Fatebound Books, the publishing imprint that could! I'm so thrilled to Vale Born has a home with Fatebound. I could say something dorky and punny about fate, but I'll leave that to Laura because she's the pun master.

My editor, David Martin Lins, thank you isn't adequate. I should be really eloquent here and write something truly profound (I am a writer, after all) but I find myself needing to sum up in a very short, succinct sentence: YOU ROCK! Any writer of any genre would be lucky to work with you, I am lucky you tolerate some of my more questionable scenes.

Paris Thompson, the recent addition to my editor team! I am so glad to have met you, and to have had your immense help on this book. Lily's final story benefitted from your keen eye and advice.

My beta team: You are all the absolute best, and I appreciate your dedication to the Vale so much!

Chris Sanchez: Where to begin! Thank you for your honest feedback that has consistently helped this series along, you're the best no matter how much you deny it!

Laura Quinn, my favorite Scottish Superfan! You comments were so appreciated, and your ideas were put into action. Thank you for being a reliable, valuable part of my beta team once again.

Raina Sachiko: I really appreciated your wish for more knowledge about how the Syrenni were faring, it's a great example for how the beta team works, because of you, it's in there! And I think further proof that this is a story we want to hear, so it's a good thing we have more to come set in the future with a focus on the Syrenni :) Thank you for your thoughts and for your excellent feedback!

Maggie Uphoff Garcia: Thank you so much for reading, for your support, and for all of your helpful feedback. It's so cool how we started our friendship through fabric, and have continued it with books.

Dawn Paterson: Even with difficult things popping up at the same time as the beta period, you managed to give great feedback, you are amazing! Thank you for your ideas, they helped me improve the story even more. I'm so glad you joined the beta team.

Gina Melchiorri: Whew, GIRL, lots of thanks due here! Thank you for being the voice of the Vale Born series as the producer of the audiobooks! I am SO EXCITED that Pull of the Vale will be out for listeners soon! Promoting with you at LA ComicCon was such a blast, thank you so much for being there for it. Thank you for the help with a certain someone's pageant backstory! I find it so serendipitous that it worked out that way, it is awesome how you have helped shape the story.

To Dogs Without Borders: Thank you for helping us adopt the little weirdo that is currently snoring next to me. Our newest addition, Grizwald, has a home because of you all, and we are lucky he found a home with us. You all have made a 7 year old's dream come true.

To That Bitch Robyn: kkdsfpjfplhd[pfi *comment redacted* sometimes stories from the forest, stay in the forest. To my sister in my heart, whether we both suddenly have praying mantis friends or we're saving all the butterflies and allowing those green little monsters to eat their way to beautifulness, it always amazes me how our lives wind along these paths with touchstones along the way that call to each other. I love your guts forever.

And to Parental Units Alpha and Beta, Carla and Jay Zilka: Thank you for buying my books and being supportive in spite of the fact that I was *ahem* not modest with certain scenes. Also I'm really appreciative you did not read said scenes …right? *laughs nervously. In all seriousness, thank you both for showing me what perseverance was through your actions, it's because of perseverance that I was able to finish this series. There were times that were not easy at all, but as Dad says "nothing of value is easily attained." Thirteen-year-old Lorin is rolling her eyes hardcore, but I've grown to appreciate the little Jayisms that Robyn is currently threatening to turn into a coffee table book.

Thank you for reading! If you enjoyed this book, I'd be very grateful if you posted a short review. Your support really does make a difference, I read all reviews personally and use them to keep bringing you great stories. Thanks again for your support!

Get updates on release information, exclusive giveaways, and insider info by signing up for my newsletter at www.lorinpetrazilka.com